THE
WITH COW

He stepped onto the
nose to nose, and he
porch light, she didn't

"You don't owe me a

"That isn't—"

"Because if we ever sleep together, Lou, it's damn well going to be because we both want to."

Her breath caught at that, because that seemed to mean there was some possibility for that to ever, *ever* happen and—

He leaned in, so close not only did her breath stay stuck in her lungs but she couldn't manage a coherent thought. His nose touched her cheek and his mouth was so close to hers, she was afraid to move.

"Your grandma's spying on us," he said under his breath.

"Oh?" She moved her head to look, but Gavin placed his palm on her cheek and kept her head in place.

"Well, don't look, dummy."

She scowled at him.

"Going to have to do something you're not going to like."

"What's th—"

His mouth touched hers. Light, featherlight. He didn't deepen it. His hand remained exactly where it was on her cheek, and still it felt like there was a rope around her lungs cinching tighter and tighter until she couldn't breathe at all.

Gavin's mouth was on hers. Soft and sweet, and she could feel the slight hint of whiskers on his chin. His hand was on her cheek, rough and callused.

It was a *nothing* kiss. Some people probably even kissed friends like that. But it shook her to her very core, so much so that when he pulled away, having done little more than press his mouth to hers, she could only stare at him. Gaping like a fish.

His smile was crooked, and he tipped his hat. "See you tomorrow, Lou."

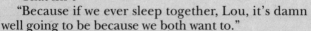

Books by Nicole Helm

Mile High Romances

Need You Now

Mess With Me

Want You More

A Nice Day for a Cowboy Wedding

The Trouble With Cowboy Weddings

Gallagher & Ivy Romances

So Wrong It Must Be Right

So Bad It Must Be Good

The Trouble With Cowboy Weddings

NICOLE HELM

ZEBRA BOOKS
KENSINGTON PUBLISHING CORP.
www.kensingtonbooks.com

ZEBRA BOOKS are published by

Kensington Publishing Corp.
119 West 40th Street
New York, NY 10018

First Printing: July 2019
ISBN-13: 978-1-4201-4696-7
ISBN-10: 1-4201-4696-3

ISBN-13: 978-1-4201-4697-4 (eBook)
ISBN-10: 1-4201-4697-1 (eBook)

10 9 8 7 6 5 4 3 2 1

Printed in the United States of America

For Traci W.
Thank you for all the ways you
share and support my books.
You're an author's dream come true!

Chapter One

Gavin Tyler parked his truck in front of the barn that acted as headquarters for Lou's Blooms.

He'd done a lot of the rebuilding of the barn himself, and it looked good. The red paint had gone on last month after a rough winter, and a Colorado spring hinted at green around the barn, the peaks of the snow-capped Rockies in the distance.

Lou's flower farm was beginning to sprout, and Gavin smiled. Lou didn't like his help, but she'd been forced to take it over the past year, and that meant he'd had a hand in building something for once.

It felt good.

He grabbed the sandwiches he'd brought over and headed for the entrance. The large barn door was open to the cool spring air, and Lou stood over a long table the length of the wall, measuring and cutting ribbon.

Her good side faced him, which meant her dark blond hair flirted with her chin, though it was tucked behind her ears. Her profile was all sharp angles that reflected her personality better than just about anything else. She wore a long-sleeved T-shirt and baggy jeans, and even though it had been a year since a fire had claimed most of her barn and some of her skin, he wasn't used to the way her physicality had changed.

She'd never been überfeminine like her sister, Em, but baggy and hidden away had never been her style either. It was hard to watch his friend retreat into this strange shell she was building for herself, and harder still that no one seemed to be able to pull her back out.

Still, he tried, because he wasn't ready to give up on her. Probably never would be. She'd been a constant in his life since she'd moved in with her grandparents on the Fairchild Ranch, the neighboring ranch to the Tylers.

And since he was a Tyler, he never gave up—not on family, not on friends.

He forced his feet forward and plastered a pleasant smile on his face. "Hungry?"

She didn't even look up. Likely she'd heard his truck approach and knew exactly who was standing in the entrance of her barn. "Whatcha got?"

"Deb Tyler special. How are the wedding flowers going?"

"Going." Lou straightened and stretched, and though she tried to do it surreptitiously, Gavin didn't miss the way she checked to make certain her bandanna was covering the burned side of her face.

She'd had a hell of a year, what with her grandfather dying somewhat unexpectedly only a month before the fire. It was more than half of why he put up with the snarly, angry caricature of herself she'd become since the fire.

Still, it required a certain amount of patience. Patience he wouldn't have thought he had, but . . .

Well, he'd found some. For her anyway.

She studied him from across the room. She kept her distance these days. Physically, emotionally. He would never have presumed she'd told him *everything* in her life, but he knew a lot about Lou Fairchild.

Including the fact that she wasn't herself, and something needed to change.

Gavin raised his eyebrows when she continued to stare at him without speaking. "Everything okay?"

"Gav . . ."

He waited. She rarely shortened his name these days. One of those soft things that had been burned to ash, like her barn and parts of her body.

"I need . . ."

She trailed off, but he waited. And waited. And waited. She held out her hand for the sandwich his mother had made her. He smiled and shook his head.

She grunted irritably. "Grandma isn't budging. She even called . . ." Lou pulled a face. "My father."

"Your father the *deadbeat*?" Gavin didn't know all the details, but he did know Lou and her sister Em had been moved to their grandparents' care as kids because their father had neglected them.

"Between losing Grandpa and . . ." Lou swallowed and pointed to her face. ". . . this," she finally finished. "I don't know who she is anymore."

Which sounded all too familiar to Gavin, but he didn't think he should point that out to her in the moment. "I could talk to her again. Assure her I'd take over as manager and we could work whatever protective clauses she wanted into a contract." He tried not to let himself *hope* for that. He had a place on the Tyler Ranch. It was a good place, a solid place. A place within his *family's* ranch. Blood rights and the like.

But he hated being second fiddle to his older brother Shane, no matter how much he loved him. He wanted to be in charge of something too. Have something that was *his*, not just the odd cattle drive but a whole spread. Just him. Running the Fairchild Ranch on the land not used for Lou's floral business, well, it would be something like a dream come true.

"I've asked her to sell. I've asked her to hire you or *anyone.* I've asked her for every reasonable alternative, and she insists only a Fairchild or a man married to a Fairchild can take over the ranch. So if Em and I aren't going to go find ourselves some husbands, she's going to make my father come here. He'd run it to the ground, Gavin. Into the damn ground."

"What did Em say about that?"

Lou pressed her lips together and turned away from him. He wasn't sure he'd ever understand why she'd decided she had to be solitary and strong when she had so many people who wanted to help her.

"You have to tell her," Gavin said, trying for the same mix of firm and gentle his mother often employed to get her way.

"I can't tell her. Our father is . . . I can't tell her Grandma's contacting him."

"Lou."

"I can't tell her. I'm her older sister. I've protected her this long and what's more . . . She's got nothing to do with the ranch. She loves running the bakery in town. Cattle and flowers aren't her problem. I've had a hard enough time convincing her of that. I'm not going to add another layer. She's separate."

"I don't think that's true."

"It's true enough. And it's final." She turned back to face him. "Sandwich." She held out her hand, a demand she didn't expect him to refuse.

He was starting to think she needed a little refusal in her life. He held on to the sandwich his mother had made for her. "What if I had an idea?"

Everything about her expression went wary. For the

past year, she'd been accepting his help because he hadn't given her a choice. She complained bitterly, and withdrew from asking him for any favors—not that she'd ever been keen on asking for help.

Still, he helped, and because he'd been there when her grandmother had refused to hire Gavin as ranch overseer, and had seen Lou's own stubbornness dug into Mrs. Fairchild's face, he'd mulled over this problem for a few weeks.

He had a solution. One he knew she'd refuse and hate, but maybe if things were this bad . . . Hell, it was worth a shot. What was there to lose?

Your dignity?

He shoved that thought away and grinned at her.

"I hate your ideas," she said.

"And you'll undoubtedly hate this one, but I don't see you coming up with better."

She crossed her arms over her chest. "Fine, what is it?"

"You could marry me."

She laughed, and it was nearly foreign for as little as he'd heard that sound from her lately. "Yeah, sure, Gav. We'll get married. Have, what, eight kids? Maybe ten. I always wanted to be a brood mare."

He didn't laugh along with her, nor did he let himself get bent out of shape. He focused on being calm. "I'm not joking."

"Then you should have gotten your head checked when that horse bucked you."

Irritation simmered through him. "I was not *bucked*, and that is so incredibly beside the point." He pushed out a breath. He wasn't calm in most areas of his life. In fact, he was known around Gracely as the Tyler with the short temper. But he'd hold his temper for Lou. "Your grandma wants you taken care of, and maybe she's . . . Look, maybe she's still reeling over your grandpa, or whatever it is, but if we get married, it won't take too long to get all the land and business moved into your name, and then we'll get divorced."

She shook her head, taking a few steps away from him. "You can't . . . I can't . . ."

"What are friends for?"

"Not marriages that are legally real and emotionally fabricated!"

"You're putting a lot of limits on friendship. Remember the time I wrecked my truck so you could blame me for the dent in your grandfather's? That was a much, *much* larger sacrifice than marriage."

"My ass."

"I loved that truck," he said, placing a hand over his heart. But she wasn't swayed and she didn't smile. "What would we have to do for it to work?" he asked gently.

"Lose our minds."

"Lou, come on. It's the easiest solution you've got. Why not take it?"

"Maybe I'm tired of you cleaning up my messes, Gavin."

"Have I ever complained?" Not once. He'd clean up a million of her messes without one complaint. "I'm going to bring Em in if you don't agree. I'll tell her about your grandmother contacting your father."

The steps she'd retreated she immediately retraced, violence all over her expression. "I'll kill you first."

"You really think she's not going to find out? That your grandma won't tell her, or that you'll be able to keep it bottled up? Lou, come on. Be reasonable."

Lou whirled away and slapped her hands on the long worktable. Then she simply stood there, her ragged breathing the only sound in the barn.

He wanted to *ease* this for her, but if he told her that, with the bald emotion coursing through him, she'd only shut down further. Unfortunately, when it came to Lou, sometimes retreat was the only viable option.

He didn't touch her, though that was what he wanted to do. Instead, he slid the sandwich in front of her. "Think about it."

"No."

"Fine. Lose the ranch and your life's work." He had to focus to make sure his voice was even and casual and didn't include the hint of temper that was beginning to light. "If you change your mind, you know where to find me."

With that, he forced himself to leave the barn and head back to the Tyler Ranch, where he'd take orders from his mother and older brother and feel about as useful as a legless horse.

You could marry me.

The words haunted Lou for *two* days. Two long, obnoxious, frustrating days. Worse, so much worse, Gavin didn't show. She spent two days waiting for his usual daily check-in, so she could give him a piece of her mind, and he didn't come.

She was furious with him. If only that fury didn't feel a lot like wanting to cry. But she didn't cry. No, she'd learned young not to show that kind of weakness.

She looked down at the pictures she'd arranged on her inspiration board. She had to admit she didn't care for the bride's taste, but that was part of the fun of doing wedding flowers. The challenge of making something she could be proud of that a picky bride would like too.

This one was certainly going to be a challenge.

She'd had to close the door against the chill of an early spring afternoon, so when it slid open with a quiet screech of metal against metal, she glanced up.

Her sister slid inside the space she'd opened, then closed the door behind her. "Jeez, it's freezing in here. You need to talk to Gavin about getting some sort of heating system."

The mention of Gavin killed the smile at seeing her sister. Gavin was her closest friend aside from Em, but having to take help from him over and over again this year had made that relationship far more complicated. She didn't like feeling beholden to him, worse when he never tried to make her feel so.

"He might be handy, but I don't think he's heating system handy. Besides, the flowers need the cool temperatures."

Em walked over and put her hand on top of Lou's. "You're ice."

"I'm used to it," she replied. "So, what brings you out? Has your nagging-Lou quota run low?"

"Desperately low," Em returned, straight-faced, as she plopped herself on the stool Lou rarely used. She preferred to stand when she worked.

Em pulled her coat collar closer around her face. "So, give me the Grandma update."

"Handled."

"Give me the Grandma update," Em repeated firmly.

"There is no update because I'm handling this." She looked at Em, trying to perfect a big-sister, don't-you-dare-question-me glare.

"This isn't a *you* problem, Lou. Grandma making unreasonable demands is *our* problem. We're in this together. Always."

It was nice Em thought so, but Lou didn't want this bleeding over into her sister's life. "I'm going to handle it. The flower farm and keeping it is my problem. Don't you have the same bridezilla I do? You should be working on your cake design. She'll have you change it five more times."

"I'm not letting you change the subject to work. I came over to discuss a few ideas I've come up with to deal with Grandma's current bout of insanity."

"We've exhausted every idea. It's been, what? Four months since she made this proclamation?" Lou wasn't a big fan of feeling hopeless, but four months of beating their heads against this impossible situation hadn't changed anything. And Grandma was starting to talk to Dad. Lou had overheard a phone conversation just last night. Grandma didn't seem to be mentioning the ranch to him yet, but she was talking to him, and that was bad, bad news.

They were running out of time. It felt inevitable she would have to face that man again, and she wasn't sure how she was going to do it. But she sure knew it fit in with the year she'd been having. Losing Grandpa. The fire. Dad seemed the only natural next step in the year of horror.

"I'm not giving up, Lou. I know she's been talking to Dad. She made sure I knew."

Lou winced. She'd been so sure she'd be able to keep it from Em, but Gavin had been right. Of course he'd been right.

"Dad is not getting his hands on this. He's not coming here."

Lou looked at Em, trying to find some semblance of her big-sister control. But Em stood there looking like Instagram come to life in her floral dress and bright knit tights and a purse in the shape of a cupcake.

She had her own problems, her adorable little sister. It wasn't easy to make a bakery successful in a small town, even with the strides Gracely had made to lure businesses and citizens alike.

Em didn't need to be worrying about this. She needed to be worrying about her business and her bottom line.

"If Dad comes—"

"Dad isn't coming," Em said firmly. "Look, I know we tried the Gavin-as-manager route and that didn't work, but that doesn't mean Gavin isn't the answer to our problems."

Gavin Tyler. Why did everything always have to come back to him these days? "Gavin is not the answer to our problems." The very thought made her itchy from the inside out.

"She wants one of us married. Married to a man who will ranch the land and take care of it like Grandpa did. So, I can ask Gavin to marry me for a bit."

She couldn't believe her sister had come up with almost the exact same plan Gavin had. "Did Gavin say something to you?"

Em's brow furrowed. "About what?"

Because her sister wasn't much of a liar, Lou could only believe her sister was as brain damaged as Gavin. "You can't be serious. You can't marry Gavin. Not for a bit, and not . . . at all." An ugly burn of something settled in her gut. Something she wouldn't analyze too closely, though the idea of Gavin and Em getting married . . .

"Grandma might buy it. We dated in high school, and Gavin's a good guy. It wouldn't be the first time he helped me out. He could take over the manager role, and we could get the ownership thing sorted.

Then he and I could get divorced and deed everything to you."

"No." Lou clutched the table in front of her and squeezed her eyes shut. It was out of the question because it wasn't Em's problem to solve, and the acrid burn of whatever it was twisting in her gut was just worry. Fear.

"Lou, the only other option is . . ." Em trailed off. "Lou," she said gravely, resting her hand on Lou's shoulder. "I've been doing some research on getting someone declared . . . incompetent."

Lou gasped. It might have been an overreaction, but she couldn't imagine her sweet-hearted sister even *thinking* such a thing, let alone researching it. She stepped away from Em's hand.

"We'd need a lawyer," Em said, clasping her hands together. "Some money to pay a lawyer, but we both know she isn't right."

"She saved us," Lou replied, because what else was there to say? They couldn't hurt Grandma that way, the woman who'd given them a life when theirs had fallen apart.

"I know she did. Now she's threatening to bring Dad here. So, maybe we need to get her help."

"Not like that."

"Lou."

"No, you can't. You can't do that to her. She's lost Grandpa and . . . You couldn't. *I* couldn't. We can try to get her to see she needs help, but I will not use some scummy lawyer to get around her. I couldn't live with myself. Could you?" Her breathing was labored, but she watched her sister. Forced herself to stay in the moment.

"If it helped you," Em said solemnly.

Lou wanted to throw up, or cry, or just give up,

but she'd come too far in life to do any of those things. "We won't do that to her. It isn't right."

"Then I'll talk to Gavin about marrying me."

"No. No, not you." She squeezed her eyes shut again. It couldn't be Em. It just couldn't.

"I don't have to listen to you. I can do whatever I need to do to make sure this doesn't happen."

"You're not going to marry Gavin." Lou let out a sigh and opened her eyes and stared at her sister. She couldn't believe this was her life, but that had been a pretty common feeling since the fire. "I will."

Chapter Two

Gavin kicked his feet up onto the porch railing of the Tyler house. Something he could only do because his mother was with Ben at their bizarre square dancing club. Deb Tyler did not like boots on her railing.

But Deb Tyler wasn't home.

His younger brother, Boone, mimicked his pose, sipping on a bottle of beer. Something that also would not be allowed if Mom was within a hundred or so yards.

"What must it be like to live like this on an everyday basis? Being thirty and not having to follow my mother's rules?"

"But then you wouldn't be eating your mother's cooking, and that is quite the tradeoff," Boone said with some uncharacteristic goodwill toward home.

Gavin shrugged. "I'd have a pretty wife to cook for me."

Boone snorted. "What's stopping you? Oh right. That ugly mug."

Gavin raised his middle finger at his brother, but mostly he sat back and enjoyed the sound of spring peepers on a pretty spring evening.

"Didn't go see Lou again today," Boone offered casually.

"And here I thought only Shane kept tabs on me."

"Don't have to keep tabs on you to notice your obnoxious mouth is around more than usual."

Gavin chose not to say anything to that and sipped his beer instead.

"What happened? You two have a little tiff?"

Gavin raised his eyebrow at his brother. "Did you want to gossip? You'll have to call up Lindsay. She'd be happy to giggle over boys with you even if she and Cal are all but living together now." Quite the thing, his oldest and youngest siblings happily attached. He couldn't quite work out the emotion that lodged inside his chest. Not exactly bad, not exactly good.

Boone snorted and pulled his hat lower on his head. "Hell no I don't want to gossip. Just making conversation."

"Watch out. I hear that's catching. The next thing you know, you'll be meddling in everyone else's life like Mom."

It was Boone's turn to flip Gavin off, but instead of a retort, the sound of a car engine broke through the quiet evening. Both brothers moved up their hats and squinted down the dusky drive, ready to jump out of their chairs and hide evidence of beers on the porch if Mom was home early.

"Is that Lou?" Boone asked.

Gavin relaxed back into his chair, being careful not to smile or let an ounce of his triumph show. Boone would jump all over triumph, no matter what he claimed about not wanting to gossip. Bad enough he'd noticed Gavin hadn't made his usual trip over to the Fairchild Ranch the past few days.

But deep, deep down, he was grinning because the only reason Lou was driving up the Tyler drive was to take him up on his offer.

Probably something a little warped in being happy

about a woman agreeing to fake-marry him, but he wanted to help. A bone-deep need he couldn't ignore.

This would help. Both of them.

"Appears to be," Gavin offered casually.

"Something going on there?"

Gavin shrugged. Until he knew how Lou wanted to play this, he figured he'd let Boone draw his own conclusions. If they suited his purposes later, he'd use them, and if they didn't, he'd tell his little brother he was an idiot.

Win-win.

"What's that mean?"

"It means go find something else to do," Gavin replied, getting to his feet as Lou stopped her truck and hopped out.

She looked pissed. Which was another sign she was going to accept his help. He was under no illusions Lou Fairchild would ever take help gracefully or gratefully. Why he liked that about her, he'd never fully understand.

She stomped up the stairs, all thunder and lightning. She had her gloves on and the bandanna strapped over the burn scars on the right side of her face, and he tried very, very hard not to smile at her.

"I need to talk to you. Alone," she ground out.

"What can you say to Gavin that you can't say in front of me, gorgeous?" Boone drawled from his seat.

"Fuck off, Boone. And scram."

"If you haven't noticed, I'm not the ten-year-old you can order around anymore."

Gavin rolled his eyes. "If you two are done?" He nodded toward the stables closest to the house. "We can go talk there."

"Fine," Lou huffed, immediately stalking that way.

"She's going to eat you alive," Boone said as Gavin strolled away.

"Don't count me out just yet." He walked at a much slower pace than Lou, and by the time he reached the stables, she was pacing the length of the middle, not even paying attention to the horses who stuck their heads over their doors looking for treats.

"I'm surprised to see you here."

"Are you?" she retorted, stopping her pacing and fisting her hands on her hips while she glared at him.

"Doesn't seem like you've left your place much that didn't involve wedding stuff since Christmas."

The glare melted into something like surprise, and then she started pacing again. "Why do you always notice stuff like that?" she muttered.

"Because I'm your friend and I pay attention."

"I'm your friend and I don't pay attention."

Gavin feigned a yawn and took a seat on one of the stools in the corner. "Yeah, that's why you brought soup over when I had the flu in February."

Her jaw dropped. "My . . . my grandmother did that," she stuttered. "Made the soup, that is, and told me to bring it over."

"Sure."

She made a humph sound as she crossed her arms over her chest. She was quiet for a few minutes, standing with her back to him. "You have to know this is my absolute last resort. And if I come up with anything, and I mean anything, before we actually . . . do it, I will take that opportunity."

"Sounds good to me."

She whirled, flinging her hands up into the air. "How can we actually do this? It's insane."

"We'll hardly be the first people to marry for reasons other than . . ." For some reason, the word *love* stuck in his throat. ". . . the normal marriage reasons." He frowned at her. "You're here, basically telling me you're agreeing to my help. You've made your decision, so why are you still trying to talk yourself out of it?"

"Because it's crazy. And insane. I don't want to do it and—"

"So why are you going to?"

She stopped. Inhaled and exhaled and kept whatever it was all bottled up. She'd always done that to an extent, but it was hard not to notice how much the cracks showed these days. She'd been through the gauntlet, so he understood it, but that didn't mean it didn't poke at him to see her struggling so much.

"Em suggested . . ." She blew out another breath, and something like a shudder went through her. She looked at the floor as she said the next words. "She suggested having us legally declare Grandma incompetent."

"Christ. You can't do that."

"I . . ." She turned away, and he knew she was struggling with composure. Which just about broke him in half, especially knowing Lou would rather saw her good arm off than cry in front of him.

He got off the stool and gently took her by the shoulders. She tried to angle her bad shoulder away from him, but he held firm enough. He knew it didn't hurt her because she'd reamed him out for being afraid to touch her a few months after the accident. If he remembered her exact words, they were something like *I may be burned, but I'm not ash that'll blow away, jackass.*

Slowly, he turned her around to face him, though she kept her chin to her chest. "Hey."

"Gavin, don't—"

"Hey," he repeated firmly, and he didn't let her go.

She didn't look at him, but that was okay. She didn't need to see his face to hear the truth in his words.

"There's no ideal solution to this, I get that, but there are a lot worse ones. So. Hang on to that. I'm going to help you out, and that's all it is. A friend helping a friend. No need for wailing and dramatic rending of garments. It could be worse."

Her head whipped up to glare at him and he smiled, because she was ever predictable, and that was a great comfort sometimes.

"I am not wailing," she said through clenched teeth.

He only smiled wider, still holding her shoulders. "Come for a ride with me."

She glanced at the lineup of horses warily. She hadn't ridden much since the fire, but before that, she used to do it as much as time allowed. Either with him or his sister, Molly. Her grandparents had gotten rid of the horses at the Fairchild Ranch in favor of four wheelers once her grandfather had been a little too feeble to get up on one and they'd been afraid he'd do it anyway. So, she'd come over to the Tyler Ranch to get her horse fix.

Until the past year. "Come on. You know you want to. Besides, it'll get everyone talking."

"We don't have to fool everyone." Her eyebrows furrowed. "We won't fool everyone. We're not that good at pretending."

"Maybe not, but we should probably try. I'm not sure my mother would approve, and if she didn't, she might tell your grandma. You know how they are. Best to let everyone think we've gone crazy for real."

Lou pressed fingers to the temple not covered by the bandanna. "Gavin, I . . ."

"Come riding," he insisted, giving her a little shake. "You know you miss it."

She blew out a breath and then pushed him away so he had to drop her shoulders. "Fine," she muttered. "Fine. You win."

Gavin could only grin in triumph.

She hadn't been on a horse in something like a year. First, there'd been the physical discomfort as her burns healed. Then, she'd developed a fear of losing her bandanna if she went too fast. Because she didn't have any horses at home to ride by herself, she just couldn't . . .

She didn't want Molly or Gavin to see her scars. It wasn't that she thought they'd treat her differently. It had been a year since the fire, and they *did* treat her differently, but not as badly as she'd thought they would. Not in the *ways* she'd thought they would.

Still, she hated the idea of anyone seeing what she saw in the mirror. She couldn't explain that feeling or rationalize it away, so she just didn't let it happen.

But here, surrounded by horses, the bone-deep *missing* of being on horseback on top of everything else she was dealing with overrode her good sense, and she worked with Gavin to saddle two horses.

"Ready?"

She nodded, taking the reins of Molly's favorite horse, Bodine. On a deep breath, Lou got up on the horse, surprised at how easy it felt for her body to move through the motions of mounting the horse after a year not doing it.

She sat in the saddle, reins in her hands, and something truly peaceful washed over her for the first time in a long time.

She glanced at Gavin, who'd gotten on his horse, Sullivan. He grinned at her. "Don't forget to pace yourself. You're liable to have forgotten everything you know about horse riding," he offered, and then he urged Sullivan into a run.

Lou laughed in spite of herself, and then urged her horse into a run as well. She hadn't forgotten *anything* about what it was like to ride, and fast. She had a second of worry about her bandanna, then went ahead and forgot all about it. She had a spare in her back pocket. If she lost this one, she could replace it somewhere away from Gavin before he saw her.

So, she let it all go, and she couldn't remember the last time she'd done that. Let her mind fly with the wind, weighed down by none of the things she should hold on to. But it felt so *good* to gallop across the beautiful Tyler Ranch, mountains in the distance, cattle dotting the just-starting-to-green grass, with absolutely nothing crowding her brain except *joy*.

She'd had a rough, shitty year, but by God, she got to live here, and that was something to be grateful for.

Gavin pulled his horse to a stop at the gate that separated their properties. Lou slowed down a few yards away from him, holding the reins with one hand and readjusting her bandanna with the other.

He sat on his horse, looking at the sunset blaze the mountains a fiery orange, but Lou took a second to look at him. Him, who was offering her a way out of this crap situation she was in, but she had to pretend to be *married* to him. To Gavin Tyler. One of her closest friends since she'd been a scrappy mess of a nine-year-old and he'd sat next to her in their fourth-grade class and laughed every time she was mean to him.

She'd eventually learned Gavin was genuine, and then the real problem had started. She'd hero worshipped him, and hated herself a little for elevating anyone that way. But it was just . . . true. He had this amazing, gigantic family. He fought for what was right, maybe a little too quickly sometimes, but he always fought. He always protected. He was the best, strongest man she'd ever known.

Which was why Rex had always held more appeal in their middle and high school trio. Rex didn't have that same core of goodness Gavin did. He'd had an edge she'd recognized, and so it had made sense to date Rex. Keep Gavin firmly in friend territory.

It was the only place he could ever belong, and yet now she was going to marry him. Even if it wasn't going to be a real marriage, it would be a legal one. She'd have to pretend for her grandma. For his mother. Jesus. Deb Tyler could smell a rat a mile away.

There were no other options.

She was going to have to look at Gavin in his faded cowboy hat, the crooked nose, brawler's face, and tall, rangy body, and pretend he was someone other than her friend. She was going to have to look into his dark eyes and smile and feign *love.* The romantic kind. Not the friend kind.

And he would grin that awful grin, and how was this ever going to work?

"You gonna stay over there all night?" Gavin called across the distance.

There was some odd flutter in her chest warning her she should. Keep some distance. Put a very careful fence around Gavin. Just like way back when, when she'd agreed to date Rex, when she'd *loved* Rex, when she'd, if she was being 100 percent honest with herself, used Rex as a buffer between all the weird adult things she'd felt when it came to Gavin.

Rex had been simple. Even him being part of the reason she'd been burned had been simple. He was a self-absorbed asshat who could be manipulated into just about anything. Including blaming her for his lying, cheating, self-absorbed asshat ways enough to help set a fire that could have killed her.

But Gavin, oh Gavin Tyler had never been simple, even back in the fourth grade.

She'd spent twenty years handling that complexity, though, hadn't she? It was all under-the-radar complexity anyway. On the surface, Gavin was simple enough. He was who he was, and there was no reason to be timid. Wary of his help? Always. But never timid.

She encouraged Bodine to trot over next to Gavin and Sullivan.

"Felt good, didn't it? The ride?"

She glanced away from Gavin's self-satisfied grin, leaning forward to run her fingers over Bodine's mane. She rested her cheek against the horse's neck and just *breathed* for a moment. "Yeah, it did."

"Don't you know by now I'm always right?"

She snorted. "You're no Deb Tyler, Gav."

He maneuvered Sullivan to face back toward the Tyler house, so she did the same with Bodine.

"Race?" he offered casually.

"Going to play fair?"

He flashed one of those grins she'd never really figured out, if only because her reaction to them didn't make any sense. That flutter again, a little giddiness mixed with a whole heap of foreboding.

"Never, darling." Then he was off like a shot, urging Sullivan to fly across the rolling path between pasture and stables.

It was silly to do the same, urge Bodine to speed across the ground they'd covered. He had a head start. She'd never win.

But she tried anyway, and she laughed while she did

it. When she pulled to a stop in front of the stables, he'd already gotten off his horse. He held out a hand to her.

"I don't need help down," she said, insulted.

"I know," he returned, not pulling his hand back. He nodded toward the Tyler house. "Everyone's watching."

She glanced at the wraparound porch on the glossy Tyler cabin, about three times the size of the ramshackle house back home. A majority of Gavin's family was assembled in chairs or on the railing or standing. They were all definitely watching. "We don't . . ." She swallowed. "We don't have to try to fool them." She didn't think they could, and somehow she was more afraid to try than fail.

But Gavin was never on the same page as her on that.

"It wouldn't hurt to try. One of them is liable to blab. Best keep it all on the down low."

"Em knows," she said, feeling so damn foolish and conflicted and wishing there were any way out of this. But then she thought of Em offering herself to marry Gavin and worse, it really was worse, talking about declaring Grandma incompetent and . . . well.

She let Gavin help her down, most of the happiness of the ride fading. She had troubles, real worries, and Gavin's hands were resting firmly on her hips. Gavin Tyler.

They didn't stand like this. They didn't touch gently, ever. It was all slaps and shoves and . . .

"It's going to be okay, Lou," he said, a gentle, reassuring smile on his face as he stood too close. Gentle was not Gavin, but he'd shown her an ocean of gentleness in the past year. Now he was making promises with those words, and the worst part was knowing he thought so, understanding he thought he could promise to fix her world for her because that was who Gavin was.

He'd never in a million years fully understand how unfixable she was. Before or after that horrible fire and these hideous scars.

But for a little while, she had to pretend, and hope it didn't break her even more.

Chapter Three

"So, what was all that stuff with Lou about?"

Gavin looked up from where he stood in the kitchen next to the coffeepot. Shane didn't drink coffee. A fact that never failed to baffle Gavin. How did anyone face sunrise without caffeine?

Not only was caffeine a necessary, life-sustaining elixir of survival, not having had it yet gave him an excellent excuse not to fully engage with what Shane was saying. He yawned, he watched the trickle of liquid slowly fill the coffee maker's carafe, and he expressly ignored Shane's question.

"I think Mom was on the phone to Mrs. Fairchild before Lou was even off that horse."

"Then why don't you go jack your jaw at Mom?"

"It was a simple question," Shane returned mildly, moving over to the sink, where he filled up his water bottle.

"It's a dumb question." Gavin was glad Shane was asking it, even more glad Mom had called Lou's grandma last night. That was all part of his plan. Make everybody buy into it.

But he hadn't anticipated this odd coil of unease

winding through him. Last night he'd had no problem putting on a show in front of his family. He'd lingered with Lou, lingered with his hands on her hips.

Hips.

She'd watched him warily, and that thread of vulnerability that made him itch was underneath it. She'd stood very still and very stiff.

And his hands had rested on her hips. Lou was just about as tall as him, sturdy. She wouldn't care for that descriptor, but it was partly in the way she held herself. Like she could take on the world while hefting all the other planets on her shoulders.

But he'd had his hands on her hips, the soft feminine flair, and she'd felt something other than sturdy. Very nearly soft. Very nearly warm.

Then he'd met that wary, vulnerable blue gaze, and there'd been a simple moment of forgetting what he was really after.

Not her—that ship had sailed years ago—but her ranch, and to do his friend a favor.

The touching was going to be a problem, for both of them, but it had to be done. Just like he'd decided to head inside after she'd left, avoiding his family as if he didn't want to talk to them about what they'd seen.

Acting squirrelly and embarrassed, touchy over it, that would definitely convince his family this was legit. Maybe get a little pissy when they inevitably asked about it today.

Lou'd voiced concerns that Mom would see through it, and normally, he would have agreed. His mother had an eagle eye, and an intuition that rivaled some kind of witch. There were very few things he'd gotten past his mother in thirty years on this planet.

But Mom also thought he had a decades' old thing

for Lou. It *could* cloud her usually very clear judgment just enough.

Shane had finished filling up his water bottle and taken one of the muffins Grandma Maisey had baked last night. He was watching Gavin fill up his thermos with coffee, so Gavin scowled at him.

"Don't you have a pretty wife to go stare at instead of me?"

"What's really going on, Gav? I know she hasn't been herself since the fire, but the fact she didn't deck you when you helped her down from that horse is downright pod-people territory."

"Lou's never decked me."

"You know what I mean. She didn't argue or even give you a shove. Something's going on. Fess up."

"Nothing is going on," Gavin said, a weird mix of success over making Shane suspect something and that dissatisfied itchy feeling digging deeper in his gut.

Shane's expression went considering, almost soft, like he was about to have some horrifying heart-to-heart moment.

Thank God Cora walked into the kitchen at that moment.

"Thought you were going to sleep in," Shane said, that soft, contemplative expression turning soft for an entirely different reason.

Gavin grimaced.

"Mm." Cora smiled right back, and it really wasn't fair his brother got the ranch and the pretty wife and all that went with it. "Couldn't fall back asleep," she said, crossing over to where Shane stood by the sink.

They shared a disgustingly *suggestive* look and then started moving their mouths closer together.

Gavin groaned. "Do you two *mind*? I'm right here."

Cora slowly turned her head to stare at him, then raised an eyebrow. "So you are." Then she very purposefully kissed Shane full on the mouth.

Gavin grunted and screwed the lid of his thermos on as he strode for the hallway. On a good day he couldn't stand watching his brother be all touchy-feely with his wife, and he wasn't quite sure why, but this morning didn't feel like a particularly good day.

Not bad. He was just edgy, and that wasn't all that abnormal. Constantly having to follow his brother's orders was a pain in the ass, and some mornings it really chafed that he'd been born just a year and a half too late to be considered the head of the family.

Anything else was just . . . just . . .

"Gavin. Wait."

Gavin stopped at the front door as Cora hurried to catch up with him. She was dressed for the day in one of her frilly outfits that meant she had wedding planning meetings to attend. Though her feet were bare and she hadn't painted her face yet.

"So, what's going on with Lou?" she asked, though it didn't have the same demand to it that Shane's question had.

"Shane's got you doing his dirty work already?"

"Dirty work?" Cora wrinkled her nose. "What dirty work?"

"Asking me about Lou. Like I told him—"

Cora waved her hand. "I don't care what you told him. I'm trying to figure out how you got her up on that horse, and wondering when you can do it again."

"Huh?"

"I know you've been friends with her way longer than I have, but it doesn't mean I don't worry. Even in the past few months she's gotten . . . Well, I don't have to tell you. I've barely seen her leave the ranch. She's bowed out on pizza I don't know how many times. How did you get through to her? Off the ranch *and* riding?"

Cora looked up at him expectantly, like there was some magic answer besides: rock bottom. Because he was pretty sure her agreeing to marry him, even for pretend, was Lou Fairchild's absolute rock bottom.

He tried to shrug the odd weight that attached itself to his shoulders. "I don't know. Guess I just wore her down."

Cora studied him, that squinty-eyed study the females in this family seemed to have. Apparently, the whole marrying Shane and changing her last name to Tyler had turned her into a Tyler woman.

God help Shane. God help all of them.

"Well, if I can facilitate anything that might help her get out more, just let me know," Cora finally said. "And if you could give my son a particularly vile chore today to make up for the fact he ate the last of your grandmother's cookies, I'd very much appreciate it."

"The oatmeal chocolate chip with the orange junk?" Gavin asked, feigning horror. Micah would no doubt have Grandma making a new batch before the day was out, Grandma was so tickled to have a stepgreat-grandson to inflict her strange pet squirrel and horrifying sword collection on.

"The very ones. He ate the last *ten.*"

"His ass is grass."

"Thank you," Cora said, giving Gavin's arm a little pat. "I better go finish getting ready, but like I said, if there's anything you think I could do to help Lou out, please let me know."

"Sure thing."

Cora retreated, and Gavin grabbed his hat off the hook, settling it low on his head before he stepped out into the cool spring morning.

Beyond the brownish roll of land with hints of green that made up most of the ranch, the earth began to move, expand, grow. Slowly, it rose up out of the ground, turning stony and determined to reach the sky. Today puffy clouds tinged pink and the mountains seemed to glow in that pearly dawn life.

It wasn't his. He'd known that his whole life, even before Dad died. When he'd been just a kid, Gavin had felt somewhere inside him that this wasn't his to have.

He glanced to the west, still dusky in places the sun hadn't reached yet. Fairchild property there over the ridge.

Maybe it wasn't his either. Maybe nothing was, but that didn't mean he wasn't going to fight for *something* to be.

Lou usually waited for summer to take naps with her flowers. She'd sprawl out in the rows of tall sunflowers or sturdy foxglove, shaded from the sun, and grab a few minutes of relaxation.

There wasn't any other place she'd rather be, any other place she could completely let her guard down and just . . . *be.*

It was too cold today, and none of the tiny sprouts were big enough to shade her from anything. But it was cloudy anyway, and hell if she wasn't tired.

She hadn't gotten a wink of sleep last night. She didn't like lying. Keeping things to herself was one thing, but straight-out lying had been her downfall since she'd been a little girl.

Where's your daddy, sweetheart?

He goes away a lot.

Did you see your daddy with this woman?

Yeah. They fight.

How do they fight?

Yelling and stuff.

Can you tell me what kind of stuff?

Hitting sometimes.

She could see the two policemen in her mind's eye. She hadn't been afraid of them like her father had always told her to be, because she'd seen a TV show with a nice policeman, and this one reminded her of the man on the show.

When they'd told her she had to come with them, it had been a relief. She'd wanted someone nice to help them. It was too hard to keep Em from crying all the time, and she didn't like changing poopy diapers. Sometimes she didn't feel very good, and Em would just cry and cry and cry.

What about Em? She's only little. She needs a car seat.

She remembered the looks on the cops' faces, and at this point she was sure she'd never forget. She hadn't had the word for it at four, but she had the word for it now. Horror.

They'd been horrified and taken her and Em away. The first time. The other times had been . . .

She moved her bandanna so it was completely over her entire face, as if she could block the old memories out. But that was the problem with this whole thing. It reminded her too much of all the ways she'd never been any good at lying.

How the truth always seemed to hurt everyone around her.

She inhaled the rich scent of earth, focused on the

cold damp that was seeping into her back. She placed her good, ungloved hand on the turned earth of a row of sprouts. She pressed her fingers into the ground, feeling the soil in between her fingernails.

She breathed, slowly in and out, and let the land pour its promises into her.

Life goes on. Season by season. No matter what mistake you make, no matter what you lose, the sun will rise, the sun will set, and winter will come, then go.

If she messed up the lie, well, it might be embarrassing, but her flowers would still bloom. If Grandma insisted Dad come back to run this place and she lost—

No. She couldn't. She couldn't let Dad ruin this gift she'd been allowed, and she couldn't let anyone else get it either. She had to be the bloom that weathered the storm, which meant believing she could do this.

She heard a truck approach. Based on the time of day and the sound of the engine, she'd guess someone from the Tyler Ranch. Gavin or Molly, likely. Maybe Cora.

If something inside of her jittered like those old giddy nerves from high school, Lou was quite sure it was just worry about the whole lie-to-everyone thing.

She didn't get up off the ground, though she probably should. She could maybe explain herself to Molly or Cora, but Gavin would look at her like she was a little nuts, resting in the dirt.

She adjusted her bandanna and then looked up at the gray, moody sky. The sky had always been there, no matter where her life had taken her, and that was a great comfort. Almost as good as the land beneath her fingertips.

Footsteps sounded, closer and closer, until someone

was standing above her. She looked up, and up, because Gavin was tall, and though she was tall herself, she wasn't standing right now. She was laying down, her gaze traveling up the rangy body clad in boots, jeans, and a sweatshirt. His face was shaded by the beat-up Stetson, always pulled low on his head.

"I really don't think my grandma is going to buy this." Because he was fantasy cowboy and she was prickly burn victim. Her grandmother might not see all Lou's faults quite the way she did, but Grandma was a reasonable, practical woman. She'd see through this.

Gavin held out a hand and Lou reluctantly released the earth between her fingers to take it. He helped her to her feet and then didn't release her.

Instead, he angled his head just so, his eyes dancing with mischief. "I've got a few tricks up my sleeve." His eyes flicked toward the house. "Your grandma's watching."

"Wha—"

"Don't look," Gavin said, turning his body just so that he kept her from being able to see the house.

He was . . . close. Like feel-his-breath-against-her-cheek close.

"Think of this like planting seeds."

"Think of *what* like planting seeds?"

"The next few weeks. We can't go gung ho into let's get married. Everyone would see through that. A week or two we dance around, let people wonder. Then, once everyone is speculating, we get caught in a compromising situation."

Lou's face got immediately hot. "You . . . you've got this all planned out," she managed, though it sounded choked even to her own ears.

"Had a lot of time to think this morning." He glanced

at the house again. "Thought it'd take some work to get your grandma spying on us, but this is the perfect opportunity."

She didn't feel him move, but he was closer. Too close for normal human conversation, and when he tilted his head—she thought to meet her gaze under his hat—his chin just barely, *barely* grazed her cheek.

She was a grown woman. Certainly not a virgin or even all that shy with men. She'd seen too much to be too worried about appearances. But something about Gavin's face touching her face was unbearably intimate.

So much so that her body actually *trembled*, and all she could think to do was stare at him, wide-eyed and shocked into being completely frozen.

"Now, we're going to stand here, just like this, for a few seconds. You're going to look at me just like that, and I'm going to smile just like this, and in, say, thirty seconds or so, you're going to jolt away."

"Jolt away? What for?"

"Your grandmother isn't going to buy you woke up one day and suddenly realized twenty years' worth of love and devotion for me. We have to make it seem like it shocked us both. You have to be a little reticent."

"Why don't you have to be a little reticent? It's not like Grandma's going to think *you* woke up and were suddenly madly in love with me."

He shifted, though he kept his face so close to hers she could see the little patch of hair on his chin he'd missed shaving this morning. Short and dark and untouchable unless she was right here, staring at it.

"You know how people are," Gavin said. He'd stiffened a hair, something she might not have noticed if they were at a normal distance. But his voice was still casual. "Men and women can't ever be friends, blah, blah, blah. And you dated Rex. So, there's no wild speculation about you, because you were with someone else."

"You dated Em."

He cleared his throat. "Ah. Yeah, well, that was a long time ago. Jeez. High school." He lifted a hand and readjusted his hat, which created some new space between them. She almost felt as though she could breathe normally without . . . smelling him.

He smelled like spring rain in the distance, a scent she had tried to avoid labeling for most of her adult life, but there it was.

"You were with Rex for years and years."

Years and years. God, what a waste that had been.

"Anyway," he said, as if this whole conversation had taken him away from his point. "I'm going to move in, touch your face, and you're going to count to fifteen, then back away."

"All this acting seems . . . over the top."

"You want to play it a different way? I'm all ears."

But what different way was there to play it? Even though Gavin's reasons didn't make 100 percent sense to her, he was right about Grandma's suspicions. They had to take it slow and careful.

She hated the idea of pretending for Grandma. Lying to her. But for the time being, the only other option was trying to get Grandma declared incompetent, and that was by far worse than lying to her.

Or you could let Em do this thing with Gavin.

But it wasn't Em's flower farm. It wasn't Em's life here. It was Lou's. She'd been protecting her sister since she was a baby, and she wouldn't stop now.

Gavin's fingers brushed her cheek, almost like he

was wiping off a smudge. His fingers rough, the touch delicate, and then they simply *lingered* there, like last night, when his hands had held her hips like he had any business with his hands below her waist.

Now they were very much above and it had that same unsettling, the-world-is-upside-down swoop of something only a shade lighter than horror.

He angled his head again, this time tipping it so his hat brim hid most of their faces from the house.

When he spoke, it was a heated kind of whisper, a tone of voice she'd never heard come out of his mouth, because good Lord, she'd have remembered *that.*

"You forgot to count," he murmured, too close to her ear.

She did jump back at that. Not a pretend jump back either. A full-fledged bolt of panic down to the heart thundering in her chest and ears.

"Now, I'll step toward you and you'll turn your back on me and storm to your barn. That expression is *perfect.*"

She wanted to say, *well, it damn well should be because it's real.* But instead, she nodded and followed his directions.

He stepped toward her, and she turned around and marched for the barn. Once in the barn she walked straight for the sink and turned on the faucet. Moving her bandanna to the side and ignoring how cold the water was, she cupped her hands under the flow of water and splashed it on her face.

The bracing blow did exactly what she needed it to do: eradicated the lingering warmth from Gavin's touch and cleared her foggy brain.

The past year had been a shit sandwich, and she'd wallowed too much in taking every last bite. Well, that was over. She was taking control, starting here and now.

Which meant not letting Gavin Tyler take charge of her life and make her feel all topsy-turvy.

Not now. Not ever.

Chapter Four

A Tyler family dinner was never dull. Or quiet. Some days Gavin enjoyed the boisterousness of three generations at one table—well, now four with Cora's son joining them.

Micah was still acclimating to ranch life, or it could be that preteens always complained about early mornings and endless chores to be done. Gavin didn't remember complaining about it when he'd been Micah's age, but he didn't dare bring it up lest his mother correct him.

He'd rather remember himself a perfect, hardworking angel.

It was Friday, so along with the normal family members—Grandma, Mom and her husband Ben, Molly, Shane, Cora, Micah, and Boone—Lindsay and her boyfriend Cal also joined them.

A full house. Much as Gavin felt stifled by the fact that his mother and brother ran the ranch, he appreciated the Tyler house full to brimming. He couldn't imagine living like Lou did, with only her grandmother's constant company and the occasional visit from Em.

He'd be bored and lonely all the time.

"So," Molly said casually, which meant whatever she was about to say wasn't casual at all. He was closest in age with Molly, who was only eleven months younger than him, and while he'd say his friendship with Shane was his strongest sibling relationship, he and Molly got along the best. Shane was rigid and too high up on his I'm-the-oldest horse, Boone was antagonistic on a good day, and Lindsay was all drama, or had been. She'd mellowed lately, matured maybe, but Gavin still thought of her as the flighty, emotional teenager. He and Molly were more even-keeled. Until they got angry. He just happened to get angry a lot more than Molly.

"I talked to Lou's grandma today."

"How is Inez doing?" Mom asked. "I went and visited last week and she was awfully skinny."

"Well, we just ran into each other at Em's and she was eating a doughnut, so that's a good sign. Especially because it involved her being out and about and off the ranch. She was also quizzing me about Gavin."

All eyes at the table turned to him, except Micah's. The boy was busy inhaling Mom's biscuits. Gavin snatched one before they were all gone. Then he smiled blandly at his sister.

"About me?" He must have played the innocent card a little too heavily based on his mother's narrowing eyes, so he took a big bite of biscuit.

"She was just wondering if I'd noticed you spending more time than usual at the Fairchild place."

Gavin pretended to consider it. "I don't think any more so than usual. I go over around lunch time most days."

"I think I'd notice if he was spending more time over there," Shane added.

Gavin knew Shane was trying to stand up for him, but it grated nonetheless. He had to clamp his jaw shut to keep from reminding Shane he wasn't the keeper of Gavin's time.

"Why would it matter if he was?" Lindsay asked. "They probably need some help over there. Their ranch hand is married to one of the teachers I eat lunch with. She said Mrs. Fairchild is basically acting like she's closing up shop. He's started looking for a new job because he's afraid she's going to sell the place to developers, or one of those big ag conglomerates."

Gavin frowned. He wondered if Lou knew all that. The ranch had always been her grandfather's domain, though he was sure Mrs. Fairchild had a hand in things. But Em and Lou had been encouraged to do their own thing, and it was very possible Lou focused so much on her flowers she didn't have a clue what was going on with the ranch.

They were going to have to speed up their little plan if Mrs. Fairchild was really downsizing. He'd known Mrs. Fairchild had decreased the ranch stock significantly, but what other things might be cut back on by the time he got his hands on it?

It'd give him the opportunity to build from the ground up, and that wasn't so bad. Better for him if he could get in there sooner rather than later though.

"Well, maybe we can offer some help," Mom said. "Inez hasn't been herself since Martin passed. Understandable, especially with everything that's gone on with Lou. I've been more helping with meals and whatnot, but it hadn't occurred to me to send over help with the ranch when Inez has hands."

"I don't see why Gavin couldn't go over there and sort things out ranch wise," Lindsay suggested.

"I've tried. I offered to take over as ranch manager, but Mrs. Fairchild isn't big on the idea of a non-Fairchild running the place."

"You offered to take over as manager without discussing it with us first?" Shane demanded.

"Yes, because last time I checked, I'm an adult who gets to make my own decisions."

Shane sighed. "That wasn't what—"

"Let's focus on one thing at a time, boys," Mom said, emphasizing the word *boys* very purposefully. "We should find some way to help Inez."

"She doesn't want to be helped."

Mom frowned disapprovingly at him, but it was true. He'd tried to get through to Mrs. Fairchild. So had her granddaughters. Deb Tyler might be a miracle worker, but she wasn't going to magically swoop in and fix this.

"Em and Lou have both tried to get through to her."

"So, you're suggesting we just let her lose her ranch?" Mom said, her inflection making it sound like a question when it most definitely wasn't.

"What I'm suggesting is, we can't force Mrs. Fairchild to view the world any differently. So, we simply keep being there for all three of them best we can." Because he didn't need his mother meddling in this and screwing him out of his chance to be in charge of something.

It was completely selfish and probably made him something of a terrible person, but he couldn't bring himself to care right now. Not after Shane had bristled over him making some choices on his own.

He couldn't live like this for the rest of his life, chafing under Shane's thumb.

"Gavin isn't totally wrong," Cora offered, earning

her some surprised looks from around the table. Mostly from her husband. "I know I don't know the Fairchilds as well as you do, but I do know something about other people trying to fix things for you. There are some things you have to fix yourself. Having people try to do it for you doesn't always actually help."

"We could invite them over for dinner," Molly suggested. "All three of them. Get Inez and Lou off the ranch and Em away from her bakery for a night where we take care of everything. It doesn't change their circumstances, but maybe drawing them out of their hiding places will remind them they have friends they can turn to for help. And if we end up talking about the ranch, well, it might give us an opportunity to talk about how we could help without them feeling like we're meddling."

Mom nodded. "That's an excellent idea. Can you figure out a day that'll work for all three of them?"

"I'll get it all sorted tomorrow."

They spent the rest of dinner talking about schedules and what days would work best. Micah was forced by his mother to share his day. Boone was badgered about seeing a doctor from just about everyone until he stormed off before dessert was even served.

Gavin might have found it funny if Mom didn't look so worried, and he had the oddly illuminating thought that Mom might be focusing on the Fairchilds because ever since Boone had come home from the rodeo circuit last year, beaten to hell and back by a bull, no one had been able to get through to him.

No, a Tyler dinner was *never* dull.

When they scattered after dinner, Gavin trailed after Molly and stopped her before she could go upstairs to her room.

"Hey, I can figure out a night for the Fairchilds to come out if you've got lessons tomorrow."

Molly narrowed her eyes. It was freaky when she looked that much like Mom. "What's really going on?"

He raised an eyebrow. *"On?"* he asked as dismissively as he could manage.

She fisted her hands on her hips. "Don't play dumb. There's something weird going on with you and the Fairchilds and I want to know what."

"Well, last time I checked it wasn't any of your business."

Her frown deepened, but her voice wasn't so much irritated as it was laced with concern. "I'm worried about my friend, Gavin."

Which grated even if it shouldn't. *Second fiddle to the friend.* "Well, then, go ask your *friend.*"

Molly blew out a breath. "I know you care about her, Gav. I know you want to . . . I don't know, help her or whatever. But you should be careful with whatever it is you're doing. I don't want to see either of you get hurt. Lou's still healing, and you . . ."

"And I what?" Gavin demanded, temper snapping.

"You've always had a soft spot for her," Molly said, her voice quiet and grave, and worse, gentle. "Lou's got too much on her plate to worry about hurting your soft spot. So, I'm saying, be careful with whatever it is you've got up your sleeve. For both your sakes."

Because she was being . . . Well, concerned rather than high-handed, worried about both him and Lou rather than just her or just him . . . He kind of wanted to tell Molly it was all an act to help Lou secure her land. That he was helping her and selfishly getting something he wanted. He wanted to confide in his sister because he valued her opinion on such things.

But the more people knew, the more they risked.

So, he did what he always did: flashed a lopsided grin and made an off-handed comment that would irritate the person trying to offer him some help. "I'll keep it under advisement, Mol." He sauntered away, ignoring her muttered curses at him.

When Lou heard a truck approach early in the morning, she assumed it would be Gavin. She ignored the jitters in her stomach and the need to rush to see if it was him and kept focused on her work.

She'd woken up to three emails from her current client with three new ideas. Lou didn't mind the difficult brides too much. They were frustrating, but she understood they just wanted their day to be special.

She really wished Pinterest would die in a fire, though.

All more important thoughts than what Gavin's next step would be on the whole convince-everyone-they-were-getting . . . closer. A shiver went through her. A foreboding one, she was sure.

"Knock, knock."

At the female voice Lou whipped around, frowning at the sight of Molly Tyler in her doorway. She looked around Molly, trying to see if Gavin was maybe behind her, but there only seemed to be Molly. "Molly. Hi."

Molly frowned. "Expecting someone else?"

"No," Lou replied, too quickly.

"You seem to be looking for someone else, and a little frowny that it's me."

"I'm always frowny."

Molly laughed good-naturedly. "Fair enough." She entered the barn and poked around like she usually did when she stopped by. Which was fairly common place. Molly focused more on riding lessons than working at the Tyler Ranch, so her hours were a little bit more flexible. She often came over for no reason, just to hang out.

But this felt different.

Still, Lou did what she always did. Focused on her work and let Molly guide the conversation.

"I have to admit I came over because I'm worried about you."

"What else is new?" Lou grumbled. Twenty years of nosy Tylers and she was used to it. It had certainly taken some time to trust, but she did these days. Even when she didn't expressly want their worry or care, she believed it came from a good place.

Sometimes she wished she could be like Em. Em was warm and kind. She knew how to deal with people worrying over her. She knew how to set people at ease.

"This time I'm not just worried about how you're doing, though there's always that. I'm worried about what's going on."

"Nothing is going on," Lou said resolutely. Because if something *was* going on with Gavin, she would say that. Deny it. Because she had to pretend like something was going on.

She wanted to beat her head against her table. Instead, she kept working on a demo for the new boutonniere design the bride wanted, an overly complicated sprig of evergreen and berries that didn't match a spring wedding at all, but who was Lou to say? It wasn't her wedding.

Was she really going to have to go through with a wedding with Gavin?

God, she could *not* think about that. She had to pay attention to whatever Molly was going on about. She'd assumed the question was geared toward Gavin, but she was saying something about . . . jobs?

"Who's looking for a new job?"

"Wow, you're more distracted than usual. I'll come back to that, but Lindsay said Gene is looking for a new position because he thinks your grandmother is getting ready to sell."

Lou fumbled with the wire cutter she'd been using to cut wire to arrange the berries. She whirled around to fully face Molly. "He can't do that. She isn't doing that."

"Are you sure?"

"She's not going to sell," Lou said firmly. Though she wondered . . . But Grandma wouldn't lie to her. She wouldn't claim she was going to have to bring Dad in only to sell. "She has other plans. That are no more appealing, but . . . No. He can't . . . I'll talk with him." How on earth was she going to bring this up with Gene?

Rumor is you're ditching us in our time of need. Grandpa would be so proud. Except as much as Grandpa had done a lot for Gene over the years, Gene wasn't family. He was an employee. Maybe a friend, but he didn't owe the Fairchild women anything with the future so uncertain and him needing to take care of his family.

"I don't understand why she won't hire Gavin to run things," Molly said casually.

Lou didn't buy the casual, but she shrugged. "I don't either. I know she likes Gavin, trusts him and your family. I know he'd do a good job. I think . . . I think grief is clouding her decision-making. I do. But there's not much I can do about that." Lou thought about Em researching ways to declare Grandma incompetent and shuddered. God, it couldn't come to that.

"So, you and Gavin are cooking something up, then?"

Her shoulders tensed before she purposefully relaxed them. Though she wasn't sure if she should act like she felt—panicked and weird—or like everything was normal. So she found something in between. "What do you mean?"

"Past few days have been a little odd."

Lou shrugged jerkily. "I don't see how."

Molly sighed heavily. "Do you always have to be so difficult?"

"Way I hear tell, I was born that way."

"You know you can talk to me. That you can ask for help, and it wouldn't change anything. You *know* that, I know you do."

Lou *hated* that kind of emotional honesty, but she'd grown up with Em's bouts with it and knew she couldn't just ignore it. Not with people she cared about. She turned to Molly, looking as apologetic as she could muster. "I know you do. And . . . I'm not trying to be difficult. I just . . . This is hard. I'm used to dealing with hard on my own."

"I get that. I do." Molly started crossing to her, and Lou held up both hands.

"Don't you dare," she warned her as Molly opened her arms.

Molly's face was all mischief. "You need one."

"I will cut you," Lou replied, grabbing the wire cutters and waving them toward Molly. "You hate hugs as much as I do."

"No one hates hugs as much as you do." And with that, Molly enveloped her in one.

"You're turning into your mother," Lou grumbled, and while she didn't wrap her arms around Molly, she let her friend hug her without pushing her away.

Molly gave her one last squeeze before releasing her. "Thank you," she said cheerfully. "Speaking of my mother, she wants all three of you over for dinner sometime this week."

"We don't need pity dinners."

"You need friendship and support. If you won't take help, at least come to dinner. I can't imagine shutting herself in that house all day every day is good for your grandma. Getting out and about, hanging out with my mom and grandma, who both understand what she's going through, might be just the thing."

"Thursday should be good," Lou agreed. Maybe Molly was right. Maybe if Grandma got out a little more she wouldn't be so grief-stricken. Maybe she'd realize this whole Fairchild man or married-to-a-Fairchild thing was crazy.

Then Lou wouldn't have to marry Gavin and make half her life this awkward lie.

As if even thinking his name summoned his being, she heard the sound of a truck pulling up.

Molly glanced at the doorway. She frowned and turned back to study Lou for a moment. "Gavin doesn't usually stop by in the morning, does he?"

Lou's cheeks heated against her will. "I . . ."

"Hey, what are you doing here?" Gavin said, stepping into the barn and looking at his sister.

"Came to invite Lou to dinner."

"Thought I was going to do that."

"No. I told you *I* was going to do it."

He shrugged, then turned his gaze to Lou, grinning. "Two invites are better than one, I guess. Here, brought you some breakfast." He crossed to her, holding out a bag.

"I *can* feed myself," she muttered, not taking the bag.

He set it on the table and moved so that he was standing beside her. He ran his hand down her back like it was the most normal thing in the world.

She nearly jumped out of her skin. No one just *touched* her like that. Casual and somehow intimate.

As if he knew what it was like to run his bare hand along her bare skin and—

What the *hell*? Her face was so hot, she was surprised the air around her didn't steam.

"You mind giving us a minute?" Gavin said to Molly.

Molly's gaze went from Gavin to Lou and then back again. She did *not* look pleased. But when she looked up at Gavin, trying to get some *clue* as to what he thought he was doing, he just had his normal cheerful smile in place.

"All right. See you later, Lou."

Lou nodded. She didn't even try to say goodbye because she knew it would come out like a garbled croak. Once Molly was gone, and Lou didn't feel like she'd been shaken off her very foundation, she whirled on Gavin and smacked him across the chest.

"What the *hell* was that?"

Chapter Five

"A success," Gavin replied. Molly's eyes had practically popped out of her head when he'd touched Lou's back.

It was incredibly gratifying, considering he knew Molly was going to be harder to convince than the rest of his family, with the exception of maybe his mother. Shane, Boone, and Lindsay were removed enough they might just shrug their shoulders and move on, but Molly knew too much about Lou. Maybe even too much about the whole Fairchild Ranch situation.

Which was why Gavin had come over here even though he'd known Molly already was. Which was why he'd made sure to touch Lou in a way he normally didn't.

Gavin looked down at his hand, curled his fingers into a fist, and then released them. He could still feel the rough texture of her coat, the way she'd all but jumped away from him, but not before he'd felt the slightest of tremors at the small of her back.

It was very strange to suddenly touch someone in a way you hadn't for twenty years. Maybe fifteen years ago he'd had a few fantasies about touching her, but he'd very determinedly gotten over that when Lou had been dating Rex.

She'd chosen Rex over him, and that was all Gavin ever needed to know. They were friends, and now they'd pretend to be a little more to help each other out. No harm. No foul.

But he couldn't seem to get the odd thought out of his head that he'd never felt that kind of electricity with anyone else, not even in the year he'd dated Em.

Of course, that hadn't been real either. He had a bad habit of swooping in, trying to solve the Fairchild women's problems for them. But he *had* helped Em, and now he'd help Lou.

That was all there was to it.

"I don't like lying to Molly," Lou said, turning away from him and hugging herself. "It feels wrong."

"I know."

She glanced over her shoulder at him, her pale eyebrows drawn together. She must not know that her bandanna was a little askew and he could actually see some of the scarring on her right cheek. He could only see a little pink slash peeking out from the blue material. Most of her burns had been sustained by falling debris as she'd tried to break her way out of the locked barn.

He curled his fingers into fists again because the usual hot tide of anger swept through him. That Rex could be so stupid and careless as to have put Lou in so much danger, so much pain.

She readjusted her bandanna, breaking him out of his reverie.

"It doesn't help. You being angry over it."

He wasn't surprised she could see right through

him. He wasn't any good at hiding things. "Well, help or not, I'll always be angry over it."

Her mouth curved, as if she was going to smile, but that didn't make any sense to him. Not when they were talking about the fire that had caused her so much suffering. Then she laughed, and he really thought she'd lost it.

"Sorry, I just got to thinking . . . If we actually have to go through with this insanity, Rex is going to be *so* pissed I married *you*."

Now *that* did make Gavin smile. "Well, now we have to go through with this insanity."

She shook her head. "It's our last resort."

"I think we're getting pretty close to our last resort."

She inhaled sharply, but she nodded. "I know. Rationally I know that. I just keep hoping for some kind of miracle."

Gavin spread out his arms. "Turns out, I'm your miracle." He wanted to make her laugh, to lift that awful weight sagging her shoulders down.

She did roll her eyes and turn back to her workbench and the bag he'd brought her. She pulled out the doughnut and ripped it in half, handing the smaller piece over to him.

He took it, but he didn't take a bite. He wasn't hungry, most especially when she licked the remnants of glaze off the fingers that had handed him his half. She did it quickly, efficiently, and he didn't breathe the entire time.

He refused to name that thing coiling in his gut, because this was Lou, and he was doing her a favor. He was doing himself a favor. This had nothing to do with tongues.

He cleared his throat, desperate to say something. Anything.

But there was the sound of a car engine outside. The engine cut and Lou scowled.

"If that's another Tyler, I'm going to lose my mind."

He didn't know who else would be out, but maybe Molly had come back. Or Mom might have come over to ensure the dinner invitation went over. Regardless, if someone they knew was going to walk into this barn, they needed to do something drastic. Because this was about Lou keeping her flower farm, and him getting something he got to be in charge of. Nothing else.

He dropped his uneaten half of the doughnut on the bag laying on her table.

"Come here," he ordered. If he'd been thinking more clearly, had more time to plan, he would have thought to voice it as a question.

She chewed her last bite of doughnut. "Ex*cuse* me?"

"Come here," he hissed, reaching out and pulling her to him. She stumbled into his chest, glaring up at him as he wound his arm around her back. "There we go. Now, we're going to get caught."

"Get caught doing *what?*"

"Kissing."

She immediately shoved at his chest, but he'd predicted that and held her in his arms.

"Are you high?" she demanded.

He shushed her, also not a good move, but he didn't have time to think. "We have to speed things up," he said, keeping his voice low so no one would overhear. "If someone walks in thinking we didn't know they were coming and catches us, you know . . ." He had to clear his throat again. "Kissing, then there's no cause to doubt we're legitimately in a relationship.

And the news of actual kissing will spread like wildfire, especially if it's a Tyler catching us."

"Gavin—"

As much as they didn't have time to discuss it, he also didn't want to keep going on about why they should. Couldn't stand the thought of trying to keep being rational when something was squeezing his chest with a vise. "Trust me, okay? Trust me."

She blinked up at him, something in her softening in a way he didn't understand. In a way that felt too good in his arms.

"I've trusted you for as long as I can remember," she said on a whisper.

It might have hurt less if she'd stabbed him with one of her tools, or gotten in a good knee to the groin. Lou didn't give her trust easily, and he had never been totally certain she trusted him. Or anyone. Tolerated, yes. Cared about, some. But trusted?

No, he thought her trust began and ended with Em, and even those two had their secrets from each other.

He'd spent something like twenty years trying to earn that trust. He should be happy, but all he could seem to think was: *why Rex?*

But that was a question from teenage him, and he wasn't that kid anymore. No more worrying why he was always second best. No more wallowing in immaturity. He had a chance to have his own place and he'd take it.

He was helping Lou in the process and that's all it'd be.

So, he had to kiss her. Which would be fine. Just a kiss. It didn't have to be anything more than mouths touching. There wasn't time to think about why he felt . . . uneasy.

He reached out and took the corner of the bandanna that covered the corner of her mouth. His fingers brushed the soft skin of her cheek as he folded it under. There seemed to be some band of pressure around his chest, made only worse when she exhaled a shaky breath.

She smelled like earth and sugar and her skin was as soft as the petals of the flowers she tended. Her blue eyes looked especially dark and fathomless this morning, and . . .

He had to kiss her. Kiss her. It was time to *kiss her, idiot.*

"What on earth is going on?"

He jumped away, and so did Lou. As if they'd been caught doing . . . anything. When all they'd been doing was touching a little. Apparently, neither brave enough to do the thing.

But maybe that would work in their favor just as well.

He glanced at Em standing in the doorway, who was wide-eyed and clearly shocked. Gavin couldn't tell if it was a good shock or a bad shock and he found he wasn't too keen on sticking around to find out.

"Hey, Em," he greeted, and if his voice was rusty at best, that only worked in their favor. "I was just on my way out. See you guys around." Then he hightailed it out of Lou's barn like a coward.

But it was an act, of course, just to get Em wondering. An act. So he and Lou both got what they wanted.

That was all.

Lou couldn't seem to breathe normally. Or wrap her mind around any of that. He hadn't even actually kissed her, but it had felt that . . . intimate. The way his thumb had brushed her face as he moved the bandanna away from her mouth.

The way Gavin's dark gaze had studied her mouth so . . . so . . . intently.

"Well," Em said.

Lou couldn't bear to look at her sister. She hadn't planned on lying to Em. Em knew too much for any lie to work. But she didn't know how to explain *this.* Because she was acting fidgety and weird, no matter how much her inner voice kept yelling *calm down. Explain it was fake.*

She cleared her throat, ready to calmly explain to Em what she and Gavin were up to.

"I guess this is why you didn't want *me* marrying Gavin," Em said, her voice carefully devoid of any emotion.

"What? Why?"

"Because *you* want Gavin for yourself."

"That isn't . . . We were only . . ." Lou tried to laugh, but it came out all weird. "No. That isn't what's going on."

"Then what's going on?" Em asked mildly.

Lou stared at her sister. Em was never mild. She was never cool and disdainful, certainly not with Lou herself. "Maybe that should be my question for you. Because you seem weirdly bent out of shape over . . ." Lou hesitated. How on earth could she label that odd moment with Gavin?

Em raised a brow. "Over what?"

"Did *you* want to marry Gavin?" Lou demanded.

"Lou."

"Well, you brought it up first, and now you're . . ."

"I'm worried about you. I'm worried about what I just saw. When I suggested marrying Gavin, I meant with him knowing what he was getting in to. Not getting tricked into it. Especially by you."

Lou's face heated. "I'm not tricking him. I'm not . . . doing anything with him. We were just talking."

"Oh, that's why you jumped apart like I'd caught you *really* going at it."

Lou opened her mouth. She had no way to explain this, especially when her sister was being so accusatory. Em, of all people.

Em, who she was trying to protect. Em, who Lou had spent her entire life trying to shield and keep safe, and she had the gall to come in here and start casting aspersions on what Lou had to do. After the year she'd had.

"Maybe there is something going on," Lou said haughtily. "And maybe it has nothing to do with this place *or* you."

Em's expression went slack in surprise if not hurt, but Lou didn't even have time to feel guilty because she heard *yet another* engine approach.

She swore. "What is this? The circus?"

"It's Cora," Em said coolly. "I thought we could meet about our bride. I can't keep changing my cake design, and I assume you have the same issues. We need to work out a way to mitigate some of this."

Lou stared at her sister, wondering how on earth this simple morning had gotten so ridiculously out of hand. How she was suddenly very close to fighting with Em, which was the absolute last thing she wanted right now.

"Em, listen—"

"Morning," Cora greeted cheerfully, stepping into the barn. Much like Em, Cora always seemed so effortlessly bright and feminine. Her blond hair was swept back into the kind of braid that looked elegant rather than serviceable. She wore a cute skirt with completely nonfunctional boots, and subtle makeup that made her look like a magazine ad.

Lou had always felt like a plodding kind of hulk in the face of her sister's effortless femininity, and now she was surrounded by two of them. With a scarred face and body to boot.

Really, this day kept getting better and better.

Cora looked from Lou to Em. "What's going on?"

"Oh, the usual," Em said breezily. "I walked in to see Gavin and Lou kissing."

Cora and Lou both screeched, though Lou assumed it was for different reasons.

"We were *not* kissing, Em. Good Lord."

"So, what were you doing?" Cora asked gently.

Lou had never dreamed she'd appreciate *gentle.* It usually made her feel uncomfortable, but her friendship with Cora had given her a clue as to ways gentleness could feel like support rather than a shoe ready to drop.

"It was just . . . He was helping me fix my bandanna."

"Because you ever let anyone do that," Em said dryly.

"I don't know what all this third degree is about, but I don't appreciate it. Are we going to deal with our bride or not?"

"Well, I have an hour. I don't see why we can't discuss both."

Lou scowled in Cora's direction, but Cora didn't wilt. Instead she looked around the barn, finding one of Lou's folding chairs and pulling it over to the workbench. She patted the chair, waving Lou and Em over. "Come on, girls, let's talk."

"Don't use your mom voice on us," Em muttered, trudging toward the bench.

Cora smiled sweetly at them both. "Then stop acting like children."

Lou and Em grumbled, but they took a seat on the workbench next to each other and scowled at Cora as she fixed them with one of her mom glares.

"Now, tell us the truth. If you and Gavin weren't kissing, and Em thought you were, what exactly was going on?"

Lou cleared her throat. This was the whole point of agreeing to marry Gavin. Fool everyone. Save the flower farm, get Gavin a ranch to run himself. Right here was the opportunity to plant the seeds of their little lie. *Necessary* lie. "There was a . . . moment, I guess." That's what she'd have to have them believe, wasn't it? Regardless of truths or lies or weirdness in the middle, everyone had to believe they'd been about to kiss, even though it had been a fabricated, made-up about-to-kiss.

"You guess?" Em demanded.

"I don't know. He was . . . It *was* innocent. It just felt . . . I don't know. Different." Which was somehow both the truth and a lie and had Lou all churned up.

"Haven't you known him for like twenty years?" Cora asked.

"What's that got to do with anything?"

"How do you suddenly find yourself attracted to someone you've known that long? I mean, I know people change and all, but isn't it weird?"

It is weird. It's very weird.

Except that . . . Whatever it was she'd felt wasn't attraction. Not *that* way. Because they were friends. They'd *always* been friends. He'd dated Em, and that told Lou everything she needed to know about his taste in women.

Not. Her.

"I mean, all the Tyler men are hot," Cora offered when Lou still said nothing.

When both Fairchild women looked at her like she'd lost it, Cora shrugged.

"What? They are. In different ways, and of course I love Shane, so I think he's the hottest, but that doesn't mean Gavin and Boone aren't good-looking. Really, really good-looking." Cora sighed happily. "It's no hardship sharing a house with them."

"What would your husband think if he heard you say that?" Em demanded, clearly as horrified as Lou felt.

"He would be horribly aggrieved," Cora said gravely. "And then he'd show me just how much he loved me, and just how lucky I am to have ended up with him." She sighed happily. "Of course, this is about Lou and Gavin. So, just FYI, if *ahem* is hereditary, the Tyler men are well endowed."

Lou jumped off the bench. "What is happening? Why is this my life? I do not want to think about . . . that."

"Don't you?" Cora asked innocently.

"No. No." She was blushing. Profusely. And acting way too squirrelly as she paced her barn, because that should be something she'd want to know. If she was playacting this insanity. She should be interested in . . .

Good. Lord.

"It seems like maybe you're a little . . . scared."

Lou scoffed. Scared? She was not *scared*. A little out of sorts, maybe. But *scared* had been being stuck in that burning barn. *Scared* had been being in charge of Em when she'd only been a baby herself. She'd had real things to be scared about.

Gavin Tyler was not one of them.

"I don't think I've ever seen you scared," Em said, a kind of awe in her voice.

Which was somehow heartbreaking and satisfying at the same time. For as long as she could remember, it had been her job to put on a brave face for Em. She'd succeeded, all these years when she'd been so sure her fake bravery had been transparent.

She let out a breath, overwhelmed by too many things at once. "Can we talk about work for a little bit?" she managed to ask without sounding belligerent. Which was what she really wanted to be. Mean and nasty and get everyone running away from her. It was safer that way.

But she couldn't do that to Em, even if she was miffed at her sister for being weird about the Gavin thing. And she couldn't do it to Cora because Cora had been nothing but a good, solid friend.

"As long as you promise to talk to us when you need to. We're your friends. We're here for you. No matter what weird moments are happening. You can lean on us. You're not alone," Cora said.

Lou managed to nod and smile. She wasn't alone, no, but that didn't mean she could do any leaning. Being the one leaned on had gotten her through this far in life.

Is it such a great life?

She pushed that thought out of her head and strode to the bouts she'd been fiddling with. "If I have to make another one of these, I'm afraid I'll threaten to shove it up the bride's nose."

Cora and Em laughed and got to talking about their frustrating bride, and Lou tried to focus on that too.

But Gavin's face far too close to hers, the smell of him—spring storms on the horizon—nearly overtaking the smells of earth and flowers in her barn, well, she couldn't quite seem to eradicate that completely.

But she would. Eventually.

Chapter Six

"Where are you headed?"

Gavin stopped midstride. He'd purposefully taken this route through the front rather than the back with the express purpose of getting stopped by Shane and asked that very question. Somehow, the demand still irritated the crap out of him. "Out," he gritted.

"Out where?" Shane asked, rocking back and forth on the sturdy porch chairs. King lay at his feet, his tail thumping happily against the porch floor. The sun had set a while ago, so it was all dark and stars.

"Gee, Mom, last time I checked I was an adult capable of going places without telling anyone where or why."

"Sure," Shane said in that equitable tone that never made Gavin feel much of an equal. "You could also just answer a question without acting like a guilty teenager."

That was the problem with Shane. He made every overbearing request sound so reasonable. He had such an easy way of making Gavin feel like a tool. The dumb kid who didn't quite measure up.

He'd been tired of it for a while now, but he dealt

with it because he loved his big brother. He was in *awe* of his big brother, and he'd wanted to prove something to Shane, or maybe even himself.

But whatever he'd been trying to prove rang hollow the older Gavin got. He couldn't keep stuck in this perpetual adolescent space Shane wanted to keep him in. Actually, Shane didn't mean to do all that. He was just used to taking care of everyone. It was his habit, his way.

That was the other problem with Shane. Gavin understood Shane didn't mean to be overbearing or a pain in the ass. Shane thought he was doing what their father would have done if he'd lived.

Gavin suddenly felt weary. Like turning around and heading to bed.

Except he had a plan. A plan to get his own place. A plan to find something that made him feel less like this and more like . . . more like . . .

Well, something else.

"Why are you out here alone?" Gavin asked in return.

"Cora's helping Micah with his English homework and I've discovered it's best for both of us if I don't give my two cents on the matter. When it's math and history, I'm in charge and Cora sits on the porch to enjoy some quiet."

It didn't surprise Gavin in the least Shane was made for this stepdad stuff. Ever since Dad had died, Shane had played the father role to four younger siblings. He was good at it. He just didn't know when to let it go. Like, say, around Gavin and the rest of the kids hitting adulthood.

"I'm just headed out. Branded Man maybe."

"As I recall, you haven't been there since you got

in a tussle with Rex Altman. Looking to repeat the experience?"

"Maybe I am." He wasn't, but lying would help him in the long run. Besides, he wouldn't mind landing another punch on Rex.

Shane pushed out of the chair, zipping up his coat. "Then I'll go with you." He made a move for the door like he was going to let King inside.

Gavin scowled. "Stay home with your pretty wife and your ornery stepson, huh? I'm just going to go for a drive or something. You don't need to babysit."

"I'm only looking out for you."

"But I don't want you to." Gavin wasn't sure he'd ever been quite that honest about it. He usually couched it in too much anger or too many jokes. This was just honest, regardless of his plan. "I want to do some things on my own, without anyone else's interference or commentary."

Shane stared at him a moment, as if thinking that over. *Considering* it, like Gavin *was* a grown man who could make his own choices. "I think you were born into the wrong family for that."

Because it was true, Gavin laughed. Why would he ever expect things to change? "Maybe I'll go see Lou." Because that was the point. Plant the seeds of their little lie.

"Kinda late for that."

Gavin shrugged, refusing to bristle. "Guess she'll tell me to go home if it is."

"Listen, Gav." Shane cleared his throat, his expression serious and far too grave for Gavin's comfort level. "For the record, I don't want to lose you here. I know you feel like you don't have enough say. We can work on that. You don't have to . . . You don't need your own place to have more room to run things."

"That isn't why I'm going to see Lou."

Shane's eyebrows raised and he rocked back on his heels. He shoved his hands in his pockets and, in typical Shane fashion, took time to mull that over.

"So. This is . . . personal?"

"Yeah, maybe it is."

"Is it, ah, reciprocated personal?"

"What? You think she's taking pity on me?" His temper boiled, and while he never took it out on Shane with a punch, man, he kind of thought about it over the idea he wasn't good enough for Lou to care about.

Wasn't he already perfectly aware of that fact?

Shane sighed. "I don't know why you have to always assume the worst. Maybe I think you're taking pity on her."

"Maybe, just maybe, we're friends and anything beyond that is just . . ."

"Just what?"

Gavin pulled his hat down low and kneeled down to give King a good scratch. "Stay," he whispered.

When he straightened, he tipped his hat at his brother. "Good night, Shane." Then, ignoring whatever Shane had to say to that, Gavin strode for his truck.

He took the back way to the Fairchild place. Taking the path that skirted their pastureland, then to the gate that would lead him to the side of the Fairchild Ranch that boasted Lou's flower farm. Mom didn't like it when they cut through, but Gavin wasn't keen on caring after his interaction with Shane.

He went through the rigamarole of opening the gate, driving through, closing it back up again. He parked his truck behind the barn, where Mrs. Fairchild wouldn't be able to see it from the house. Not because he didn't want her to see it, but because if she by chance *did*, he wanted her to think he was trying to hide.

He hadn't been upstairs in the Fairchild house since high school, but he could only assume things hadn't changed. Mrs. Fairchild's room was on the west side, while Lou and Em's tiny closet-size rooms were on the east. He'd never been in Lou's room. Only seen Em's room through the hallway because Mr. and Mrs. Fairchild had been very strict about where boys were allowed to go.

Luckily, he didn't have to remember which window was Lou's. One was dark and one had a cozy warm glow behind the curtain.

The fact he knew one could climb up to the window because of Rex wasn't exactly a happy thought, but he was glad for the knowledge anyway. He focused on the steps to get up to the second-story window rather than consider that his asshole of a former best friend had once done this very thing to get into Lou Fairchild's pants.

Gavin allowed himself some cursing as he leveraged himself up on the railing, then tested a few spots on the overhang of the porch to find the best place to pull himself up on.

Once he found a good place that felt like it'd bear his weight, he did something of a pull-up and then pushed himself up and onto the small roof that sheltered the front porch below. He took a minute to breathe, looking out over the Fairchild Ranch.

Everything was dark except for the stars that stretched out forever. All sparkle and shine. He wasn't a particularly reflective man, but he took a moment to breathe in the cold spring night air. Took a moment to just . . . be. When did he ever do that?

When his thoughts turned to his father, a man he could idolize because he'd been a good man and died before Gavin had grown up to find his reasoning or old-fashioned ideas lacking, wondering what Dad would think of all this . . .

Well, he decided that was a good time to scoot over to the edge of the roof and reach over and knock on Lou's window.

"What the hell," Lou muttered as her window shook. Like someone was knocking on it. Did they need to prune the tree again? Surely it hadn't grown that fast. It'd only been a month or so.

Maybe it was some poor bird. Or a rabid squirrel. Whatever it was, it just kept knocking against her window.

Irritated with her nightly ritual of seed catalog browsing being interrupted, Lou crawled out of bed and whipped the curtain back. When she saw a *human face,* she shrieked and jumped back, her heart racing and her hand grasping for anything that could be used as a weapon.

But it started to dawn on her the face was familiar, not menacing. "Damn it, Gavin, what the hell is wrong with you?"

She moved back to the window and tried to pull it open quietly, hoping her scream hadn't woken up Grandma down the hall.

"Are you insane?" she demanded of Gavin.

"Remove the screen. Let me in."

"You could have texted. Why are you lurking in a second-story window like a total creeper? You—"

"Lou? Lou, is everything all right?" Grandma's voice wavered from the hallway.

Lou dropped the curtains and practically lunged across her room to flip the lock. "Everything's fine. I just . . . uh, stepped on a . . . thing."

"A thing?" Grandma's voice was skeptical more than worried.

"Oh, look at that." She desperately searched her floor. She glanced at the window, thankful the curtain covered Gavin. Though Grandma would be concerned about the window being open.

"Lou—"

"A pinecone! It was a pinecone." Oh, wow, that was the worst lie ever.

"A pinecone." Grandma clearly didn't believe her. "Louisa, open this door."

Lou took a deep breath, trying to calm her erratic heartbeat. Between the scare and Gavin and . . . She blew out the breath, unlocking and opening the door and forcing herself to smile at Grandma. "Sorry to have scared you."

Grandma poked her head in, looking all around the room, frowning. "Hmm," was all she said.

Lou was desperate to add more to her story, but it would only make her sound like the lying liar she was. She might be a terrible liar, but she'd learned a thing or two about how not to be so obvious. So she kept the likely insane smile on her face and waited for Grandma to decide everything was okay.

Grandma eyed her carefully. "It isn't like you to shriek."

"I suppose it isn't," Lou agreed. "Long, long day. Bridezillas in my head. I should probably go to bed."

Grandma made another hmm sound, but she finally nodded. "All right. Good night."

"Night." Lou closed the door, practically collapsing

against it. Then she glared at her window. She marched over to it, flinging the curtain back.

He was standing on the porch roof, which meant she could basically only see his head where it peered around the corner of the house. The light from her room illuminated his features.

The jackass was grinning.

"Go home."

"Take the screen off. Let me in. I have a plan."

She didn't move for the screen. She stood there scowling at him. "You could have texted, you—"

"I could have, but I wasn't sure you'd like the idea."

"So you just thought you'd make sure it happened whether I liked it or not?"

"Yes."

"You're a jerk."

"Probably. But if you let me in, this jerk will help you keep your flower farm and keep your father far, far away." He gave her an imploring look that made her want to smack him.

He wasn't an innocent little boy. He was a . . . He was a . . .

She grunted in frustration and removed the screen from its track. Looping his arm under the open window, Gavin carefully stepped from the roof at the front of the house around the corner to her window-sill. He pretzeled his body through the opening.

Now Gavin Tyler was standing in her room, and she was in her pajamas. Braless. She crossed her arms over her chest, and then she realized something even worse than that.

She didn't have her bandanna on. She whirled around and grabbed it off her nightstand.

"You don't have to do that," Gavin said, his voice

quiet and, well, it almost felt comforting to have him say it.

Except that was stupid. "I do have to."

"It doesn't bother me. Nothing about your scars bothers me."

"They bother *me*." She turned to face him, bandanna securely hiding the scarred side of her face. Defiant and ready to fight this to the ground, she stared at him coolly. He didn't get to dictate how she felt about showing her scars to the world. Or him.

He studied her, and she was reminded of how he used to do that when they were kids. Gavin wasn't a *studying* kind of guy, ever, but every once in a while, in those rare moments where he was still and quiet, he'd look at her with a kind of warmth, almost an understanding.

It had made her feel itchy then, and it made her feel damn right diseased now.

"Why are you here?" she demanded through gritted teeth.

"Well, your sister certainly thinks something is going on after this morning, which likely means my sister does as well. I figured we'd go for gold and get your grandmother thinking the same, and possibly my mother, depending on how we can time this."

"Then why did you *sneak* into my room? How are they going to know?"

"Because I'm going to spend the night."

She laughed for a good minute before she realized he was serious. "You can't spend the night here. What will everyone think?"

"What everyone will think is the point, obviously."

Lou could only stare at him, her mouth hanging open. Spend the night. Get caught. He wanted to . . . "My grandmother can't think we . . . we . . . No."

"What? Is she under the impression you're an untouched virgin after dating Rex for eight years?"

Lou's cheeks heated. She couldn't remember the last time she'd *blushed* before the past two days and all this insanity with Gavin. Now she was doing it every five seconds and she didn't appreciate it.

"I don't know what impression she's under, but if I have to talk to my grandmother about . . . about . . ."

Gavin raised a brow, oh so slowly, oh so slyly. "About?"

She couldn't say it in front of him. She didn't know why. Maybe because they were alone, and this was her bedroom, and she didn't have a *bra* on. But she couldn't utter that simple three-letter word with Gavin Tyler in her bedroom. "Where exactly do you think you're going to sleep?" she demanded instead.

Gavin studied the room, then seated himself in a rickety old chair she kept in the corner, more for piling things on than actually sitting. Grayson inched out from under her covers, delicately leaped from bed to floor to Gavin's lap, all in one graceful movement.

"I don't think I've met this one. What's its name?" he asked, as if this was somehow *normal*. Him in her room, meeting her indoor cat, petting it like . . .

She looked away. "His name is Grayson."

"What kind of name is Grayson?"

"The kind from a book."

"You and my mother," he muttered.

"Apologies from the literate."

"Ha, ha."

She turned to face him, because this was all fake and for the sake of her farm and *not* seeing Dad. "Isn't this a little fast? People will think night spending is too fast. We only just got a few people thinking we're . . ."

She was really going to have to start being able to say the words.

And I will. When I'm wearing appropriate underwear for the situation.

"We've known each other twenty years, Lou. I don't think anyone's going to accuse us of moving too fast."

Lou let out a very measured breath. Gavin was being calm and reasonable about this, and she could too. Even with her cat curled up in his lap while he ran his big, rough hand from the cat's head to its tail.

"You can't sleep in that rickety old chair." He could sleep on the floor, but she didn't have extra bedding or pillows in here, and she couldn't sneak out into the hall because Grandma would hear that. Lou could maybe face the embarrassment of having her think Gavin had spent the night . . . for reasons . . . in the morning.

But not while he was still here. No.

"Where are you suggesting I sleep, Lou?" he drawled, looking so damn pleased with himself she wanted to wipe the grin off his face. Because she wouldn't do it with her fists, she'd have to do what he was doing.

Prove that this was no big deal. A friend helping a friend. They were helping each other. All they had to do was pretend, and how hard was pretending when you were just friends, after all? Pretending wasn't the same as lying.

She lifted her chin, feeling a bit like a brawler getting in the ring. "There's room."

He shifted on the chair, just a hair, and though his expression was mild, something in him tensed. "Room?"

"In my bed. You can sleep in my bed."

He cleared his throat and she tried very hard not to grin at that.

"But, uh . . ." He cleared his throat again. "Then where would you sleep?"

She smiled sweetly at him. "Well, right next to you, naturally."

Chapter Seven

She was evil, and she wasn't going to win. He nudged the cat off his lap and stood. He unzipped his jacket, smiling blandly. "Sure."

She lifted a shoulder. "Sure."

"What time does your grandma get up in the morning?" He pulled his phone out of his coat pocket, then shrugged off the coat and draped it over the chair. "Gotta time my exit perfectly."

"Usually it's around four thirty. She still hasn't gotten used to not being up to make Grandpa breakfast." Lou frowned and fiddled with the corner of her bedspread while Gavin set the alarm on his phone for four twenty-five. "I don't know that she ever . . . that we ever . . . I don't know how to talk about it with her or . . . Well."

She was trying to be strong, but Gavin knew better than most what it was like to lose someone, and not just have to feel that grief yourself, but worry about all the ways that loss touched and changed your family. He'd been lucky to have so many siblings, to have such a strong mother and grandmother. And, in some ways, to have only been ten.

Lou was an adult with an elderly grandmother

and no support from her parents, and a sister she felt responsible for and always had. She understood the full weight of the world in a way Gavin certainly hadn't at the time he'd lost his father.

But regardless of the details, he understood the *feeling*. "It's been a while, but I know what it's like. I'm happy to listen, but you don't have to try to explain it to me."

"I know you do." She nodded, attempted a smile that was pathetic at best. "It gets easier, right?"

"Yeah."

"You're not just lying to make me feel better?"

"I think it's different, because you had a lot more years with your grandpa, but . . . It gets so it doesn't feel like they *should* be there. Sometimes it'll hit you a little sideways that they aren't and you wish they were, but the seconds, the minutes, the hours, they all get a little easier."

She nodded, and he couldn't help but feel important in some way. He hadn't taken her pain away, couldn't do that, though he wanted to, but he thought he'd offered a kind of comfort or reassurance and that was . . .

What friends did, was all. Certainly nothing to get sappy about.

"She went from her parents' house to this house with him, and I just can't imagine what she's . . ." Lou turned away and shook her head. "Anyway, you'll have to get up pretty dang early to catch her."

"That's okay. Perfect, really. Sneak out of here around four thirty. I'll dawdle a bit, walk in my door around five, which is right around the time *my* grandma or mom is up starting breakfast."

"You're going to tell them you were here when they ask where you've been?"

"No, I'm going to lie. Badly. Then Mom will start snooping, inevitably talk to your grandmother, and ta-da."

"Ta-da," she repeated tonelessly.

"Indeed."

"Well, anyway. I guess we should sleep then. Four thirty comes around pretty fast."

"I guess it does."

Neither of them made a move for the bed at first. Lou stood with her back to him still, and he stood next to the chair staring at the bed. It looked unreasonably small even though it was bigger than his bed at home.

It wasn't any different than sitting next to each other on a bench. A picnic table. Sharing a seat on the school bus.

If he went through all the times they'd been as close as they'd be on the bed, all those times over twenty years and he hadn't thought twice about it. He just had to convince himself lying in her bed was the same.

Sitting in the same booth when they went and got pizza. Being in the back seat of a truck together.

He moved forward, feeling somehow awkward and ungainly as he placed his phone on the little table next to the bed. The soft-looking, frilly-decorated bed. That he was going to crawl in next to her.

Giving her a reassuring hug at her grandfather's funeral. Parking himself on the foot of her bed when she'd been in the hospital.

He took off his boots.

"I'm going to turn out the light," she announced.

Thank God.

It was much easier to sit on the bed, then move into a normal lying position with the room dark. Although the way the curtains fell, a swath of moonlight illuminated the empty side next to him.

He couldn't help but stare at that silvery glow against the floral-printed sheets that smelled like . . . like . . . well, like a woman. He hadn't been in a woman's bed in an embarrassingly long time, and though the Tyler house was filled to the brim with women, there was enough ranch life to make it easy to avoid.

He couldn't avoid flowers and pretty scents and soft fabrics when he was in a *bed.*

Which dipped when she finally crawled into it. Gavin immediately turned his attention to the ceiling. This was fine. Normal. Like lying on towels at the beach, not that he'd ever been to the beach. But . . . it'd be like that.

He glanced over at her out of the corner of his eye without moving his head. That stupid bandanna had to be really uncomfortable to sleep in. For heaven's sake, it was *dark,* aside from that little stream of moonlight over her. Aside from the beacon of blond hair, she was a lumpy shadow.

"You don't have to wear this," he muttered irritably, shifting onto his side so he could untie the bandanna. "I can't see anything anyway, and I'll be gone before the sun's up." He tried to untie the knot without touching her hair, but it was impossible. Light, silky strands seemed to entwine themselves around his fingers as he pulled the fabric loose.

He let it drop and pulled his arms back to his sides. She didn't say anything, though she did shift in the bed. The whole mattress moved, and no matter that there was all this space between them, that she had her back to him, he was lying on a mattress that moved when she moved.

He looked up at the dark ceiling and tried to think of anything besides all the *weird* jangling around for space inside him. Then it dawned on him, all the times he'd been a little too mired in his middle school crush on her, he'd just been an ass to her.

"Sweet dreams, Louisa."

Even though he was prepared for the blow, the way she whacked her arm against his chest still caused him to release a whoosh of breath.

"Night, asshole," she muttered without any heat.

He didn't sleep much over the course of the next few hours. He was a little too afraid to move, and way too afraid of what his dreams might look like when everywhere he moved he could smell *flowers.*

Judging by Lou's even breathing and occasional movements, she *was* asleep instead of tense and weirded out, like him.

When his alarm went off, he practically jumped out of bed, relief coursing through him. He shoved his feet into boots and glanced at Lou's form in the bed. She didn't move, so was either asleep or pretending.

This morning, pretending was fine with him.

Now, he had to put his plan into action. It'd be far easier to do if he didn't see what Lou looked like first thing in the morning. Sleep rumpled and—

He moved for his phone, fumbled it, and just barely caught it before it crashed to the ground. *Close one.* Of course, when he stepped forward to grab his coat, the damn cat chose that moment to slink between his legs. Gavin stumbled, catching himself on the rickety chair, making enough noise to wake the dead.

"Could you make any more damn noise?" Lou groaned, pulling the covers over her head.

"Sorry, darlin'," he drawled in his best attempt to be obnoxious. "I know you need your rest after that wild and crazy night."

"Go away," she said, muffled underneath the covers.

"Yes, ma'am." He picked up his hat and fixed it on his head. He felt like he should say something else, but hell if he could work out what. Best to get downstairs, make some noise, and feign surprise at being caught.

He stepped into the hallway cautiously, being careful to pull Lou's door closed as quietly as possible. The Fairchild house was old, and every floorboard seemed to creak under his weight. He moved down the stairs, wincing at every loud groan.

He was *trying* to get caught and yet that didn't make this whole thing any less nerve-racking. Where would Mrs. Fairchild be? Would he have to make a commotion to get her attention?

What the hell would her response be? He'd dated one granddaughter already. The Fairchilds had even liked him and his family, and they'd been very protective of Em. Of course, that had been in high school. Surely now that he and Lou were adults, things would go diff—

"Stop right there."

Gavin froze. He had no idea where Mrs. Fairchild's voice came from until she slowly stepped out from behind the open pantry door.

"Gavin," she said.

"Mrs. Fairchild."

Her eyes narrowed as she studied him. Gavin tried not to squirm. He hadn't even done anything, but she made him feel as if he had.

"Sit down, young man."

"I, uh, really have to get back." He didn't have to feign his nerves because he hadn't expected a *conversation* where he had to sit down. He'd expected surprise, maybe embarrassment. Not . . . confrontation.

You're an idiot.

"I said, sit down."

So, Gavin sat.

"This is my second granddaughter you've had your paws all over, apparently."

"That was a l-long time ago." Christ, she'd always made him stutter. "E-Em, that is, was a long time ago."

"Hmm." She picked a wooden spoon off the counter, slapped it lightly to her palm.

Gavin was almost positive the eighty-year-old woman in front of him was threatening him with physical violence.

"Nothing happened," Gavin said, and though it was the God's honest truth, Mrs. Fairchild and her wooden spoon-palm slapping was enough to make him sound guilty.

"Something wrong with her, then?" Mrs. Fairchild asked casually.

"No!"

"Maybe you're turned off by those scars. Can't bear to touch her."

"Jesus, no. No. Lou's beautiful."

She pointed her spoon at him. "Don't take the Lord's name in vain at my table, Gavin Tyler."

"Yes, ma'am."

"I will say this once and only once. If you mess with her, this year of all years, well, let's just say no one will find the body."

"Mrs. Fairchild, I'd never do anything to hurt Lou. Surely you know that."

"She needs a partner. Someone to support her without suffocating her. She needs someone she'll share some of that weight with. Someone who understands she's gonna take more than her share of that weight on herself. Someone who cares about her regardless of getting a ranch out of the deal. That going to be you? I've got my doubts."

"After knowing me my whole life, watching me be a friend to your girls, that's what you think of me?" It wasn't that he'd thought he'd get some kind of welcome-to-the-family parade if he pretended to have spent the night, but he really hadn't expected Mrs. Fairchild to think so little of him.

It hurt, in a lot of ways. Because he'd always liked her. Because maybe Lou thought all those things. Because . . . Hell, was he destined to be thought that little of no matter what he did?

Something in her expression softened, but her words weren't soft in the least. "Doesn't matter what I think of you, Gavin." She set the spoon down on the counter. "Now, how do pancakes sound?"

Lou had grown up on a ranch from the time she'd been nine years old. She'd started her flower farm at eighteen, which meant early mornings as well.

She still wasn't human before two cups of coffee, even if being human only meant dealing with her flowers. Because she hadn't been able to fall back asleep in the thirty minutes since Gavin left, she'd probably need three cups this morning.

She crawled out of bed not thinking too deeply about who had shared that bed with her last night. Or at least trying not to.

She put on her bandanna, and then some jeans and a bra, because you did not appear in Grandma's kitchen dressed for bed, regardless of what time it was.

She glanced at the bed and tried not to stare at the fact that there were two pillows lying side by side, each with little head indentions in them. She couldn't begin to understand that little pang of yearning that swept through her. Didn't want to understand.

She quickly stripped the bed. She'd get the sheets into the washing machine right now. It was even more important than that first cup of coffee. She hefted the sheets and pillowcases into her arms and headed downstairs.

Lou stopped suddenly at the bottom of the stairs when she heard two voices. Her grandmother was talking to someone at five a.m.

Ignoring the load of linens in her arms, Lou moved forward to the kitchen. There was Gavin, sitting at her grandmother's kitchen table, shoveling pancakes into his mouth. She must've made some kind of noise because he looked up.

He widened his eyes, not in surprise but as if he was trying to impart an important message. He mouthed the words *help me*, if she wasn't mistaken.

"Grandma, what's going on?"

"It's only polite to provide breakfast for overnight guests, Louisa."

Gavin choked on whatever bite he'd been taking.

"Sit down and eat your breakfast, then," Grandma said, waving her into the kitchen. "No use standing there."

Lou felt as though she were frozen in place for a few seconds before she finally managed the wherewithal to move to the laundry room. She dropped the sheets on the ground and tried to come up with some sort of topic of conversation or way to get Gavin the hell away from the breakfast table.

She moved cautiously back into the kitchen, where Grandma had put a plate of pancakes and a mug of coffee at Lou's normal seat.

"I don't really feel like ea—"

"Sit down," Grandma instructed, as if Lou hadn't been speaking at all. "Drink your coffee and eat your breakfast. I haven't seen hide nor hair of Gene, so I'm going to go check on things. You two enjoy breakfast and your morning after conversation."

Mortification did not begin to cover what Lou felt at her grandma uttering the words *morning after*.

Grandma shoved her feet into her muck boots and then headed out the back door without another word.

Lou still couldn't get herself to move, though she did manage to look at Gavin, who was supposed to be gone. "What is going on?"

"Well, your grandmother threatened me and said no one would ever find my body, so I had breakfast with her. Because I rather like my body, and hope, should I die, it's found and laid to rest. Now, I have to go. It was one thing sneaking into my house and trying to get caught, but being late to ranch work is going to earn me an ass chewing I'd rather avoid." He stood up, though he shoveled one last bite of pancake into his mouth. "Can you cook like your grandma? It'd add another tick in the pros-of-marrying-Lou column."

"Bye, Gavin."

"Be a good little girl and eat your breakfast, Louisa."

"Maybe I'll kill you and make sure the body isn't found."

He grinned at her, settling his hat on his head. "Good luck with your grandmother, darlin'." He tipped his hat at her.

She briefly considered throwing a piece of pancake at him as he strode for the door, but that would waste her grandmother's delicious pancakes.

She ate in silence, wondering why on earth Grandma would've threatened Gavin. Obviously, her grandparents had been a little overprotective when she and Em were teenagers, but Lou was a grown woman now.

There was no reason to act like having an overnight guest was worthy of a death threat. Disapproval she'd expected, not taking anything out on Gavin.

Lou finished up her pancakes and coffee number one. By the time she'd downed her second cup and gotten the bedding in the washer, Grandma was stepping in the back door, stomping her mud-covered boots on the mat before working to get them off.

Lou watched her with a pang of anxiety. She hadn't been able to ignore the fact that her grandparents had been getting older over the past decade. She lived with them, and she loved them, but Grandpa's death made everything she noticed seem that much scarier. The fact that her grandmother was struggling to get off her boots, something she'd likely been doing since she could walk, just about cracked Lou's heart in two.

"Sorry if I disappointed you."

Grandma looked up at her, clearly surprised by the apology. "What makes you think I'm disappointed in you?"

"I know how you feel about . . ." Lou cleared her throat. "Erm, certain behaviors."

Grandma rolled her eyes. "If there's one thing I've learned in my eighty-one years, it's that the world changes whether I want it to or not. What I think is right, what was right for me, might not be right for everyone. Much as it pains me to admit that. Whatever you two were up to last night is your choice to make. I don't have anything to say about that."

But she could feel something like disapproval radiating off her grandmother and Lou just couldn't let that go. She'd disappointed her grandmother with her relationship with Rex. She'd known that at the time, but she'd been young enough not to worry too deeply about it.

She worried now. "Gavin's a good person."

"The Tylers are a fine family. Even that wild bull rider one. Deb is one of the best people I know, and she raised her kids right. Gavin *is* a good person, but Louisa . . ." Grandma sighed, finally freeing one foot from one boot. She sighed heavily as she leaned against the wall. "You've been through the ringer this year. *We've* been through the ringer. Don't rely on the closest man simply because you need a little rest."

Lou didn't know what to say to that in the least. Mostly because that wasn't even close to what she was doing, and she rarely witnessed her grandmother be so wrong about something.

"I know I can depend on you and Em, rely on you both. I have. Gavin isn't about . . . resting."

"So, after twentysome years of friendship, you're just in love with Gavin?" Grandma asked, dark eyes quizzical and disbelieving.

Lou didn't want to say no, because that would ruin their whole plan. It also wasn't comfortable to say she *didn't* love Gavin. He was one of her closest friends. There was a kind of love there. Maybe not the same, but similar.

But she also didn't want to straight-out lie to her grandmother when a *yes* to Grandma's question wasn't exactly the truth either.

Grandma gave her an odd look. "He spent the night last night. I thought you'd jump to an emphatic *yes*."

"Gavin is complicated. It's always been complicated. And I spent a lot of years ignoring how complicated it was on purpose." The staggering truth to all that hurt a little too deep.

"And now?" Grandma asked suspiciously.

What Lou really wanted to say was *and now you're forcing my hand and making me do this crazy thing because you won't be reasonable.* Lou wanted to yell at her grandmother for making this difficult and not admitting that she was deeply mired in the grief of losing Grandpa.

She wanted to shout, but she couldn't. She couldn't fight with her grandmother or declare her incompetent. She couldn't beg for something when Lou knew she was the real reason she was in this mess.

Lou was the reason her grandparents had had to be parents all over again in their sixties. Lou was the reason Grandpa had worked too hard and too long. Lou had been the reason she and Em had to live here and change her grandparents' planned future, and she couldn't ever forget how much she owed her grandmother, no matter what she felt.

"Now, I'm figuring this thing with Gavin out. I'll no doubt make a million mistakes in the process of figuring it out, but it's long past time." Which felt way, *way* too close to the truth.

"And you have to figure this out on your own?"

"What other options are there?"

Grandma was quiet for a while, studying Lou in that way Lou always felt was disappointment.

"I suppose that's up to you to figure out," Grandma said softly before she looked down at her still-booted foot. She seemed to grapple with some big thing, and all Lou could do was stand there and watch.

It was horrible.

Finally, Grandma looked up and met her gaze, head-on and proud. "Well, looks like I could use a little help here."

Lou felt like sobbing. In all the years she'd lived

under her grandparents' roof, Grandma had never, ever once asked for help with something that was hers to do. She'd taken care of everything. She'd led them all.

Now she needed help with her boots.

All Lou could do was cross the room and help her, and try not to cry.

Chapter Eight

Everyone was sitting around the breakfast table when he got home. Everyone. From Grandma to Micah. Boone had even graced the table when he usually slept past seven, something he only got away with because his injuries weren't healing all that quickly.

Though Gavin highly doubted that's why Boone slept in.

"Well, some of you are up early," Gavin greeted.

"Lots of work to do today. Everyone's pitching in," Shane said with enough edge to have Gavin bristling.

"Just where are you coming from?" Mom asked before Shane could tell his brother to do something inappropriate.

"Just went out for an early . . . breakfast."

"In the clothes you had on when you left last night?" Shane returned, pouring himself some orange juice.

Gavin looked down at his clothes as if surprised to find Shane was right. "Would you look at that? Better go change."

"Aren't you going to eat?" Mom asked, though it was one of Mom's patented questions within a question.

She didn't want *that* answer, but she wouldn't come straight out and ask you the other question either.

"Like I said. I already ate. Went out for an early breakfast."

"What did you eat?" Molly asked in that same tone his mother had just used.

"Huh?"

"What was this magical breakfast you had?" Molly said, eyes wide and overly innocent.

Gavin surveyed his family. All eyes were on him except Micah's, who was focused on the food, and Ben, who was staring deep into his coffee cup. Gavin would hand it to his mother's new husband. Ben knew when to keep his nose out of things.

But Mom, Grandma, Molly, Cora, and Shane were all watching him as if looking for something that might explain things. Even Boone looked at him speculatively.

They expected him to lie, and they were ready to pounce and pull apart the lie. Or, more likely, slowly, throughout the day, pull apart the lie bit by bit until he finally gave into his temper and yelled the truth.

Maybe he was a contrary asshole, but he didn't want to give them the satisfaction. "Mrs. Fairchild made me breakfast. Best pancakes I've had in a while." He patted his stomach. "You should get her recipe, Mol."

Gavin didn't wait around to see what the responses would be. He headed upstairs. He'd take a shower and try to beat everyone out to the stables. Shane could shove his *lots of work to do today* where the sun didn't shine.

He grabbed some fresh clothes out of sloppy piles in his dresser. He nearly jumped out of his skin when he turned and his mother was standing there in the door. Silently.

"Christ, Mom."

She only raised an eyebrow.

"Sorry." He glanced up at the ceiling. "Sorry, God, and all that."

She studied him for another second or two before she sighed and crossed the room to stand in front of him. He'd been looking down at his shorter mother since he'd hit his growth spurt in middle school and still, sometimes, it felt all out of whack how much taller he was than this woman who'd raised him with the kind of iron will reserved for legends.

"You remind me so much of your father."

Of all the things she could have said to him in this moment, that was definitely the thing he was least prepared to hear. "I, uh, thought that was Shane's department."

"Oh, Shane has the look of him. Of course you do too. In a lot of ways, Shane takes after me a little too much. He wants to fix things for people. He carries that weight. You carry it too, but it's different. More like your father did. He . . . He knew how to help people with the kind of space that made them think they were helping themselves."

Gavin could only stare down at his mother. Her brown eyes were soft and a little shiny, and he felt like he'd been dropped into some weird moment people had before they announced they were dying or something.

"Mom, is everything—"

"It's a special gift, Gav. But a lot of times it's the kind of thing that gets taken advantage of, and oftentimes it gets overlooked. Because you've given them the illusion it wasn't you at all. People don't notice it, and it leaves you . . . vulnerable."

"Uh, thanks, I guess? But I'm not vulnerable, Mom. I'm fine, and I'm a little confused why you're all of a sudden worried about me."

"You know I love Lou."

Something in her tone had him stiffening.

"She's one of the strongest women I know, and that's saying a lot. She's been through hell and it hasn't made her cruel. I respect her immensely."

"Why does it feel like you're going to say *but*?"

Mom placed her palm against his cheek. "But you're my sweet boy, and I worry."

"What is there to worry about?"

"You've always given a lot of yourself to her. It never bothered me. But something about this . . . Well, it worries me. How fast you're moving. How strangely you're behaving."

"Because I don't want everyone butting their noses into every little detail of my life?" He stepped away from his mother's hand. "Shane might handle it okay, but I don't think the rest of us particularly have. I just want to do something all on my own. Is that so much to ask?"

"No, it isn't. I suppose I made mistakes with all of you."

Gavin cringed. He'd poked at Mom's soft spot: Boone running away, Lindsay wanting to live far away from Gracely—though she'd recently come home to stay—and Molly's failed marriage, which had kept her away from Gracely for a few years. "I'm not saying you've made mista—"

Mom held up a hand. "When three of your five children leave, you've made mistakes."

"They all came back. Lindsay's home. Molly's happy. Boone is Boone and will probably bolt again, but that's not on you, and I hope you know that."

Mom's mouth quirked. "Yes. Well. See what I mean? You've asked for something inherently reasonable and now you're giving *me* a pep talk."

Gavin opened his mouth to say something to that, but he didn't have any words. He didn't think it was any great heroic characteristic that he didn't want to hurt his mother's feelings after how hard she'd worked to raise five kids on her own.

"Now, like I said, it's a reasonable request for us to butt out. I'll do it after I say this one thing. I'd hate for you to lose Lou's friendship, because it would hurt you so deeply. So, I'll worry, even if in the process I keep my mouth shut." She smiled sadly and started retreating for the door, but Gavin couldn't let the conversation end like that.

"I don't need you to butt out. I need, on occasion, my decisions or actions not to be questioned or dissected."

She stopped her retreat and looked at him speculatively. "Have you said any of that to Shane?"

"I said something similar last night."

"He might need to hear it again. And again."

Gavin laughed without much mirth.

"But here's a trick: talk to Cora. I'm not sure you'll get through to him. You're his little brother. That's . . . Well, you know how serious he takes that. But Cora might be able to explain it in a way he can't hear from his brother and could maybe understand coming from his wife."

"Well, that's downright brilliant. Why didn't you tell me that earlier?"

"You didn't ask." Mom came over to him and wrapped him in a tight hug. "I love you. I am very, very proud of the man you've become, gratified you've taken after your father, and happy that you're your own man too. We'll try to do better about respecting that." She pulled back and looked up at him. "How's that?"

"Pretty dam—darn good."

She rolled her eyes and shook her head. "Now, why don't you stop dawdling with all this talking and get to work, huh?"

"Yes, ma'am." He cleared his throat, uncomfortable with the emotion clogged there but needing to let it out regardless. "For the record, I love you too, and I'm very lucky to have you."

Mom put a hand to her heart and rubbed her palm against her chest. "Well, now. I appreciate that." She blinked a few times, but Deb Tyler didn't cry unless someone was dead. "I'll see you out there."

"Yup."

What a weird-ass morning.

Lou stood and stretched, her back groaning in protest. She'd been planting seedlings and weeding her daffodil and tulip rows all afternoon and her body ached.

It was a good ache, all in all. A hard-day's-work badge, Grandpa would have said. She looked over at the stables. All the horses were gone, but that was where he would've been this time of night a few years ago.

She tried to shake away the melancholy, collecting her buckets and tools and heading for her barn. She took a minute to look at it in all its renovated and repainted glory. Mostly thanks to Gavin's ceaseless help, no matter that he had his own work to do over at the Tyler Ranch.

She'd been too wrapped up in grief and her recovery from the fire to truly appreciate all the help he'd put into rebuilding Lou's Blooms. Now he was going to marry her for a while so she could keep it.

She knew he got something out of it too. After all, it was his dream to run his own spread. But it didn't stop her from feeling a well of gratitude she didn't have the slightest clue what to do with.

As she was dumping her weed bucket, she heard a car and shaded her eyes against the slowly setting sun. Thank God the days were getting longer and warmer.

Em's clunker approached, though she didn't turn off the engine or get out. She opened her window and poked her head out. "The Slice Is Right for dinner?"

Lou wiped her hands on her work pants. "Sure. Gotta shower and get dressed."

"Hurry up, then. I told the Tylers we'd meet them there around six."

Lou hesitated. "The Tylers?"

"Yeah. Molly and Gavin for sure. I'm pretty sure Cora, Shane, and Micah are all coming, though at least Cora. I think they're going to try to convince Boone too."

"Aren't we going over for dinner with the Tylers tomorrow night?"

"Yeah, but that's not pizza." Em frowned. "You're not wanting to avoid the Tylers for any specific reason, are you?"

"No."

"Certainly not because Gavin apparently had breakfast here this morning?" Em smiled sweetly.

"I have no problem with Gavin being at The Slice Is

Right or Grandma's kitchen table at five thirty in the morning," Lou replied loftily.

"Well, la di da. What exactly does that all mean?"

"It means I'll go get cleaned up. Sit tight or go say hi to Grandma."

Lou walked over to the house. When her phone buzzed, she pulled it out of her back pocket to find a text from Gavin.

Wear something pretty.

She scowled and typed her response. Bite me.

Think of the gossip, babe.

Call me babe again and the gossip will be Gavin Tyler is missing a piece of important anatomy.

All right, darlin'.

She would never in a million years admit, most especially to him, that it made her laugh. That she felt something like *happy* as she rushed through a shower. She moved to pull on a pair of jeans, but Gavin was right. If she got a *little* prettied up, it might cause a few whispers in Gracely. Enough that their impending wedding, if going that far proved necessary, wouldn't come totally out of left field.

So, she rummaged around in her closet. Unfortunately, most of the clothes she had that covered the scars on her arms were of the work variety. All her cute clothes had been purchased prefire, without concern for burn-victim Lou.

That thought dimmed some of her earlier happiness, but eventually she found a flowery maxi dress and a chunky sweater to throw over the spaghetti-strapped top. The sweater was the kind of weave that left big holes in the fabric, but Lou examined herself in the mirror and couldn't see any of her arm scars showing through.

Feeling unaccountably nervous, she threw on some mascara and lip gloss. It was nothing. Em was always dressed far cuter and nicer, with way more makeup. This was hardly akin to putting on a ball gown.

Still, Lou felt like a pig in lipstick, or gloss, as the case may be.

She shoved her feet into her usual go-to-town boots, then rolled her eyes at herself. She had some cute purple flats Em had bought her for her birthday a few years back. She rarely wore them, so they had to be in her closet somewhere.

It took a few minutes that would make them late, but she finally found them and slid her feet into them. She grabbed her purse and refused to look at herself in the mirror. Her scars weren't showing, and that was all that mattered.

She fingered her bandanna, making sure it was in place as she went back downstairs. Em was sitting with Grandma on the porch, and they both stared at her like she'd grown a second head.

"What?" she demanded irritably.

"My. Don't you look pretty," Grandma said.

Lou shrugged. This was the point, but much like this morning and finding Gavin at the table, it didn't make it *comfortable*. "I just . . ."

"It's good to see you put your best foot forward again," Grandma said, reaching over to pat Lou's arm. "But at least warn me if I'm going to be making breakfast for three again."

Lou's cheeks heated. "No . . . no."

Grandma shrugged, as if it was no skin off her

nose. Was this the grandmother who had repeatedly passed judgment on all and sundry who had sex out of wedlock—TV or movie characters, people she knew, and so on?

Lou didn't even know *what* to do with that. Was her grandmother really that desperate to see her and Em married she'd forgo her strict moral codes?

It shouldn't be a surprise, considering Grandma was thinking about bringing Dad back. She was absolutely *that* serious about everything.

"Well, you girls have fun. I think I'm going to sit out here a bit longer and read."

"You could come with us," Em offered.

"No. I'll save up my energy for our trip over to the Tyler place tomorrow. God knows Maisey and I will end up fencing or racing."

Bizarre but true. Gavin's Grandma Maisey and her grandmother couldn't seem to get within ten feet of each other without challenging each other to ridiculous feats of strength or agility.

"You could just say n—" Lou stopped talking at her grandmother's imperious, raised-eyebrow stare.

"Bring me back a slice, dears. Have fun."

Em leaned down and kissed Grandma on the cheek, and Lou mirrored the movement. They walked to Em's car, Lou's stomach a maze of knots and nerves.

"So," Em said into the silence of her car as she turned the key in the ignition.

"So."

"You really slept with Gavin," Em said, as if she couldn't believe it.

Probably because it is *impossible to believe or allow yourself to think about.* "I really did," Lou forced herself to reply. They had slept next to each other. In the same bed. Technically, that was *slept with.*

"So." Em kept her eyes on the road as she drove them off the gravel and onto the highway that would lead them into Gracely proper. "Was Cora's theory about the Tyler men's endowments on point?"

Lou's cheeks heated so fast she had to lift her non-gloved hand to cool it down. "I . . . I can't talk about this with y—" Then it dawned on her who she was talking to. "Wait. You dated Gavin for almost *two* years."

Em opened her mouth, then closed it. She tapped her fingers on the steering wheel for a few seconds. "Well, yes."

"You're telling me you two never . . ." Lou could only stare at the odd look of guilt on Em's face.

"I was fifteen."

"But . . . you didn't even . . ." Lou fidgeted. She didn't want to have this conversation with her little sister. She desperately wanted to know the truth. "I'd think even a virginal fifteen-year-old would have an *idea* about things below the belt."

"We just . . . weren't like that," Em said, in that voice Lou had always known meant *lie.*

"What were you like, then?" *It doesn't matter.*

"Does it matter?"

No. Not at all. "It wouldn't have, if you hadn't made me think differently this entire decade."

Em chewed on her lip, then shook her head. She adopted that fake smile she used on obnoxious brides. "We're almost there. Now's hardly the time to discuss—"

"Em."

Em blew out a breath, and her fingers tightened on the steering wheel. She didn't look at Lou. "Okay, so the truth is Gavin and I weren't exactly . . . I mean, it was more of a . . ." Em pulled a face and then seemed to come to terms with whatever it was she wanted to say. "Do you remember Lane Beaumont?"

"Vividly," Lou replied, unable to keep the venom out of her voice even though it had been something like ten years since she'd seen that creepy piece of shit. "He all but stalked you."

"He didn't . . . I'm not going to argue about that. But the truth is, after Grandma and Grandpa forbade me to even be his friend, I made some poor choices."

Lou's heart all but stopped. She knew everything about Em. Every rule she'd broken. Every poor choice she'd made. She was her protector. "What kind of poor choices?"

"The sneaking-out-and-seeing-him-on-the-sly kind."

"Emily Anne Fairchild, he was an eighteen-year-old pervert."

"Well, I was thirteen. And stupid. I thought it was romantic. As an adult, looking back, I get it was creepy, but in the moment, it felt like love. So, I'd sneak out with him. For a year."

"How . . . how?" Grandma and Grandpa had always been strict and careful, and she had protected Em. Always. *How?*

Em shrugged, pulling into a space in the parking lot of The Slice Is Right. "He had all sorts of sneaky tricks up his sleeve. Ways to lie, places to say I was. Making sure things added up. He was a pro."

"He was a predator."

"I don't know. Maybe. He was gross, yes. I do think he liked me. I mean, he spent a year trying to . . ."

"Trying to *what*?"

"Have sex with me. I got to the point I felt like I kind of had to if I wanted him to still love me. So, we had sex."

"Em." It hurt physically. She'd spent so much time

trying to protect and shield her sister from exactly that kind of thing. How miserably Lou had failed. And all this time she hadn't *known*.

"I didn't like it. I said I didn't want to do it again for a while, and . . . Well, at that point I was a freshman. His younger brother was a sophomore. He said he'd make sure all of Gracely High knew I'd spread my legs for *anyone*."

Lou couldn't even find her voice. She was shaking with rage, desperate for the ability to go back in time and fix this. Beat Lane Beaumont to a bloody pulp.

"I still wouldn't give in. I was scared of that, scared of what Grandma and Grandpa would think. They were so good to us. I don't know why I thought they'd send me back to Mom or Dad, I just did."

"Yeah, I . . . You could have told *me*." She understood that indescribable fear of disappointing their grandparents. Hurting them in a way that would cause them to turn their backs on her. Lou wasn't sure she'd even fully grown out of that fear. It was just she was an adult with choices now.

"Except I felt the same about you. I knew everything you did to protect me, and even if I couldn't put it into words, I knew how important it was to you that I was safe. I was afraid you'd hate me."

"Em."

"I was fifteen by that time. Stupid and full of hormones and . . . The thing was, I was scared to tell anyone. I was scared of everything. Then Lane just kind of stranded me in this place we used to meet, and I had to walk back home. Thankfully, it was out on the other side of the Tyler place, and Gavin was coming home from basketball practice and saw me."

"Jesus, Em. *Jesus*."

"So, of course, Gavin being Gavin, he insisted I tell

him what on earth I was doing and why I was so upset. He promised he wouldn't let that rumor spread. I thought he was full of it."

"I never heard . . ."

"As far as I know, no one did. School went on as it always had, except I started to hear rumors that Gavin and *I* were dating. When I talked to him about it, he'd just shrug and say we might as well go along with it for a while. I never did figure out exactly what he did, but at that point I was too relieved to care."

"So, I'm supposed to wrap my head around Lane doing all of those disgusting, horrible things to you *and* the fact that you and Gavin only . . . fake dated. And I was completely clueless."

"I purposely kept it from you. I was careful and calculating. That's not a failure on your part, Lou."

Isn't it?

"Besides, Gavin and I kind of tried. Not at first, but you know, we kissed a few times. But I just hero-worshipped him, and I think he always thought of me more in the sister category."

"Why didn't you tell anyone when you broke up?"

Em shrugged. "It didn't seem important. Even though we hadn't had like a *romantic* relationship, we'd spent a lot of time together. He was graduating high school and it was time to move on, but it still felt kind of sad. If I'd explained the whole thing, I couldn't have treated it like a breakup and please, again, remember, I had just turned seventeen. I was all hormones and emotions and no sense."

Lou didn't know how to process any of it. It was like finding out half her life was a lie. She'd been so sure she'd spared Em awful things, but it wasn't true. She'd been sure she understood all the people in her life, but she didn't. At all.

"Come on, let's go inside, huh? It's not a big deal. It's all over, and I've dealt with it. It was my stuff to deal with." Em reached out and gave Lou's bandanna a gentle tug. "Unless you're ready to let me in on your stuff."

"I don't have stuff. Not like that."

"I know strangers might stare," Em said in a low, serious voice, her fingers still on Lou's bandanna. "I get that it isn't fun. But the people who love you don't care about scars. You don't have to put up these shields with us."

"It's not about the people who love me. It's about how *I* feel."

"You keep saying that, but I'm having trouble buying it."

A little outraged, Lou opened her mouth to argue, but Em was climbing out of the car.

So, Lou had to follow. She hopped out and felt just . . . so damn stupid. Dressed foolishly, this bandanna over her face, all the ways she'd failed Em, and then somehow, biggest of all in her mind right now, Gavin had lied and kept things from her too. He wasn't the open book she'd always believed.

She trailed after Em, trying to find some numb place to focus on so she could get a hold of all this roiling inside her. They stepped into the warmth and spicy scents of The Slice Is Right. Not too busy on a Wednesday night, but not as dead as Gracely had been for most of her adulthood.

Gavin was sitting in a booth, clearly boxing Boone in, while Shane, Cora, and Micah sat across from them. They were chattering and, if she had to guess, trying to irritate Boone. Trying and succeeding. Molly approached the table, pulling up a chair. She caught sight of Em and Lou standing at the entrance and waved them over.

Gavin looked over the back of the booth. He grinned at her. She thought she'd known everything about Gavin. Heart and soul. That only *she* had secrets and pieces of herself she kept hidden from everyone.

But it wasn't true, and she wasn't sure what to do with that.

Chapter Nine

When Lou just stood at the entrance to the pizza place, looking at him like he was some kind of blood-soaked ghost, Gavin wasn't sure what to think.

Em moved for the table, and after a few seconds Lou did too. She wasn't dressed in her normal ranch wear. She had a skirt on, and even makeup, if he wasn't totally mistaken.

He tried not to grin too widely that she'd actually done what he'd texted her to do. He slid out of the booth and gestured Em in to sit next to Boone. Then Lou to follow her.

Em greeted the group cheerfully, but Lou slid into the booth, her eyes on him and him alone.

He couldn't begin to figure out what was going on in that pretty blue gaze of hers. Still, he perched himself on the very edge of the booth next to her and casually looped his arm over her shoulders.

He pretended not to notice as Cora and Shane shared a speculative glance, and as Molly frowned. What he *did* notice was, Lou didn't stiffen under his arm. She just kind of turned her head and stared at him.

So, he smiled. She blinked.

What the hell?

The conversation around them ebbed and flowed. Cora and Em talking about some bride they were both working with. Molly and Boone arguing about horses while Micah dropped not-so-subtle hints to Shane about how he needed a dog.

But Lou was silent, and mostly just staring at him, and it made it hard for Gavin to pay attention to the conversations around him. He leaned his mouth close to her ear, kept the smile on his face for the sake of everyone around him even though he felt more worried than jovial. But a smile and a whisper would make everyone think they were flirting.

"Everything okay?" he whispered.

She didn't even jump, just looked up at him with those big blue eyes, the right one only concealed by the bandanna at the very corner. "Yeah. Fine."

"Why are you looking at me like you found out I killed your dog or something?"

"That's not how I'm looking at you."

Gavin realized the table had grown silent around them, and that all eyes—even Micah's—were on him whispering in Lou's ear. Much as that worked in their overall favor, Gavin would rather they didn't pay too much attention to what they were saying.

"Jukebox," he said under his breath, squeezing out of the booth in the small space he had with Molly sitting in a chair at the end of the table.

"I—"

But he didn't give her a chance to argue, just took her hand and pulled her along. But she didn't tug her hand away or refuse to come. She docilely followed him across the pizza parlor to the jukebox.

A few couples and families glanced at them, but no one he knew too well.

"Did you want to actually talk about something or is

this just for show?" Lou asked, and it somehow didn't sound accusatory or disapproving. She sounded like she was genuinely interested in his motives.

He didn't know what to do with this new, weird, acquiescent Lou. "Well, I wanted to let you know, I drove separate so I could drive you home."

"Oh. That's a good idea."

A good idea. Lou had just accused him of having a good idea. The world was ending. "Okay, Lou, you're freaking me out."

"Why?"

"*You* just admitted *I* had a good idea."

She crossed her arms over her chest. The sweater was all . . . holey, for lack of a better word, and he could see the fair hue of her skin through every hole. It was strangely mesmerizing.

"I can admit when you have a good idea," she said defensively.

He forced himself to look up from her arm and meet her gaze. "But you typically don't."

She shook her head. "I'm just out of sorts. Keep doing what you're doing." She glanced at the table. "It's going great." Her eyebrows drew together. "Oh, but then, you have practice, don't you?"

"Practice?"

She lifted her chin, almost as if she was accusing him of something. "Pretending to be someone's boyfriend. Almost two years of practice, apparently."

Gavin's eyebrows rose, and he glanced back at the table at Em. She was laughing with Molly. "She told you," Gavin murmured, slowly turning his gaze back to Lou. "After all this time?"

"She did."

"Why?"

"I don't know. We were talking about . . ." Lou

blushed, and even though she'd been doing that a *lot* lately, he couldn't quite get over it. He couldn't remember ever seeing her cheeks get all pink like that. Couldn't describe the way his stomach seemed to fill with helium and start to float away when she did.

"We were talking about what she thought you and I did last night," Lou said in a rush, determined to say it, but not all that determined to dwell on it.

"Ah."

"And she said something about . . . something, and I just had always assumed you two had . . ."

"We didn't."

"Yes, well, she explained that. The whole thing."

The whole thing. He still couldn't figure out why she hadn't slugged him yet. "So, when are you going to start yelling at me?"

"I'm not mad at you."

"*You* aren't mad at me? I expected you to read me the riot act about not telling you when it was going on." Possibly throw a few punches. Ones he'd let land because, well, it'd probably make her feel better.

But Lou just stood there looking contemplative, and maybe a little sad. Not even a flash of anger. "I might have. I probably would have if I'd found out sooner, but some of the things Em said . . ." Lou wrinkled her nose. "About not wanting to disappoint Grandma and Grandpa or . . . me. Well, as much as I wish I had known so I could have gone and beat that piece of shit to the ground, I understand why she didn't want to tell us. If you had told me, it would have hurt her. So, I can't be mad about that."

"The only reason I *didn't* beat that piece of shit to the ground was because he folded so quickly when I threatened him, it wasn't even worth it. I just did what

I'd want someone to do if it were Molly or Lindsay in that situation. Of course, then he just spread the rumor Em and I were together. I could have ignored it, but it seemed safer for Em if we went along. I didn't figure too many guys would try to mess with her if people thought she was dating me."

Her mouth almost curved. "You did have a reputation for fists first, talk later."

Gavin chuckled. "Well, it worked in our favor. So . . . is that it? You really don't want to yell at me?"

She shook her head. "No. I'm glad you were there, that someone was. I tried so hard to protect her from that kind of thing, and to find out I failed . . ."

She sounded miserable, utterly gutted. So, he took her hand and gave it a squeeze. "Listen, I know you want to beat yourself up, but Em handled it okay. I mean, look at her. Assholes have a sixth sense about who they can take advantage of, but she didn't let it continue."

Lou looked down at her shoes. "We still talking about Em here, or are we moving into Rex territory?"

"Hey, I was friends with Rex. Best friends for a while there," he said, because the last thing he wanted Lou to feel was some kind of shame for Rex's mistakes. "I get Rex's appeal, or at least I did then. That wasn't the same . . . exactly." He might not understand how she could have wasted eight years of her life on the man Rex became, but that didn't mean he didn't understand why she'd picked him in the first place.

She snorted. "Uh-huh."

He really didn't want to stand here and talk about *Rex territory*. "The thing is, everything that happened with Em, it was kind of a coincidence and all, but it laid the groundwork. I'd already done it, so it made sense to do it for you. It gave me the idea for this anyway. I'm a pretend-to-have-a-relationship-with-Fairchild-women expert."

He expected her to laugh or roll her eyes, but she kept that solemn gaze squarely on him. "But Em said you tried. For a while, you both tried to make it real."

"We did. There just wasn't . . ." He felt very uncomfortable with this line of conversation. "Oh look, the pizza—"

"Why?"

"Why did I try? I . . ." Gavin rubbed a hand across the back of his neck. Talk about your thorny territories. "She was pretty. We got along. It felt like there should be something there. It made sense to try, if we were going to be around each other a lot anyway."

"We're going to be around each other a lot anyway."

Gavin could only stare at her. She couldn't be saying . . . No, no. He wasn't going down this road again, where he read into every little thing, trying to discern whether she liked him. He wasn't fifteen anymore. He wouldn't go back there. "You wouldn't want that," he said firmly.

"No," she said, this weird tonelessness to her voice he didn't understand. "You wouldn't either."

Gavin wanted to agree with her. He *did* agree with her. He had *no* desire to try for anything real with Lou. He understood enough about himself, and her, to know that if that ship had been meant to be, it would have sailed a long time ago, or some other metaphor that made sense. Point was, Lou had picked Rex back in high school, and that was that. Gavin had moved on. Way, far on. He wasn't a lovesick teenager anymore, and he had a ranch to think about.

"Come on, lovebirds," Molly called. "Get over here and eat or there won't be any left."

"Right," Gavin muttered. "I'm starved," he lied, because right now his stomach felt like it was full of too much lead to be remotely hungry.

The pizza tasted like ash, but she choked down two pieces and pretended to laugh at Gavin's jokes and Molly's teasing.

She went through every motion she could think of because it took a lot of energy, and she'd rather spend it acting like everything was fine and dandy rather than try to understand her conversation with Gavin.

Gavin. She'd always known Gavin was one of the best men she'd ever known. She didn't have a lot of *good* men in her life. It was Grandpa and the Tylers, beginning and end of the list. So, it wasn't a surprise exactly that he'd stepped in and been Em's knight in shining armor.

But there was something about finding out about it *now*, when he was also doing a little saving of *her*, when she was adult enough and mature enough to think about what all the things he did entailed.

First, the fact that he'd had the kind of compassion to care about Em's reputation, her feelings . . . it humbled Lou. Yeah, he might have couched it in thinking about what he'd want for his sisters, but it was still a *thing*. A big thing, especially for a seventeen-year-old. His decency then and now. As an adult, a mature, reasonable adult, it awed her even more now than it had when she'd been a hurting, incapable-of-trusting-anyone-fully nine-year-old.

And, as a mature, reasonable adult, she realized

how much Gavin was giving up by offering to do this thing for *her*. Yes, he got his own spread out of the deal, but he was offering to platonically marry her for the time it would take to get everything moved over to her name and safeguard the ranch—which might take months, months and months.

Months and months where he wouldn't be trying anything with anyone. Voluntarily. She supposed he could sneak around with someone if the . . . need struck. Maybe he'd even done that when he'd been with Em.

But it was a small town, and she didn't know how Gavin would have managed that without getting found out. How he'd manage it now, especially.

She didn't have the right to find the thought horrible, when it was a convenience marriage, but it didn't change the fact that the thought of him cheating on their fake relationship made her feel ill.

He'd tried with Em, for reasons as simple as prettiness and liking each other. Surely she and Gavin shared half of that at least. If they tried . . .

She wanted to laugh at herself. Yes, she was going to magically fall romantically in love with Gavin, and they would have a real marriage. Have the kind of marriage her grandparents had enjoyed, have a family and run a farm and ranch together.

Talk about your fairy tales. She'd never, ever believed in those. She wasn't going to start at thirty.

"Earth to Lou." Lou practically jumped when Em gave her a little elbow to the ribs.

"What?"

"Ready to go?"

"Oh. Sure." She glanced at Gavin, then quickly away. She felt like her thoughts were telegraphed all over her face.

They all piled out of the booth, chatting and moving toward the door. Once in the parking lot they started to disperse, but Gavin took her hand in his, linking their fingers together.

It was amazing that even though she wasn't that much shorter than him, his hands could be so much bigger than hers. That something as simple as fingers touching could have her stomach tied in weird little knots.

They offered their goodbyes, Shane, Cora, and Micah heading off to their truck, Molly and Boone heading toward hers.

"I'll drive Lou home." Gavin smiled at Em. "Save you a trip out to the ranch and back, unless you were planning on spending the night?"

"Were you?" Em asked sweetly.

Gavin didn't even balk. He ignored Em and looked down at her. "Up to you, Lou."

Part of her wanted to refuse. Let Em drive her home and wait to be alone with him until she could figure out what her insides were doing with all these . . . thoughts.

But that wasn't the plan, and there was some old part of her she thought had died in that fire if not before, that wanted to follow that fleeting confusion until she burned up in it. Just like when she'd first been dating Rex and every wild, impossible thing he'd suggested had been exhilarating and irresistible.

She needed to go home with Em.

"I'll just hitch a ride with Gavin then," she said, her voice sounding a little scratchy to her own ears. She tried not to cringe and instead sound oh so casual. "Like he said, save you a trip."

"Uh-huh." Em smiled at them and then surprised Lou by giving her a quick hug. "You two are awfully cute," she whispered and then walked off to her car.

Lou couldn't begin to examine all the pangs that gave her. She didn't like lying to Em, of course, but then there'd been some weird flutter and . . .

Lou shook her head and walked with Gavin to his truck, still hand in hand.

He opened the door for her, then just stood there, waiting for her to climb in. She swallowed at the completely unaccountable nerves jangling in her stomach. But he hadn't given her much room and she had to brush against him to crawl up in the passenger seat.

He was just so . . .

"They watching?" he murmured, leaning way closer than he needed to.

Right, because this was all a show and Gavin was the expert. She looked over his shoulder. Molly and Boone's truck was turning out of the parking lot, but Em and Shane's vehicles were in line behind them, and Lou could definitely see Cora's face practically pressed to the passenger-side window staring at them.

"Some of them."

"Good deal." He pulled away and closed the passenger door carefully. Lou buckled her seat belt and tried to get a mental hold of herself.

Gavin got in the driver's side and started his truck. He didn't say anything, though his expression seemed perfectly at ease. He even hummed along to the radio as he pulled out of the parking spot.

Lou moved her gaze straight ahead. Of course she was feeling churned up. This was a bit of a weird situation, and finding out Gavin had once helped Em this way was a big revelation, even if it didn't mean anything..

Except he never really dated Em.

Well, what did that matter? He'd dated plenty of other women. Some she'd met and some she hadn't.

Now he's giving up that opportunity for you.

She almost couldn't bear it. She knew she didn't deserve it, and quite honestly, the only reason she continued to move forward was because she knew how much he wanted to run his own place. He was doing this for himself as much as her.

But he was giving up other women. Giving up sex, for the foreseeable future. Today was some awful perfect storm of having to consider these things. What would it be like?

Oh sweet Lord, you cannot let yourself imagine that.

Maybe he wasn't actually thinking he'd give up anything. Maybe he figured because it was platonic, he'd just do whatever he wanted.

"If we actually end up getting married, I don't want you cheating on me even though it's fake," she blurted out over the soft strains of some old country song coming from the speakers.

"I wasn't . . . I wasn't planning on it." He spared her a quick, puzzled glance. "Where did that come from?"

"It's just I've been the butt of that particular town joke, and I don't want to do it again." It had been bad enough with Rex long after she'd realized she hadn't loved him anymore but long before she'd had the balls to end it. She couldn't imagine enduring the gossip when it was Gavin. When it was fake. When it would look poorly on him and hurt her and—

"Lou, I wouldn't—"

She had to keep going or she wouldn't get it out. "But if you needed . . . well, you know, people have needs. And if you needed something like that—I mean, we could . . ." Oh, God, what was she doing?

"We could . . ." Gavin trailed off, but Lou couldn't bear to look at him.

She was trying to be nice. She was trying to be *considerate.* To offset the possibility of that kind of embarrassment. For both of them. For their families. But she couldn't handle what that might look like to him. "Just, you know, if you had to."

"You're not saying what I think you're saying."

Frustrated by the horror in his tone, she glared at him. "I'm trying to be nice!"

"Oh, good, I've always wanted someone to offer sex *to be nice.*" His expression was stormy, his words acidic, and that made something she didn't understand roil uncomfortably in her gut.

"I wasn't offering . . . that. I was offering . . ."

"Oh, I'm all ears. What were you offering?"

She couldn't believe he was being a jerk about this. "Never mind."

"Oh, no, please, enlighten me. I'm dying to know what you were offering with that little line of thought."

Lou felt small and stupid in the force of Gavin's temper. He rarely used that quick one on her, at least without some warning, but here it was. That hard edge to him she'd never feared, because it wasn't like Rex's. It wasn't anything like the men she'd encountered before coming to the Fairchild Ranch.

Which had always made it easier to witness. Simple to defuse. Except she wasn't usually the cause like this, and she had no way to defuse anything except the truth. "You've given up a lot for us. Sacrificed things. Em's little confession just got me thinking about all the things we haven't considered. The implications beyond the fact that it would get us both what we want."

Gavin pulled up to her house and let out a long

breath. His gaze was on the house, and she didn't know what else to say. "You should never feel like you owe me something you don't want to give. I suggested this. I'm getting something out of this. After all these years of friendship, you really think I can't . . ."

"It's not that."

"Then what is it?"

"I don't know. I don't know." She pressed a hand to her chest. Something like panic beat there, and she tried to rub it away.

He turned off the truck and opened the driver's side door.

"What are you doing?"

"Walking you to your door," he replied, but it had none of that light fun his voice usually included when he was doing something to prove to everyone they were a thing. He was all fury and . . . hurt wasn't the right word, but something in that family.

She scrambled to follow him up to her porch, stepping up onto the stairs before he could and standing in front of him so he'd stop his forward motion. "Gavin, I'm sorry if—"

He stepped onto the same stair so they were practically nose to nose, and he was so *fierce* in the glow of the porch light, she didn't know what to do.

"You don't owe me anything. Ever. Got it?"

"That isn't—"

"Because if we ever sleep together, Lou, it's damn well going to be because we both want to."

Her breath caught at that, because that seemed to mean there was some possibility for that to ever, *ever* happen and—

He leaned in, so close that not only did her breath stay stuck in her lungs but she couldn't manage a coherent thought. His nose touched her cheek and his mouth was so close to hers, she was afraid to move.

"Your grandma's spying on us," he said under his breath.

"Oh?" She moved her head to look, but Gavin placed his palm on her cheek and kept her head in place.

"Well, don't look, dummy."

She scowled at him.

"Going to have to do something you're not going to like."

"What's th—"

His mouth touched hers. Light, featherlight. He didn't deepen it. His hand remained exactly where it was on her cheek, and still it felt like there was a rope around her lungs, cinching tighter and tighter until she couldn't breathe at all.

Gavin's mouth was on hers. Soft and sweet, and she could feel the slight hint of whiskers on his chin. His hand was on her cheek, rough and callused.

It was a *nothing* kiss. Some people probably even kissed friends like that. But it shook her to her very core, so much so that when he pulled away, having done little more than press his mouth to hers, she could only stare at him. Gaping like a fish.

His smile was crooked, and he tipped his hat. "See you tomorrow, Lou."

She couldn't manage to repeat the sentiment. She could only stand in the glow of the porch light and watch him drive away.

Chapter Ten

"Oh, well, there he is."

Gavin turned from his spot by the coffeepot to find his youngest sister on the threshold. "Shouldn't you be off warping the young minds of the world with ideas that they can follow their dreams of art and joy?"

"It's spring break, genius."

"Then shouldn't you be at Cal's?"

"I don't have to spend every waking moment with Cal."

"Isn't that funny? You could have fooled me." He'd always enjoyed teasing his baby sister. She was the easiest to rile up, but this morning it wasn't nearly as satisfying as it usually was.

"Well, while we're standing here talking about significant others, let's talk about yours."

Gavin turned his gaze back to the coffeepot, willing it to brew faster. "What about mine?"

"I apparently missed quite the dinner last night."

"Did you? I mean, pizza is good and all, but I don't know what's so exciting about it."

"You and Lou were all over each other."

He wanted to correct her, because they had hardly

been *all over each other*, but if the gossip was working that fast, he supposed it was all well and good. "And?"

"*And*, jackass, that's new. As is you being late enough to miss Grandma's breakfast."

"Not that new." Well, not sleeping well at all was a *little* new.

Lindsay sighed. "Oh my God, get your coffee already, and when you're done, could we *please* have an actual conversation?"

"I don't have time for actual conversations. Big day. Lots of work. Already late." He poured coffee into his thermos and yawned. He needed to work off this edge inside of him he couldn't explain. Focus on something other than Lou's insane behavior last night.

And that kiss. You have definitely been focusing on that kiss.

Which really needed to stop considering it had been at most a friendly . . . lingering peck. He turned away from the coffeepot, screwing the lid on the thermos. Lindsay blocked the exit from the kitchen and he sighed. "Why are you making my life difficult? Go make Cal's life difficult."

"Gav," she said gravely, reaching up and putting her hands on his shoulders.

"Linds."

"Do you have time for me to be happy for you for like ten seconds?"

Even though he wasn't happy in the way she thought, and was actually kind of pissy about *everything*, his lips quirked into a smile. "If your ten seconds starts now."

"I like you and Lou. A lot. I mean, separately too, but together especially. Rex was such a tool, and you are very much not."

Uncomfortable with the comparison, and with the

praise when this wasn't what Lindsay thought it was, Gavin could only manage being a little bit of a smart-ass. "Your blessing is noted and compliment filed away for later use."

Lindsay dropped her hands and chewed on her lip, her expression going serious over happy. "Are you going to see Lou today?"

"Yeah."

"I hate to be the bearer of bad news, but Gene's wife told me he found a new job. I don't think he'll be with the Fairchilds much longer."

"Seriously?"

Lindsay nodded. "Maybe Mrs. Fairchild would let you help out now that you and Lou are seeing each other. Maybe it'd be like keeping it in the family."

"Yeah. Yeah, maybe. We'll give it a shot."

She gave him a quick hug, then moved out of the way so he could get out to work. "Well, I'll see you at dinner tonight."

Right. Dinner. With the Fairchilds and his family. Knowing Gene was going to quit.

He strode outside, lost in his own thoughts. Gene quitting was a blow to his timeline. A blow period. If the Fairchild Ranch got even farther behind or in the red, Gavin wouldn't have much left to work with. Just as bad, if not worse, it put Lou in danger of losing her place and having to deal with the father she so desperately didn't want to deal with before they could really convince everyone they were a thing.

They had to put their plan into motion quicker than they'd expected, and Lou's *if* we end up having to get married was going to have to turn into *when.*

It settled sharp and uncomfortable in his gut. He was prepared for the eventuality. He'd made the offer knowing full well what he'd sacrifice and what he'd gain. Somewhere between selfish and selfless, he knew what he was doing.

But that stupid conversation last night. The way she'd looked at him just because he'd done a favor for Em once upon a time. Like that changed anything. Like that meant she should . . .

He shook away that thought. He couldn't dwell there when there were real problems to dwell on. How was he going to convince his family, and Lou's, and Lou herself that setting the marriage wheels in motion needed to start *now*?

"Oh, look, princess has decided to join us," Boone greeted from where he leaned against the fence.

"Funny coming from the guy sitting on his ass spectating rather than lending a hand. Or are your legs not the only thing that are busted?" It was too harsh, and Gavin immediately regretted the words, but he wasn't in much of a mood to admit that.

"What crawled up your ass and died?" Boone demanded.

"I don't know, maybe it's whatever's been up yours for the past six months."

"All right," Shane interrupted. "I don't need to know anything about what's up anyone's ass. Let's finish getting the truck loaded, huh?"

Shane and Gavin worked to load the hay bales onto the truck bed. With the snow finally melted almost everywhere, Ben and a few men would be off checking fences, and another crew would be checking for what spring repairs would need to be accomplished before calving season really got underway.

As spring did its thing and the grass started growing again, they'd slowly start cutting back on the daily cattle feeding. But they still had a way to go for that, so Boone would drive Gavin and the hay out to the pastures and he'd spread some feed for the herd.

It was the kind of mindless work he'd prefer on a day he wasn't thinking about all the ways the next few days could blow up in his face. Then again, why not start right here? If Shane or Boone laughed in his face or demanded to know why, well, it'd give him a training ground of sorts to work on his story.

"I'm going to propose to Lou," he blurted, lifting a bale with a grunt and throwing it onto the truck.

"Propose what?"

Gavin spared Boone a glare.

"That's . . . fast," Shane said far more equitably than Boone.

"Twenty years isn't fast," Gavin muttered, throwing the last bale onto the truck.

"You look awfully green for a guy who knows what he's doing," Boone offered, not doing anything to help Gavin's snapping temper.

Shane tossed Boone the keys to the truck. "You come talk to me when you're ready to propose and tell me how sure and confident you feel."

"You weren't?" Boone replied, as taken aback by that as Gavin himself was.

"Hell no. Even when you love someone and you're sure you want to spend the rest of your life with her, it doesn't mean marriage is some easy decision. There's lots to consider, and quite a few pitfalls."

"Then why the hell did you do it?" Boone demanded.

"Because I love Cora, and Micah, and the in-the-now positives outweighed any potential pitfalls. I was sure. I'll always be sure. Doesn't mean it's not scary." Shane clapped Gavin on the shoulder. "Come on. I'll come with you."

"Don't you have other things to do?"

Shane shook his head and climbed up into the bed. "I'll handle it. Grab another pitchfork."

Gavin did as he was told as Boone got in the truck. Gavin handed Shane the tools, then climbed over the bales himself. He settled in a corner in the back opposite Shane.

"So. Proposing," Shane said as Boone started the truck and began driving toward the north pasture. "You sure about this?"

"No," Gavin said. Because why not give an honest answer? Shane didn't know the whole story, but everything else could be honest.

"Marriage is a big step," Shane said in that maddening older-brother voice.

"No shit, Sherlock."

Shane chuckled. "Do you think she'll say yes?"

"I don't know." Because this was coming at them a lot faster than he'd planned and Lou was never quite predictable about anything, let alone this whole scheme. They'd managed to convince everyone they were involved smoothly enough, but ready to get married?

"You could wait."

"I could."

"But you won't?"

They reached the pasture, and Shane hopped out to open the fence. Boone drove the truck through and Shane locked the fence back up before getting into the truck. Gavin poked one of the pales with his pitchfork, trying to work out how to explain it all to his older brother.

The worst part was, he wanted advice. He wanted someone to talk to about the whole thing—not just what to do, but that whole bullshit conversation last night and what went on in women's brains, because he for sure didn't understand a thing.

He wanted to ask why some wisp of a kiss that shouldn't have registered anything had felt like being ripped apart and stitched back together.

He'd rather cut his own balls off than voice any of that last part, but maybe he could cop a little to the first and get Shane's take. "Maybe it's not the best reason to rush into marriage, but they're going to lose that ranch if Mrs. Fairchild doesn't change her mind about some things. I could wait, I could, but I could also do it now and maybe step in and help." Both he and Shane moved forward in the bed and started to pitch hay into the field.

The cows began trotting over, following the trail of feed, and Gavin wished that for a day or two his life could be as simple as a cow's.

"I love Lou," he managed, which was true. Friendship love and all that. He loved Em too. They were part of his life, the very fabric of it. A teenage crush and a certain amount of adult attraction didn't mean it was the kind of love you wrote poems about or whatever. "I'm not sure timing matters. At least, not to me."

"You're right, it's not the best reason to get married," Shane obnoxiously agreed. "But I'd venture to say it's not the worst reason either. As much as I know you want to run your own place, you wouldn't be inserting yourself in this if you didn't think you could save Lou some harm. I think the trick is making sure you're upfront about that. Marriage should never be built on a lie or an omission."

"You should write a book with all these marriage wisdom gems."

"Well, I would, but apparently I'm going to be running this place all on my own."

"Don't forget Mom, Molly, Ben and . . . well, maybe even Boone."

"Sure. They're no Gavin Tyler, though."

"Whatever," Gavin muttered, uncomfortable with the praise and the foreign emotion clogging his throat.

"I know you get pissed when I sound like a dad, but I'm proud of you, Gav. You're a good rancher and a good man. I know if you get the chance, you'll do good with the Fairchild place, and I know you'll be a good husband."

"Yeah, you had nothing to do with that," Gavin offered, his voice rusty against his tightening throat.

Shane cleared his. "When I tell Cora about this later, she's going to ask if we hugged."

"You married a perv." When Shane rolled his eyes, Gavin shook his head. "Let's not and say we did."

"Deal."

Lou wasn't in the mood to figure out why the tulips in her high tunnel were blasting. Not that it mattered in the grand scheme of things. They weren't usable or salable regardless of what had caused the blooms to come out so abnormal.

After a bad night's sleep and the news Gene was quitting, Lou didn't have the emotional energy to deal with this blow in a healthy way. She was a little tempted to lay down in the middle pathway and throw a full-blown toddler tantrum.

She only had two-and-a-half weeks before the upcoming wedding, and the farmers market where she had held a booth started just about the same time.

She'd wanted to quit on it last summer, but sheer spite had driven her out. Let everyone look at Lou the burn victim selling her flowers at the farmers market.

Her spite seemed to have died in the winter. She just wanted to stay home and hide away from everything and everyone.

"Here you are."

She turned to find Gavin stepping through the door of the high tunnel. He had his hat pulled low on his head so she couldn't make out his expression, but something about him seemed tense.

She stared at him for a moment. Gavin wouldn't back down or give up on something he wanted, no matter how hard it got. He'd fight through it all. In the past that kind of thinking had defeated her. Everyone handled things better than her, but she'd been through a fire that had threatened to end her business and could have seriously ended her life and there was something in that . . .

She wasn't perfect. Half the time she wasn't even very good, but she'd certainly paid her dues. Why shouldn't she keep going? Keep working? Why should she hide away instead of going after and getting some of the things she wanted?

Gene had quit. He was only giving Grandma a week to find a replacement. Grandma could be in the house right now calling her father. Or Lou could step up and do something about it.

"We have to talk." They were going to have to speed up this marriage thing. The idea tied her stomach into knots, but they'd agreed to this plan. Gavin had *suggested* this plan. It wasn't like she was taking advantage of him. He was getting something out of it.

"Picnic lunch," he said, his tone oddly gruff. "No talking until then."

"Gav—"

"Come on now. Time's a wasting." He grabbed her hand and started pulling her toward the door.

"I'm filthy!"

"Doesn't matter."

"Why are you—"

He opened his truck door. "In you go."

She crossed her arms over her chest and planted her feet on the ground. "I won't go a step farther until you tell me what the hell's going on."

He flicked the brim of his hat so it went up and he could stare at her. He flashed one of those devious grins that had her stomach doing somersaults she usually ignored very resolutely. "Want to bet?"

"What are you going to do? Lift me up and force me into the truck?"

He stepped toward her, as if he was going to make a move to lift her up. She didn't trust that odd glint in his eye, so she sidestepped him and climbed into the truck primly.

"You're being weird," she informed him when he climbed in the driver's side.

"That I am." He turned the ignition on the truck and backed out of the spot, turning around and heading toward where he presumably came from: the Tyler Ranch. He even cut through the property, which Mrs. T frowned upon, though all her kids did it now and again.

"I'm coming over for dinner. I don't think we need to have lunch together. I don't have this kind of time. But we do need to talk."

"We do, and we need to do it before dinner tonight." He kept his gaze on the gravel path that led him back to the ranch. He'd left the fence open, and drove back through. He didn't head toward the house or any of the pastures or even the stables. He followed the fence line back into the small wooded area that straddled the Tyler and Fairchild properties.

All the Tylers and Fairchilds had played back here as kids. Partly because it was away from the prying eyes of adults, and partly because it was next to the Tyler family cemetery, where they'd tried to scare one another to death. Because it wasn't enclosed pastureland for the cows, unlike most of the other places on the ranch, it was a safe space to run around and act like fools.

Something in the air seemed heavy almost, and she couldn't find her voice even though they'd just agreed they needed to talk. She wanted to ask him where they were going, or tell him that Gene had quit, or anything important.

But instead she sat there letting the silence stretch around them. She watched Gavin out of the corner of her eye and couldn't read this serious, grim side of him. At least not when it came to her. Sometimes he looked like that when things were bad with Shane or Boone. He'd looked like that a lot last summer, when he'd been so mad Deb was planning on marrying Ben.

But what could *she* have done to get that kind of reaction from him? What could be happening that had to do with them . . . Oh, God. Maybe he wanted to call the whole thing off.

Oh. God. Oh, *God.* She'd mentioned sex stuff last night and now he wanted to get the hell out of Dodge. Or maybe her kiss was so repellent, he'd decided he couldn't even pretend. Maybe all Rex's stupid comments she'd always brushed off as him trying to be mean were true. She was a frigid bitch destined to be a spinster for life.

"Come on."

Lou blinked out of her horrible reverie of past mistakes and potential new ones, realizing Gavin had parked and already gotten out of the truck. She didn't want to get out. She wanted to rewind time and shut her stupid, stupid mouth.

But Gavin was out there collecting things from the truck bed and she had to follow. Better to face the music than delay the inevitable. He would let her down easy, and the Fairchild Ranch would be gone forever.

When she got out of the truck, he was already striding toward the trees all anxious, purposeful energy. She could only trudge after him, dread making each step feel like a supreme effort.

But he led her into the woods and then she stopped dead, forgetting everything else. Him, Gene, life.

"Gav," she breathed. It was beautiful. The entire little wooded area was practically carpeted with the tiny purple blooms. "I haven't been out here in . . . years." Back in middle school she, Em, Molly, and sometimes Lindsay had had their girl meetings here. They'd pretended to be fairies or gossiped about boys, but it had been a long time since Lou had ventured into this little spot of Tyler property, and she'd forgotten this utter *magic.*

"Figured we better have a good story if we were going to do this so quick, and I assume Gene quit today."

"Yeah, but what's that got to do with a good story?" She turned to face him. He'd spread out the blanket and put the cooler down on it. He couldn't have looked more like a picture-perfect dream, standing there in the dappled sunlight. Tall, rangy cowboy complete with hat in the middle of a little woodland clearing covered in wildflowers.

He held out a little velvet box. The jewelry kind. *The engagement ring kind.*

Lou had to swallow, and remind herself this was all a scam. Playacting and lies and pretend. The butterflies in her stomach and the tears in her eyes were the stupidest thing she could have done, because this was just a *joke* at best.

"Well, you've certainly created quite the story." God, her voice sounded hoarse. "This is . . ."

"Your dream proposal, if I remember right. It'll help with the whole why-are-you-getting-engaged-now thing if I seem extra-romantic. Of course, I think your dream man back then was Rex, but we don't need to share that."

"You . . ." Surely she hadn't yapped to Gavin about things as stupid as proposals. And he'd remembered? And . . . "I don't think Rex was ever my dream man," she muttered.

"I don't know why you picked him, then."

"Too many awful reasons to get into," she returned before she thought better of it. Because her brain didn't work anymore. Gavin Tyler was standing in the middle of a field of violets with an engagement ring. Fake or not, it was a dream. One she'd never known what to do with, most especially now.

His eyebrows drew together, but he seemed to push whatever questions he had about that away. "We'll announce it tonight at dinner." He stepped forward and held out the box.

She took it because she didn't know what else to do. Dying of curiosity, she opened the lid. A slim gold band that had little purple jewels, amethyst maybe, encrusted around it rather than one stone in the middle as was typical. It was beautiful. Unimaginably so.

"It looks . . . real," she managed to say because it was so sleek, so sparkly. So . . . perfect.

"Well, that's because it is."

She all but dropped the box like it had burned her, but managed to grab a hold of it before it fell. She looked up at him, shaking her head. "I don't want you spending money—"

"I bought it a long time ago."

There'd been a time not all that long ago when she would have told anyone who asked, Gavin Tyler couldn't surprise her, but this was just another surprise in a long line of them these past few weeks.

Chapter Eleven

Gavin wanted to chop something down. Or run a marathon. Or shovel a hundred metric tons of shit rather than do any of what he was doing. His muscles were tensed against his will, his gut twisted beyond measure.

It felt like nerves, except nerves didn't make any sense when you were fake proposing.

"Well, you should put it on. I'm not sure it's going to fit."

"Gavin, why on earth did you buy a ring a long time ago?" she asked. Her expression was baffled but soft. There was no accusation, and if she felt nerves or concern over this thing, she didn't show it.

It should ease *his* nerves that she was going to just agree. That she understood Gene leaving meant they had to speed things up. He should be relieved this was going to be simple.

His stomach roiled uncomfortably, and at least if he talked about Stephanie, he wasn't talking about this thing they were doing.

"I almost proposed to someone once a long time ago, and it was too embarrassing to have to return the thing. So I just kept it. Figured I could hock it if I ever really needed the money, but I haven't yet. Now, it works for this."

"Who did you almost propose to?" He could see her doing the mental calculations, going through the list of former girlfriends. "Stephanie."

It was no surprise she'd figured it out. His long-term relationships weren't exactly legion, and any woman he'd dated seriously had been brought into the group. They all hung out, and he didn't keep his girlfriends separate. Not that there'd been that many since Stephanie. Why the hell were they talking about this? "Yeah. Look, it's not import—"

"You were going to propose to Stephanie? You wanted to *marry* Stephanie?"

"Well, I kind of did propose, but then I rescinded the proposal. Well, she had some ultimatums I didn't want to agree to." He shrugged. That had been that. What was the big deal?

"Gavin. My God. How did I not . . . How . . ." She seemed something like hurt, maybe that he hadn't told all and sundry about his failed proposal. He should have been irritated. Instead, he found himself explaining.

"I didn't tell anyone. About the proposal part. Not even Shane. He was dealing with his own weird female problems at the time and . . . I don't know. I like keeping things to myself, having certain things I don't have to run the whole Tyler-Fairchild judgment gauntlet on. Good thing too, or I'd never have lived that breakup down."

"Tell me the story."

"It's old news."

She stepped forward, one hand clutched around the now-closed velvet box while one hand reached out and wrapped around his forearm. "Tell me the story," she repeated.

It was stupid to want to tell her. To get this old thing off his chest. But she was looking at him imploringly, her hand gripping his arm tightly. He was helpless to try to keep it all in.

"Well, right before we broke up, we were talking about getting married. Her father was going to hire me as overseer at their spread. Man, the Phillips Ranch. Overseer of that place? Hell. I would've married a chicken. So, I told her I'd buy a ring. I proposed, and she said she had some, oh, how did she put it? She had some *conditions.*"

"Conditions to saying yes?"

"Conditions to getting married. Top of the list was, uh, no female friends. I had a problem with that one. She had a problem with me having a problem with it. I took the ring back. She told me it was the most hideous thing she'd ever been given, and that was that."

"Female friends," she echoed, blinking. Her blue eyes were so *earnest.* "You mean me."

"Don't be so conceited."

She narrowed her eyes at him.

"Well, not *just* you. You *and* Em."

"She didn't want you hanging out with us," Lou repeated, as if she couldn't wrap her head around it.

"It bugged her that Em and I had dated. It didn't seem to matter that it hadn't been real dating. And she . . . Well, she really didn't like you for some reason I never understood. It wasn't the most unreasonable request. Hell, if she'd wanted to hang out with a bunch of guys her age, especially ones she'd dated, I'd have been asking for the same or having some reservations. It wasn't so much that she said she wanted me to never hang out with you guys, just not alone. She wasn't unreasonable. I was."

"She didn't trust you. *You.*"

Gavin shrugged. "I understood. I mean, in the moment I was pissed, but when I calmed down, I understood. I might even have apologized later, tried to propose again, but shamefully, it made me realize I wasn't so into Stephanie as I was in to the idea of running the Phillips Ranch, and that wasn't right." There'd been more to it, but in the light of what they were going to do, explaining to Lou Stephanie's insane allegations he was more in love with Lou than he'd ever be with her didn't seem particularly prudent.

"No, I suppose not," Lou muttered. She dropped his arm, opening the box back up and pulling the ring out. "Well, Stephanie was wrong. Not to trust you, and about this ring. It's the most *beautiful* one I've ever seen." She shoved it resolutely on her finger and held it up to the sun.

It glittered and dazzled as she stood in the middle of the fairy-talesque wildflower field and *shit.*

It crystalized something he'd known and tried to ignore for a long time, even when Stephanie was telling him just that. When he'd been in that jewelry store however many years ago, he hadn't been thinking what Stephanie would want. He'd been thinking about someone else entirely.

Wasn't he always?

"I think we should be a little honest," she said, marching over to the blanket. "Tell our families we would have waited, but with things in flux at the ranch it made sense to rush things a little. We've been friends for so long and we . . . we love each other and blah,

blah, blah, and even though it's fast, we know it's right. No one could argue with that."

She plopped herself down on the blanket and opened the cooler, immediately pulling out the food he'd haphazardly packed for their impromptu picnic. Gavin couldn't seem to make himself move.

The sunlight haloed her blond hair gold even with the bandanna tied over half of it. She sat on a blanket in the middle of wildflowers, and in all his denials—long, complicated years of them—this simple moment was like a microscope to things he'd rather keep in the murky, confused dark.

She was the ideal. Everything he was doing was for her and her alone, and running his own ranch was just the excuse to be here, doing this.

He had to close his eyes against the sharp stab of pain that awful realization caused. He'd promised himself a long time ago he wouldn't be here again, because wasn't this exactly where he'd been fifteen years ago? Quietly doing everything for her, hoping she'd notice. She'd chosen Rex instead, and he'd been so sure he'd moved on.

But rehashing the whole thing with Stephanie just reminded him he was pathetic at best. The only one he'd ever really wanted was Lou, regardless of how hard he'd tried to make that not the case.

And he was going to tangle himself up with her? Entwine their lives completely for months if not a year? What kind of *idiot* was he?

He couldn't back out of this. Wouldn't. Wouldn't hurt her that way, wouldn't give up this thing he wanted for the second damn time in his life. But he had to . . . be careful.

She looked up at him. "Are you going to eat?"

Right. Eat. They should eat. But first . . . "You know all that stuff we were talking about last night?"

She visibly tensed as she looked away. "Uh, yeah."

"We should be careful. Keep all the lines drawn. The marriage stuff will be one thing, but then we're going to have to weather the divorce stuff too. We should just make sure we're . . . friends still."

She was silent for the weirdest, longest second of his life, then she just nodded. "Yeah, totally."

Totally.

Lou had no idea what had happened in that field. Maybe it was just the reality of the situation fully hitting them that had caused Gavin to get so quiet and tense.

Gavin. Quiet. She wasn't sure she could ever remember a time when she'd sat at a meal with him and he hadn't chattered along endlessly. Gavin hated silence. He hated awkward silence most of all.

But eating lunch in that fairy-tale clearing had been nothing but an awkward silence. Followed by uncomfortable, heavy silence all the way back to her place.

When he pulled to a stop in front of her barn, he didn't move to get out of the truck. He just offered some weird, forced smile. "Well, I'll see you at dinner."

She wanted to ask him if he was okay, but she was way too afraid the answer would be things she didn't want to hear. Second thoughts. Wanting to back out.

If she was a good, selfless person, she would ask anyway. She would let him back out, but she couldn't. So, she nodded and hopped out and waved as he drove away.

Waved, the ring a strange, heavy weight on her

finger. It was a little loose, so she'd have to be careful with it. She looked down at it, furious all over again that Stephanie had been jerk enough to criticize it.

Oh, it had been years ago. They'd been in their early twenties. Lou had probably done a lot of jerky things then too. It was just if she'd done them, she'd done them to Rex. Not someone like Gavin.

What was eating him? Maybe he really did want to back out. Did she have any right to ask this of him even if it *had* been his idea, even if he *did* get something out of it?

And what the hell was the whole thing about lines and staying friends and . . .

She'd never in her life been confused by Gavin. She'd always understood him, or at least been under the impression she'd understood him, but the past few days were certainly showing her that had been something of an illusion.

What other things was he hiding? She'd thought the Em thing could be the only thing, but now there was a Stephanie thing, and surely there were other secrets lurking in those odd silences today.

She looked at the barn and then at the house and then back down at the ring on her finger. A proposal in a field of wildflowers. A fake proposal, perfect down to the ring.

I don't know why you picked him then.

Such an odd way to talk about her going out with Rex. As if she'd plucked the jackass from a pack of men instead of said yes because he'd asked.

Lou took in a deep breath, letting it fill her lungs and expand her chest. Well, this was bound to be hard. It was lying, which she wasn't any good at, and Gavin wasn't much better. It was trying to figure out how to play things. It was stressing her out, and likely the reason for Gavin's behavior too.

She had to be smart about it. Not let the little things get her down. It wasn't all that different from healing and rebuilding after the fire. One day at a time, and each day got you a little closer to things feeling more on track.

Is any of this on track?

She shook that thought away and headed for the house. She'd tell Grandma now and alone, before dinner tonight. Maybe it would solidify some of her nerves into certainty if she knew Grandma would definitely sign the ranch over to them now that they were engaged.

Grandma was in the kitchen, holding the phone to her ear. "They're not going to magically—" Grandma stopped talking and stiffened, which was how Lou knew immediately she was talking to Dad. "Why don't you call me tomorrow, all right?" She paused. "Yes. All right. Russel? I love you, all right?" Grandma listened to whatever he said in return and then she hung up.

Lou tried to remember any of the pep talk she'd just given herself outside, but she couldn't think past the panic crushing her chest.

Grandma didn't turn to face her, and when she spoke, everything came out sounding . . . tired. "Is everything okay, sweetheart? You don't usually come in this early. Feeling well?"

"Why are you talking to him?" Every word shoved the knife of betrayal deeper.

Slowly, Grandma turned. Her expression was grim but determined, a kind of battle light Lou hadn't seen in her eyes since before Grandpa had passed. "I don't think I'll stand questioning over talking to my son, even with my granddaughter."

There was something worse than panic inside her now. Panic and fear and disgust and all those old feelings she'd spent something like twenty years trying to bury. She couldn't let all that old stuff win, and now she had a weapon. A talisman.

"Gavin and I are engaged," Lou said, shoving her finger out into the air between them. "I want you to hire him to replace Gene. Dad doesn't need to be involved."

"Sit down," Grandma said, as if Lou was simply an overexcited teenager.

"You said if Em or I got married—"

"Sit down," Grandma ordered with a snap.

Lou sat before she fully realized she'd intended to.

Grandma lowered herself into the chair across from Lou, the kitchen table between them. She took Lou's hands. She tapped the ring. "If this is honest and real, I am so happy for you, and I will honor what I said. I'll hire Gavin to replace Gene and we'll move the ranch into both your names."

Oh, thank God.

"But that doesn't mean you shouldn't deal with your father."

Lou recoiled, pulling her hands out from under her grandmother's. "What do you mean?"

"I know he hurt you."

"Apparently, you don't." Lou scrambled out of the chair. "He . . ." She didn't want to get into all the things her father had done to them. All the things she'd done in response. She was an adult. She'd moved past her childhood issues, and if she hadn't, well, it was too late.

It was too late.

"He wants a chance to—"

"To what?" Lou demanded. Grandma looked exhausted and beaten down, but that little voice whispering at her to calm down and think of Grandma, was drowned out by the beating, horrifying panic inside her. "To make up for twenty-nine years of failure and abandonment? For the neglect or for disappearing? For not . . . for not . . ." She could barely get the words out. "He didn't even come to Grandpa's funeral."

"Your father and your grandfather had a very complicated relation—"

"I don't care! He should have been there. He should have been there for you. For us. For the man who worked to the bone to raise *his* daughters. Why are you doing this?"

"We all make mistakes, and the older we get, the more they weigh on us. Your father has a chance to . . . He can't change the past. He can't make up for it, but he wants to try to build a future. I've lived twentysome years without seeing my son. Barely speaking to him. The boy I gave birth to and raised. I did that more for your grandfather than I did it for myself."

"How can you forgive him?" Lou demanded. It wasn't fair to feel betrayed, but it snaked around her heart and took hold anyway. "I don't understand."

"He's my son."

"He's my father. That doesn't help me understand anything."

"Maybe when you have kids of your own you will, or when you get to be eighty. I understand why you're angry. If I were your age and in your shoes, I would feel and say the same things. Louisa, sweetheart, don't misunderstand me. I will never, ever blame you for being angry with your father. But let me tell you from the place of having lived a lifetime, forgiveness isn't for them. It's for you. Don't you think there will come a time when you want to forgive him, if only to lift the weight off your heart?"

Maybe sometime after I forgive myself. "Never." She pushed away from the table. "I have work to do."

Chapter Twelve

They were late. In the whole of his existence, he had never known Mrs. Fairchild to be late anywhere. So, when her truck rumbled up at five past, Gavin's stomach sank at the fact that Lou wasn't in it.

Em got out, then rounded to the driver's side and helped Mrs. Fairchild to the ground. She'd survived a rough year with Lou's fire and Mr. Fairchild's passing, and it had certainly taken its toll physically as well as emotionally.

But where was Lou?

Em and Mrs. Fairchild walked across the yard, and Mom opened the front door as they crested the porch stairs.

"Lou's coming in her own truck," Em offered, but her attempt at a cheerful smile failed.

"Oh. Okay." Gavin tried desperately to appear casual instead of worried. "Everything all right?"

Em leaned in a little as Mom ushered Mrs. Fairchild inside and Grandma Maisey immediately pounced to start talking about . . . push-ups? Jesus.

"Lou's upset about something, but she wouldn't talk about it, and the freeze between her and Grandma."

Em shuddered. "I don't know what went down, but it was big."

Gavin looked inside, but Mrs. Fairchild had already disappeared deeper into the house. He glanced back at Em. "Did Lou tell you?"

"Tell me what?"

"Nothing."

"Um, yeah right." She poked him hard. "Tell me what?"

"Just . . . I'll tell you when she gets here, okay?"

Em scowled, but as she studied him, something in her expression softened. "Okay," she agreed far too easily. She moved inside to follow her grandmother, but Gavin couldn't bring himself to follow.

He wasn't in much of a mood to pretend period. He most definitely wasn't going to go in there and pretend alone. He pulled out his phone, trying to decide whether he should text her.

When he heard an engine, he glanced up, some band of pressure in his chest loosening. Except it wasn't Lou's truck. It was Cora's car.

She pulled into the drive, then hopped out, offering a little wave as she hurried up to the porch.

"Sorry I'm late. Wedding dress emergency in Benson. I cannot wait until this wedding is over. Usually the really complicated ones aren't this early in the season."

"It's okay. Lou's not here yet either."

"Oh." Cora paused in her move for the front door. "Is that why you look . . ." Cora cocked her head, studying him. "You look worried."

"Get involved with a woman, have a perpetual look of worry about you. I learned that from Shane."

Cora smiled at that and instead of continuing to the door, she joined him where he was standing at the railing. He was sure it was obvious he was watching the horizon where the Tyler and Fairchild properties met. If it was one of his siblings he might have pretended otherwise, but he didn't really feel the need to act cool with Cora.

"You know, Tylers are a little overwhelming."

He slid a grin her way. "Aren't we just?"

"And while I'm one of you now, I've still got some Preston in me. Which means if you want to unload, I could actually listen without suggesting a solution."

"I don't believe you."

She leaned against the railing, raising an eyebrow. "Try me."

"Shane's a pretty lucky guy."

"Well, thank you. Are you trying to compliment me away from digging into your problems?"

Gavin sighed. He couldn't tell Cora what was really bothering him, wasn't even sure he would if he could. But he needed to get something off his chest if only so he could pretend through what promised to be a bizarre evening.

"I'm just worried about making everything work. With Lou. I don't want to screw it all up." His personal feelings were definitely going to screw things up if he wasn't careful.

"Oh, well, that I'm intimately familiar with."

"You couldn't screw things up with Shane if someone put red hot pokers . . . Well, since you're a lady, I won't finish that."

"I've learned to trust that, but it wasn't easy in the beginning. You know what happened with Micah's father. I had some trust and worth issues I had to work out, but it took time dealing with that fear of messing it all up."

"I was never abused, Cora. My life has been pretty damn simple."

"Simple lives can leave scars too. It doesn't have to be a tragedy, though I wouldn't go so far as to say life's been *easy* for you. You lost your father young. You all bear that mark in different ways. Believe me, I'm intimately acquainted with Shane's scars regarding that. I could make some assumptions on yours that would make my therapist applaud. Instead, I'll let you in on a little secret."

"Aren't I lucky?" But it didn't come out as sarcastic as he might have liked. Truth be told, he could stand to be let in on a secret or two.

"You'll never get what you deserve until you believe you deserve it, just a little bit. Your family loves you because that's what good families do. Your friends support you and like you because, well, same, and you're a good guy, but that big old world out there? Ranches and love? You have to believe you've got something to give for it to give anything back."

"It still might not."

"You're right, it might not. But if you never believe, and you never try, it definitely won't."

Gavin didn't have the first clue what to say to that. Why it felt like some sort of lightning bolt of truth. Luckily, Lou's truck appeared over the rise and Gavin didn't have to.

"Let me tell you one more thing, because Lou reminds me so much of my sister. Well, a ranchier, meaner version of my sister—and I say that with so much love. She's had to be too strong for too long, likely because of real life and a mix of her own issues. She needs to handle a lot of things herself, so she doesn't need a knight in shining armor to swoop in and save her, but I bet she could use a shoulder to cry on or lean on sometimes."

"Funny, that's what Mrs. Fairchild said to me." But he watched her approach and wondered if Lou would ever let him be that shoulder. He doubted it.

"Well, then, we must be right." She gave him a little nudge. "I'm going to head inside. I'll try to keep them occupied so you and Lou can talk a bit."

"Thanks. Really. Thank you."

She smiled big and bright. "Anytime."

She disappeared inside, and Gavin wondered what it would take to get Lou to smile at him like that. He watched her stormy face as she approached, having parked next to her grandmother's truck. He wasn't sure he could get any kind of smile out of her when she looked like that.

Gavin thought about what Cora and Mrs. Fairchild had said about Lou needing a partner, not a knight in shining armor. That was hardly news to him, but there was a certain crystallizing of that fact when he heard other people say it to him.

When he thought about his mother saying he helped people without them realizing they were being helped.

Maybe you're perfect for each other.

Yeah, that's why they were here, thirty and having never shared anything more than a fake kiss.

"Hey," she offered, taking the stairs with more force than necessary.

"Hey. You okay?"

She shrugged jerkily. "Yup."

He could leave it at that, but no matter how much he wanted to keep his emotional distance, he couldn't let her look like she was going to shake apart with rage and not get some of that off her chest.

And, if he was upfront and honest with himself, he wanted to be the one to take care of her. She'd hate that. Even more than him wanting more from her than this fake thing they were doing, but it didn't eradicate the desire to help her. To be that shoulder she could lean on.

"You want to talk?"

She gestured at the door. "We have dinner and an announcement to make."

"Doesn't mean we couldn't talk for a minute or two before we go in. Em said you had a fight with your grandmother."

"Don't worry. It wasn't over you. She said she'd hire you now that we're engaged. We're all good there."

"Okay. That doesn't explain why you're upset though."

"I'm not upset."

"Lou. Does that bullshit work on *anyone* when I never understood the term *mad enough to spit nails* until seeing your face?"

"I'm not in the mood to joke, Gavin."

He didn't want to touch her—well, it wasn't that simple. He desperately wanted to touch her, but he shouldn't. Keeping lines uncrossed and all that. Making this easier on him when they finally had to call it all off. Self-preservation.

"I'm not trying to *joke,* Lou. I'm trying to get you to tell me what's wrong. We're about to announce our engagement to both our families. You haven't told Em and I haven't told anyone. So, we have to at least put on a happy face."

Lou smiled, a horrible, blank, empty smile. "Here is my happy face, Gavin."

He took her by the shoulders then. Screw self-preservation when she looked like one wrong move would break her apart. "Tell me."

She looked away, her jaw working, but there was a wavering in her determination to sweep inside and do this thing.

"If I'm going to be your husband, fake or not, you're going to have to let me in on some things. Even if we're not romantically married or whatever, it's still a partnership. Give a little, Lou. You might just find it eases things a bit."

He was probably right, but the thought of crying in front of him was too mortifying to bear. She'd shed her share of tears over the past year. She was tired of them. Done with all the sadness and hard stuff.

She wanted life to be *easy* for a while. She wanted to feel . . . Oh, hell, she didn't know. But not churned up. Not hurt.

She swallowed at the lump in her throat. She wasn't a big talker. When she had problems, she dealt with them. And when Em had problems, Lou tried to deal with those too.

She looked at Gavin. His expression was pained, almost. His hands were comforting on her shoulders, like he could lift some weight off them if she let him.

"She wants me to forgive my father." The words were out in a choked whisper before she'd fully thought them through. They didn't even make sense, but there they were. Out of her mouth and into his ears.

"Your grandma."

"Yes. She said she'd give us the ranch, but that didn't

mean I shouldn't . . ." Lou shook her head, keeping a ruthless iron control on the tears threatening. She'd spent a lot of years learning not to cry, hadn't she? "She wants me to . . . She's talking to my dad and she started going on about how I should too, and asked when I'd forgive him, and I just . . ."

He gave her shoulders a squeeze, easing some of the tension she'd been carrying there since this afternoon. Still, he didn't say anything.

"Well? Aren't you going to tell me I should?" she demanded, needing something to fight against. To yell at. "Don't you agree with her? Aren't I just a hysterical woman who's always wrong?"

"Lou, I can't . . . I don't know what your father did that needs forgiving, which means I can't tell you what I think." His dark eyes were compassionate, and she wasn't sure what she'd expected his reaction would be, but it wasn't . . . that he'd have no opinion. "Why don't you tell me?"

"Dinner?" she croaked, motioning toward the door.

"Cora said she'd try to give us some time to talk. So, why don't you tell me what your grandmother expects you to forgive your father for, and then I can tell you what I think."

It didn't matter what he thought. Why should she tell him or want to know his opinion? Her opinion was the only one that mattered.

But there was something so comforting about his strong hands gently massaging her shoulders, everything about him just ready to listen.

"He . . ." She cleared her throat, trying to sound stronger when she told the story. "He used to leave us. By ourselves. I don't know when it started, I just remember being four or five and having to take care of

Em all by myself. And he'd just be gone when I woke up from a nightmare or because Em was crying."

"Jesus, Lou."

"I tried so hard to take care of Em, but I was young. I didn't know what to do."

"Of course you didn't. I don't even think I was tying my own shoes yet."

"A couple of times the police would be looking for him for some reason. Then they put together we were alone and after a few times . . . Well, that's when we got put with my mother."

This is all your fault, Louisa. Couldn't you just handle it? She squeezed her eyes shut against the memory. In retrospect, she figured Dad was high or drunk or something while he yelled those things at her as the police dragged him away and took her and Em in the opposite direction.

They'd spent the night with Family Services, then Mom had picked them up the next morning, none too happy. "Which was worse," she whispered, almost forgetting where she was now, so lost in those old, horrible memories.

"How . . . how was it worse?"

He sounded horrified, and she couldn't . . . She couldn't get into *that.* "It doesn't matter. I think I've seen him a handful of times since then. He showed up here once when I was . . . twelve maybe. Made a bunch of promises and was gone within a week. When he came back for my high school graduation, I told him I never wanted to see him again, and I haven't. Not even for Grandpa's funeral. Why should I forgive him?" She met Gavin's sympathetic gaze.

She didn't want to wipe it off his face either. She didn't want the ground to swallow her up whole in her embarrassment. She wanted to lean into that hard, sturdy chest. She didn't know what to do with *that*, so she just stood there, even as his hands moved from her shoulders to her cheeks. "How can *she* forgive him?" A tear slipped over her and trailed down her cheek. She wished she hadn't said it, except it felt good to say it to someone.

"He's her kid."

When she tried to whip her head out of his grasp, he held on firm, his long fingers curling around her head. He kept her right there, looking into her eyes.

"Let me finish," he said, so serious and like he knew what the hell he was doing or talking about.

She wished she could muster half of that.

"Look, I think it's . . . Remember when Mom and Ben were engaged and they got in that big fight about Boone? Obviously I'm not a dad, so I don't get it, but parents have complicated feelings about their kids, even when their kids have done some shitty things. Maybe your grandmother needs to forgive him because that's what's right for her. That doesn't mean it's what you need or what's right for you."

"I don't know how she can forgive him." *I don't know how she can forgive me.* "He hurt us." *I hurt everyone.*

Gavin pulled her into his chest, his arms wrapping around her and holding her tight. She managed a breath that might've been more of a sob, but she was holding on to him tight and he wouldn't see the tears now streaming down her face. If she could breathe normally and turn away when the hug was over, he'd never have to know she was crying.

"I get it. It feels kind of like a betrayal, because you and Em were the ones being hurt, but . . . Maybe she can forgive him, and you can't. Because you're two different people who need two different things. If you talk it through, maybe you can learn to respect each other's choices even if they're not your own."

He held her there for she didn't know how long, but she got control of her tears. She didn't know how she could talk to her grandmother about this when her grandmother would no doubt see through her better than Gavin did. But she still felt better, somehow, for having discussed it. For having cried over it a little bit.

He pulled back, though he kept his hands on her arms and studied her face. Even in the dusky half-light, he had to be able to see the tearstained cheek not covered by the bandanna. It was so strange not to care.

"Why was living with your mother worse?"

She looked away. "I don't want to . . ." Except, this had felt good. She hadn't wanted to talk about this, but having someone else validate her feelings, without invalidating Grandma's . . . That was something.

But, God, how could she possibly tell Gavin about that awful year with her mother?

"Maybe some other time. We should really get inside." She forced herself to smile at him. "Thanks for this."

"That's what fake fiancés are for." He grinned at her, but there was something . . . sad there. She couldn't recall very many instances of noticing *sadness* in Gavin's expression. Without thinking it through, she reached out and cupped his cheek, wanting to ease something for *him.*

He had to have just shaved, because his jaw was smooth against her palm, plus he smelled like soap instead of ranch. And . . . she met his gaze. Everything about him was so strong and sturdy. So good, and he looked so handsome in the fading daylight.

She wanted to kiss him. That was this thing inside her. The irregular pulse, the tingling skin, that yearning ache deep in her core. She wanted to feel his mouth on hers. More than that gentle peck from the other night that had been fake.

She actually, *actually* wanted to kiss Gavin. Figure out the taste of him and . . .

He stepped abruptly away, and she stumbled forward at the loss of someone to lean on.

"Better get in to dinner," he said, jerking the door open.

"Right." Because this was only ever going to be fake. He didn't want to cross lines, and that was, of course, for the best.

But she didn't know how to explain away the wave of disappointment that washed over her anyway.

Chapter Thirteen

Gavin stalked into the house. He shoved his traitorous, shaking hands in his pockets. He'd been dreaming that Lou had been looking at him like . . .

You will not fall for this bullshit.

He wasn't going to do it again. It wasn't as if time was suddenly going to change how things were between them. He couldn't let himself be fooled into feeling that way again. He had to be strong. He had to be certain.

When he walked into the dining room, still too severe and plodding, everyone had already taken their seats along the long, ancient dining room table. Mom had used the nice tablecloth, and things were set up in that just so way that meant Mom and Grandma had put some extra work into this.

When Gavin stopped in the entrance, all eyes turned toward him. He wanted to turn tail and run like a damn coward, but Lou was right behind him and she came to stand at his side.

It was the perfect time to announce everything. After all, they were standing here and everyone was looking at them with some amount of concern in their gazes.

Gavin didn't dare look at Lou, but he reached out and only fumbled a little as he slid his arm around her waist. He didn't pull her closer, though he probably should for the show of it. He just couldn't act quite *that* much in his current state.

He forced the biggest, happiest smile he could muster and looked out at his family and hers.

"Well, we have a little bit of an announcement."

A few people at the table looked at one another, but mostly all eyes remained on him and Lou. Too many pairs of speculating eyes. Gavin opened his mouth to say the words, but he couldn't get past the flutter of panic stuck in his esophagus.

The silence stretched on, and the more it did, the more Gavin couldn't seem to get any part of his body to work the way it should, most especially his voice.

"We're engaged," Lou said brightly as she slid her arm around *his* waist so they were standing there holding on to each other in front of everyone they loved. "Gavin and I are going to get married."

When Gavin looked at her out of the corner of his eye, he saw her holding her free hand, wiggling the ring he'd bought for someone else but also, somehow, her. It twinkled in the light like some kind of joke.

Gavin and I are going to get married.

He knew what he'd been doing from the beginning and still Lou saying those words in front of everyone he loved made his stomach churn.

But he only had a second to feel that heavy sense of impending doom before Em's squeal nearly pierced his eardrums and Molly and Lindsay's laughter filled the air.

Em jumped out of her chair and rushed toward them, her eyes suspiciously bright, her arms wide open. Gavin figured she'd engulf Lou in the hug, but she grabbed on to both of them, pulling them together and toward her.

"I can't believe it," Em said, holding them both tight. "I mean, I totally *can* believe it, but . . ." She gave another little squeal and loosened her grip so she could look up at both of them. "I'm so happy for you two. This is absolutely perfect. I've been waiting forever for this to happen."

"We haven't been dating that long," Lou said, her voice sounding tinny.

Em smiled at Gavin, giving him the uncomfortable, horrible feeling she knew just exactly how long he'd been helplessly head over heels for Lou. His family had always joked about it, but Gavin had been able to chalk it up to the fact people couldn't let male-female friendships alone.

But maybe they all knew. Maybe he was the most transparent man on the face of the planet no matter how he'd tried to deny any feelings he had over the years.

Worse, so much worse, maybe Lou knew it too. It was the kind of embarrassment he wasn't sure he could survive.

But he had to. He would, because he wanted to run the Fairchild Ranch. This wasn't just his ridiculous need to help Lou because he was the idiot in love with a woman who didn't love him back. It was about getting something he'd always wanted.

"Come eat. Come eat," Mom said, waving the three of them back to the table. "And tell us how quickly we can expect an actual wedding, considering how fast this engagement was."

Gavin ushered Lou over to the two empty chairs at the end of the table, trying to smile at his mother's clear chastisement. "Haven't given that part much thought," Gavin offered, pulling out the chair for Lou, then taking his own.

"I think we should just go to the courthouse. Something simple. Quick," Lou said firmly.

The outraged screeching from the female population of the room was very nearly deafening.

"Lou. We spend all year talking about what we'd do differently if we were our brides," Em said. "You can't be serious about not having a wedding. I've had ten wedding cake designs saved just for you for I don't know how long."

"Well, we can have a little dinner or something after. Like this." She looked around the table, then up at him, clearly hoping for some help.

So Gavin smiled at Em. "We don't want anything fussy. That's not us. Courthouse, dinner, that'll be fine."

"I can put together a small, nonfussy, Lou-and-Gavin wedding," Cora said. Not in the same demanding tone Em had used, but in a far deadlier one. Careful. "I *want* to do that for you, if you'll let me."

Gavin looked from Cora to Lou, and something heavy in his chest shifted. He'd made a lifetime out of studying Lou's expressions, and while he didn't understand all of them, there was a clear flicker of yearning on her face before she cleared it.

"N—"

"We can do that," Gavin said, interrupting her clear refusal. She wanted a wedding? He'd give her a damn wedding, even if it was small and fake. Because, yes, he was *that* much of a sap. "How fast could you put something like that together, Cora?"

"I'll have to look at my schedule. But something small, with Em baking for us, and Lou doing her own flowers if she wants . . ." Cora mentally calculated.

"If we did it on a Sunday evening? A couple of weeks. The biggest issue would be clothes."

"Gavin could wear my suit from our wedding," Shane offered. "We're the same size. It'd be about right."

"With some help with the sewing, I bet I could get you into my wedding dress, Lou," Mrs. Fairchild said, her voice a little scratchy.

"Between the two of us, we'd have it done in no time," Grandma Maisey said with a determined nod.

"We can have it here, like we did with Deb's. Smaller scale, of course. Quick ceremony. Shane and Boone can barbecue. Em will do desserts. The grandmothers and Deb can do the sides," Cora continued. "If you want anyone to stand up for you, they can wear whatever they'd like if you don't want to worry about clothes. I can line up some kind of officiant. A photographer might be tough, but Em takes great pictures."

"Yes. All of us can take pictures, and use one of those wedding apps, and you can just use whatever the best ones are."

Gavin shared a look with Lou. He found his discomfort from the porch was gone, steamrolled right out of him. "What just happened?"

"I think we just planned a wedding," Cora offered with a grin. "But if you want to nix anything, it's all up to you guys. If you want the courthouse, that's fine. We just want you to know that if you want something, we'd all be more than happy to pitch in and make it happen."

There was a little spark of hopefulness in Lou's eyes before she looked away, so Gavin took her hand under the table and gave it a squeeze.

"A wedding it is."

Because he could give Lou some things she wanted without sacrificing his self-respect. He'd been down this road before, hadn't he? He'd remained friends with her while she'd dated Rex. He'd been there all these years. Why should it change now? If she saw through him, she'd seen through him for years and had never said anything. Why would she say something now?

They'd have their wedding, for Lou, for their families. He'd get his ranch, she'd keep her farm. He'd sure as hell protect her from her douchebag of a father, and when the time came for them to get divorced, they'd still be friends. Friends with the things they'd both wanted.

Letting *feelings* give him second thoughts was childish, and he wasn't a child anymore. He wasn't the second son on a ranch with too many of them anymore. He finally was close to what he wanted, and that was where he'd find that worth Cora had been talking about earlier.

Mrs. Tyler had busted out some wine and Lou was happily buzzed on two glasses. It made the whole pretending-to-be-a-happy-couple thing way easier.

"Wait a second. We haven't heard the proposal story," Molly said.

Everyone had finished dinner and dessert, but they were still situated around the table having raucous conversation after raucous conversation. The grandmothers and Deb and Ben had taken the dirty dishes to the kitchen, refusing all the young people's help and encouraging them to sit and chat.

So, they had. It was something Lou had always enjoyed in the past, a nice, loud dinner with the Tylers. Whenever she spent this kind of time with the whole clan, she always felt a little jealous of Gavin. That he had this big family full of noise and movement and life, and he never had to contemplate the meaning of the many silences like she did.

But the wine helped with that too. She just *enjoyed* it. Enjoyed being a part of it and didn't worry if she was an outsider, because she was going to marry Gavin.

She looked down at the ring on her finger. Her brain kept circling around the real parts of this whole proposal thing. The ring, the field of violets. That kiss the other night that had been for the sake of her grandma but had been real nonetheless. The moment on the porch.

"Yes. I want to know," Lindsay was saying. "Is Gavin a secret romantic? We know Shane's not. Between Boone and Gavin, my money's on Gavin."

"He shoved it at her and grunted, I bet," Boone added, his smile completely for the sake of pissing off Gavin.

Lou frowned a little. She'd been around the Tylers most of the past twenty years, and she'd always been envious of the way all five of them got along. Oh, there were bumps and issues, of course, but they were all different, and they always had someone to turn to.

She and Em were close, but if they got in a fight, they could only retreat to their corners. Grandma wouldn't take sides, and neither would Molly, because she'd been friends with both of them. Being annoyed was done all alone.

But the Tylers chose sides and ganged up and teased, and she'd always liked that about them.

Until now. She didn't at all like them teasing Gavin about something that, for all they knew, was very personal and important.

"It was the perfect proposal," Lou said defensively. "It was sweet and romantic and thoughtful."

Boone cringed, and it was possible she felt Gavin cringe next to her as well.

"Did he get down on one knee?" Em asked eagerly.

"No. No, but you know the wildflower field out in the clearing between our properties?" When Em and Molly nodded, Lou continued. "He took me out there, and the violets are blooming everywhere. I got out of the truck and looked around, just kind of . . . awed, you know? And when I turned around, he was holding the ring box."

"Oh," Em said, dabbing at her eyes. "That *is* perfect."

"We used to go out there when we were kids and play pretend wedding," Molly said, an awed note to her voice. She looked at Gavin like she was putting some great puzzle together.

It made Lou want to squirm, so she quickly kept talking. "Picnic lunch and everything. And this ring—isn't it beautiful?"

"It suits you down to the bone," Em said emphatically.

Gavin pushed back from the table. He had that weird smile on his face, one she'd noticed before but never taken any time to parse. "Well, this sounds like a bunch of girl talk, so I'm going to have to pass. Shall we retire to the stables, gentlemen?"

Normally, she would ignore the tenseness underneath all that fake joviality because it didn't have anything to do with her, but she saw for the first time that if the situations were reversed, if she were tense and pretending not to be, Gavin would do something. He would step in and ease that tension away, probably without her even realizing he'd done it.

She wanted to do the same for him. He'd said it outside. This might not be a *love* marriage they were planning, but they were still going to be partners. It meant they had to talk to each other, rely on each other.

The tough part was, she didn't know how. She was so used to reaching out in a protective way. Protecting Em from the world's cruelties or trying to ease Grandma's load, but she never simply eased something for someone in this way that she wanted to be there for Gavin.

"Micah's got algebra homework, so I'll have to pass," Shane said, pushing away from the table as well.

"We could go out to the barn for a little while, though," Micah said hopefully.

"Not this time, buddy."

Micah groused with Shane as they exited the dining room, but it was a sweet kind of parent-kid thing.

"I better head out too," Cal said, standing. "Early morning."

"I'll walk with you," Lindsay said, taking his hand as they walked out of the dining room.

"And I'm going to get to work on that wedding of yours. Do you have time for a meeting tomorrow?"

"I can talk and work if you want to stop out whenever."

Cora nodded. "Okay." She walked over to their side of the table and squeezed them together, much like Em had at the beginning of dinner. "Congratulations, you guys."

"Thanks," she and Gavin muttered in unison.

"Well, I'll go help Mom and them, huh?" Molly said, getting up as well. She paused at the door between the dining room and the kitchen. "I'm really happy for you guys too."

It was so strange to actually *feel* the happy, instead of reminding herself this was all a sham. But she didn't want to be reminded it was fake or why they'd had to do it. She just wanted to feel good.

Grandma appeared from where Molly had gone and smiled at Em. "I think I'm ready to head back, sweetheart. You ready?"

Em got up from the table and nodded. Grandma looked at Lou, and most of that happiness faded away because Lou didn't know what to say to her grandmother right now. She didn't want to talk about Dad or forgiveness. She wanted to pretend for a few short minutes that her life was as simple as this.

"I'll be home later."

Grandma nodded, and she and Em headed for the door, leaving just Lou and Gavin. Gavin was still standing there next to his chair, and she was still sitting in hers. The air was silent and heavy, and worry began to creep into Lou's mind. She opened her mouth to say something, but Gavin did it first.

"I'll walk you out."

Even though she was the only one left in the room because Boone had disappeared without a word a while back, it took Lou a minute to realize Gavin was talking to her.

Dismissing her.

She looked up at him quizzically, but he didn't look back, just forward. After a second or so, he started walking out of the dining room toward the front door.

When she finally got her wits about her enough to move and follow him, he was holding her coat out in the empty entryway.

He smiled, but it was one of those old empty ones she hadn't seen from him in quite some time. He held out the coat for her to slip her arms into.

She stood where she was. "You know I could spend the night here. It would cement things."

"I sleep on a twin. Wouldn't be all that comfortable or reasonable."

"Oh. Right, well, why don't you come home with me? We got engaged today. We should probably spend the night together."

He was hesitating. She didn't know what that was about, and that niggle of worry settled deeper and deeper.

"Gavin."

His gaze finally met hers, and it did nothing to fight off the worry pressing down on her chest.

"Are you having second thoughts?" she asked on a whisper.

He dropped his arms, though he kept her coat in his fingers. He stepped forward, eradicating the distance between them. He looked right into her eyes. "No. Look, no matter what happens, I won't back out. You have my word on that."

"What could happen?"

He seemed taken aback by her question, but he shrugged. "I don't know. Fights or . . . weirdness or whatever. Just stuff. But I'm not going anywhere. You can trust me on that."

For the first time in maybe her whole life, she believed someone wholeheartedly when they said they'd stick around.

Chapter Fourteen

Gavin wasn't sure how long he was in the stables by himself before Shane appeared, but he was about six beers deep, on top of the wine from dinner, with a nice little buzz going on.

"Here you are."

Gavin held up the half-empty bottle in his hand. "Here I am."

"Isn't like you to drink alone."

"Sometimes a man has to do what a man has to do."

Gavin could *feel* Shane's disapproving gaze, but like so many other *feelings* in his life right now, he ignored it. He didn't care about Shane's judgment right now. He cared about some way to ease all this . . . *shit* inside him.

If he understood why he was panicking now, he might be able to handle it without getting a little drunk. But he'd been fine and dealing until today, and he didn't know why he was suddenly so . . . so . . .

Terrified. He hated that word, but it was the only one that fit.

"So. What's eating you?"

"The emptiness of this bottle."

Shane surprised him and crossed to where Gavin's

box of beer cans sat half empty now. Shane grabbed two beers, handing one to Gavin before settling himself on a rickety old chair that had once been part of Mom's kitchen set.

The siblings had been holding their own family meetings out here since they'd been kids. They didn't do it much these days, especially now that they'd all settled into Mom marrying Ben. There just weren't too many things they didn't need Mom not to overhear anymore.

But it was still the place Gavin came when he didn't know what to do. When something ate at him and there was no way to let it out.

Usually, that was to brood about how Shane was in charge and all he'd ever be was second fiddle, but today it was Lou. All Lou.

She'd defended him. His proposal. Talked about how great it was as if he was somehow great, and he knew this was about the whole *pretending* thing they were doing, but no one ever stepped in and stood up for him. When you were the second oldest of five, there was no one rushing to your defense.

After a few moments of silence, Shane finally spoke. "I know I said that proposing is pretty scary and I understood why you were so nervous this morning, but this is different."

"Well, as you might remember, after the proposing comes the marrying."

"And marriage is a big deal. It's hard and scary and complicated. But typically, when people get engaged, there's enough excitement and sex. The reality doesn't settle in quite this quick."

"So, what are you saying?" *You're blowing it. Typical.*

"I'm saying, if there's something you need to get off your chest, I can listen without . . ." Shane cleared his throat. "My wife may have suggested I offer to listen without rushing in to fix it for you."

Gavin laughed, and it lightened his mood just a hair. "I don't have a problem. Not a fixable, definable problem. I just . . ."

"You're scared."

Gavin bristled, hating to be called out on this, but it was true, wasn't it? It was a truth within a lie he could actually discuss with his brother. Because as often as he felt he existed in Shane's shadow, he loved and respected his brother beyond measure.

"Okay. Maybe, *maybe*, and this is probably the beers talking, but maybe you're right. Maybe I'm scared."

Fucking terrified.

"I was scared too."

"You didn't act it."

"I've gotten pretty good at hiding the scared. Been practicing since Dad died. We got to see a really great marriage when we were kids, and I think because it's crystalized that way and we never had to see it as adults to pick it apart, we probably put some pressure on ourselves to match up to that ideal relationship."

"I don't think that was Molly's experience." Molly's marriage had been not great from what little she'd told them about it when she'd moved home after the divorce.

"It's different for girls." They shared a look, and Shane continued. "Don't you dare tell her I said that."

Gavin sipped the beer Shane had given him and thought about what Shane had said. He'd never really thought about marriage in the context of his parents, but . . . there was some truth to everything Shane said. Gavin had only witnessed good, caring marriages. He'd never really known Molly's husband, so he'd never witnessed that. He hadn't been a fan of Mom and Ben's relationship, but he'd gotten over most of his issues there, and Ben *did* care about Mom. That much was obvious. Then there was Cora and Shane.

There was a mutual love there, a tenderness he didn't particularly want to admit he wanted, but he did.

Which he would never say aloud if his life depended on it, but the point was, he had a respect for the institution of marriage. A deep belief in love because he'd seen it too much to deny its power.

He'd tried to manufacture that with Stephanie, and it hadn't worked out. Now he was manufacturing the outside of it with Lou, knowing the inside of their marriage was friendship, not deep, abiding love.

At least the reciprocated kind. She'd looked at him with a certain kind of curiosity on the porch when she'd arrived, but he understood this was . . . Maybe she'd convince herself she had a thing for him. Maybe she'd try to make it work for real because he was *here,* but he just couldn't let that happen.

And he couldn't talk to Shane about it. Or anyone. He just had to keep plodding along and hope it didn't kill him.

"Maybe it's just sort of generic panic. The kind that goes away with time."

"Maybe," Shane agreed equitably. "It also might be the legitimate kind you should communicate with her."

Gavin shrugged. Yeah, he'd tell Lou he was desperately in love with her. Then she could what? Reject him? Try to make something of it and then realize if she didn't feel the way he felt by now, she was never going to?

Nope. He'd hoped back in high school. He'd spent too much time hoping the Tyler Ranch would ever feel like part his to run. He'd wasted too much time on hope. He was thirty. It was time to focus on choosing, not hoping. Acting, not waiting. Deciding, regardless of what anyone else said or felt.

"I'll be fine."

"Okay. Just don't let this be because you think you can't hack it."

He turned to face Shane full on. "Excuse me?"

Shane sighed and rubbed a hand over his neck. He shook his head and put the beer down on the ground and stood up. "Never mind."

"No, explain that."

"I promised Cora—"

"Fuck that."

"Don't start. I'm not going to fight with you because you're pissed off I'm right."

Gavin stood too, barely noticing his beer can tipped over and was spilling onto the ground. Fury pounded through him, twining with all that fear and alcohol to make an awfully potent combination of rage. "I can't hack what exactly?"

"You can hack any damn thing, asshole, but you convinced yourself a long time ago that you couldn't. Sometimes you blame Mom for that and more often than not you blame me. Hell, I bet you blame God sometimes, but the truth of the matter is, you're here, my number two at this ranch, not because life and fate are cruel enough to make you younger but because you chose it."

Gavin didn't think the action through. He simply reared back and punched Shane right in the jaw. Shane stumbled back, but he stayed on his feet, planting them and curling his hands into fists.

"I'm not going to hit you back, Gav. I promised Cora I wouldn't butt in or fight. But you're damn lucky I made that promise."

"Yeah, I'm shaking in my boots. Maybe you should go ask Cora permission to hit me back, or maybe she'll be man enough to do it for you."

Gavin expected the blow, but it didn't make his brother's fist connecting with his face any more comfortable. Unfortunately, due to the placement of his beer cans, he also stumbled with it and fell right on his ass.

Shane stood above him, furious and with a nice red mark already blooming on his cheek. "You feel better, now that we've both acted like children?"

"I feel great," Gavin shot back, feeling exactly like that: a child. He put his fingers up to his swelling lip and it came away bloody. A child with a split lip.

"Are you still going to feel great when all this gets back to Lou? After everything she went through with Rex and that fire, you think marrying a guy who can't solve his temper with anything other than his fists is still going to be the kind of guy she wants to marry?"

With that, Shane left, leaving Gavin with an even worse sense of fear and dread than he'd had before.

Lou was up long before dawn, doing all the things Grandma normally did. Turn over the wash, breakfast preparations. She'd also checked to make sure Gene had shown up. She was a little afraid he'd just disappear into the new-job ether.

But he'd been there, taking care of their tiny herd. Seeing everything so diminished reminded her how important it was she do the farmers market this year. That plus all the florist stuff should help fill the income gap.

Please God.

Now, she was trying to emulate a breakfast her

grandmother would make, and while her grandmother had taught her basic kitchen concepts, Inez Fairchild did the cooking in her house and Lou was *no* expert. Especially after last night.

She hadn't slept much. There'd been too many things to turn over in her mind. First it had been all the weird with Gavin. Then it had been the awful conversation with Grandma.

In the end, Gavin was right. She needed to have a conversation with Grandma about being in different places. Lou would try not to feel hurt Grandma could forgive Dad, and Grandma would have to learn to live with Lou not forgiving him. Forgiveness was personal. Individual.

But not doing something her grandmother asked of her was really, really hard.

She turned at the creak of the stairs, swallowing against the nerves. She wasn't big on face-to-face apologies. Or facing down much of anything that wasn't a threat.

Since when is Dad not a threat?

"Since now," she said aloud to herself. She was thirty years old, and if her father was part of the boogeyman in her dreams, it was long past time to face that. Not in forgiveness. She didn't want to forgive.

But she wanted peace between her and Grandma. Always.

Grandma's eyebrows immediately rose as she stepped into the small kitchen. She crossed her arms over her chest. "Well. What's all this?"

"I made breakfast," Lou offered with an awkward flourish. "It's not as good as you, but I don't have the practice."

"Hmm."

"Um, so go ahead and sit down." Lou gestured

toward the table, then went about fixing Grandma a cup of coffee the way she liked it. She loaded up a plate with the omelet she'd put together and set both things in front of Grandma.

"It's not my birthday."

"I know that," Lou muttered, fixing herself her second cup of coffee and loading up her own plate. She took the seat across from Grandma and watched as Grandma took a bite of the omelet. She didn't flinch or spit it out, so that was good.

"Um. So, about Dad . . ."

Grandma paused with a bite halfway to her mouth, then went ahead and finished the motion. Chewing as she watched Lou.

"I can't forgive him." Because as much as she blamed herself for her failures, the older she got, the more she had to hold her father responsible. She shouldn't have had the kinds of responsibilities thrust upon her that she had. She'd failed them, but she'd been too young. "But I'm trying very hard not to be upset that you have."

Grandma nodded slowly. "Okay."

"Gavin had a good point when I was talking to him about it. I know you think forgiveness is important, but . . . I don't think it weighs on me the same as it does you. I think we're different people who need different things, and I hope . . . because I love you so much and am so grateful that you took such good care of us and—"

"Don't you ever say you're *grateful* for me raising you, girl. As if I made some great sacrifice. Do you know what it was like for us to have a . . . a . . . second chance, almost? To raise you girls right after all the mistakes we'd made with Russel. I . . . Don't you ever thank me for that. It was our duty and our pleasure and we loved having you girls every second. Maybe a few teenage seconds we didn't love, but only a few."

"You sacrificed a lot for us," Lou said past the lump in her throat.

"Love requires sacrifice. Giving up something for someone you love isn't always a bad thing. Which is why . . . Lou, I'm going to ask you to do me one favor. And it's a big one."

"Okay?"

"I'd like you to invite him to the wedding."

It was like Grandma hadn't heard a word she'd said, and that really hurt. "I can't—"

"I don't expect you'll regret not forgiving him in this moment if you're not ready. But I do think you might regret excluding him from the big things. A wedding, no matter how small, is a big thing. He doesn't have to walk you down the aisle or be involved. You could exclude him from the reception if you want. But I think he should be there to watch you marry a good man."

"A far better man than he'll ever be."

"Maybe he should see that."

"As revenge or solace?" Lou returned, because she wanted the revenge, but she had the sinking suspicion Grandma wanted the solace that he hadn't screwed her and Em up completely.

"Does it matter?" Grandma asked blandly.

Lou looked down at her plate, trying to blink back her blurry vision, but instead, a tear slipped out and fell onto her plate. She stared at the little drop of water next to the egg crumbs.

Grandma moved her chair next to Lou. "Louisa." Grandma reached out and brushed the stray tears off Lou's face with her wrinkled fingers. "I don't do this to hurt you."

"But it hurts," Lou managed to say.

"Oh my girl, surely you know by now that life hurts." Grandma sighed and leaned her forehead against Lou's temple. Lou kept staring at the teardrop on her plate, trying to figure out how to know what the right thing to do was.

She wanted to make Grandma happy, but she knew she couldn't bring herself to. Where did that leave her? With no one to protect, the person she most wanted to please asking her the impossible . . . She didn't know how to deal with this wave of emotion swamping her.

Grandma wrapped her hand over Lou's. "I kept him at a distance for my husband, and for you girls. Well, my husband is gone, and you girls are grown. So, I have to do this for me, and for my son. I hope you'll be able to forgive me."

"And I hope you'll be able to forgive me that I can't get to the same place you are."

"You don't need my forgiveness for that." Grandma gripped her chin and made her turn to meet her gaze. "You're right, or Gavin's right. Maybe you don't need the forgiveness like I do. I'll respect that."

"I don't want him at my wedding." Maybe she should give in, because it wasn't exactly a *real* wedding, but she didn't want him seeing Gavin . . . period. Maybe it was a silly overreaction, but she didn't want Gavin looking at that man and picking out similarities. Putting them into the same pool of worthless.

"All right. Will you have a conversation with him when he comes to visit?"

Visit. Here. Lou closed her eyes, but Grandma still held her hand and pressed her forehead to Lou's. She was asking her to do something hard, but she wasn't pushing away when Lou said no. She was holding her through the refusals, the disagreements.

She always had, and at this point Lou had to finally accept she always would. Why had it taken her so long to truly accept that?

"Okay," she managed to rasp, because she didn't owe her father anything. But she owed her grandmother everything.

Chapter Fifteen

Gavin didn't hear from Lou all day. Usually that meant he'd head over to the flower farm at some point, but there was a ton of ranch work to do, and Gavin was exhausted.

And maybe he didn't really want her asking about his split lip. Not with Shane's awful words still rattling around in his brain.

He also hadn't seen Shane all day. He'd been out in the pastures before Gavin had woken up, and all Gavin's instructions for the day were related to antibiotic inventory.

Shit job for a shit brother.

By midafternoon, he'd double-checked all their lists and inventory. They were set for next week. He'd skipped lunch, so his stomach rumbled, but there was something nice and punishing about being out here by himself and starving.

"Figured you'd be out in the fields."

Gavin turned to find Lou standing in the entrance to the barn, the light haloing her golden hair. Her bandanna was purple today instead of the usual blue. He almost asked her about it, but she immediately frowned.

"What happened to your lip?"

"Ah. Would you believe I got in a fight with a raccoon and won?"

"I might have if you'd lost."

He smiled, but that hurt his lip, so he ended up wincing. Lou crossed to him. "What happened? You didn't . . . you didn't get in another fight with Rex, did you?"

"I wish. At least I'd feel justified."

"Justified for what?"

He blew out a long breath, though that hurt his lip too. But he certainly deserved the little sting, didn't he? "I got into it with Shane."

"Shane hit you? *Shane?* I think the raccoon story is more believable now."

"Ah yes, because Shane is a perfect saint. Why would he ever hit his brother? Too good for all that."

Lou's eyebrows knitted together. "Shane doesn't lose his temper like you do. What is up with you? You're not usually so . . . edgy."

"I'm not edgy. I'm irritated that you'd waltz in here and just assume everything is my fault."

"First of all, I wasn't doing that. You're putting thoughts in my head. Second, wasn't it your fault?"

"Yes! Of course it was my fucking fault," he returned, all the more angry and irritated she was right. "But it'd be nice if just once someone didn't *assume* that."

"Well, I think you'd have to spend a few years, you know, not hitting people for people to assume things differently. Besides, I *didn't* assume that. I just said Shane hitting you is out of character for him."

"Oh, right. My choice." As if he *chose* to fail. As if it felt good to never be able to hack it when Shane always did. Shane didn't understand him at all. Maybe that was why he was so angry.

"Huh?"

He didn't want to explain it to her. Didn't want her *here.* In the long-running course of their friendship, he dealt with her problems. Helped her. Listened. He wasn't interested in going vice versa on that. "Why are you here?" He knew it came out too harsh, but hell if he was in the mood to try to be anything else.

"I hear engaged people like spending time together."

"Trust me, no one will like spending time with me right now."

"Well, I hear married people have to deal with that anyway." She plopped herself on the chair he'd been using while he'd done the inventory.

"I'm going to go get lunch."

"It's like three."

"I was busy."

"What's your deal?" she demanded.

"I don't have a deal. I have a split lip and an empty stomach, which means I'm in a piss-poor mood and you should make yourself scarce."

"As if your piss-poor moods scare me. I'll come inside with you and hang out while you eat."

"Why don't you go find Molly to talk to?"

"I don't want to talk to Molly."

"You're giving me a headache." He raked a hand through his hair, trying to find some semblance of calm because his shitty mood wasn't her fault. "Can you please leave me alone?"

Her expression softened and she got out of the chair and crossed to him. She reached up and gently touched the corner of his mouth, right next to the part of his lip that was swollen.

He didn't dare look at her, instead picked a spot on the far wall to stare at. He held himself very still and didn't let himself lean into the soft, comforting touch. Fingertips weren't that exciting anyway. Even when they were gentle and represented some level of care.

"I'm not going to leave you alone. I have to start acting like a wife."

"I don't want a wife."

"Sorry, you're stuck with me." She grinned up at him, and somehow that made him forget he was supposed to be looking elsewhere. "What's really bothering you?"

She never asked him things like that. Never looked up at him with big blue eyes like she wanted to ease his burden. He didn't want it. Didn't want anyone easing anything. Shane was wrong. He hadn't chosen *failure* or second fiddle, but he did choose to deal with his shit on his own. Without dumping on anyone else.

Blue eyes wouldn't change his mind on that. "It's not important."

"You said it yesterday. We're going to be married, regardless of the reasons for it. That makes us partners. If I was sulking like a child, you wouldn't let me go."

"So, I'm sulking like a child?"

"Kind of." But she smiled at him like that would ease the blow.

The worst part was that it did. Her touching him, her calling him out on his shit—a lot more gently than Shane had—it soothed some of those roiling feelings inside him.

"You need to apologize to Shane. I know you well enough to know you wouldn't be this irritated if it wasn't at yourself. Apologize. You'll both feel better.

And you have to listen to my advice because I listened to yours."

"Mine?"

"You told me to talk to Grandma about forgiving Dad. So, I did this morning."

Thank God. He could change the subject far away from him. Maybe she'd stop touching him. He should make her stop touching him.

He couldn't seem to move his limbs.

"And talking went well?" he asked, his voice sounding pained even to his own ears.

"I don't know about well. She wants me to invite Dad to the wedding. She wants him . . . here, I think. I can't want that. But we're trying to respect each other's different wants. Just like you said." She looked sad, but not like yesterday. Not that heavy panic and anger. Just a little melancholy.

He was reaching out to touch the corner of her bandanna before he even thought about it. Touching the fabric in between his fingers, his thumb brushing against her jaw as he did it.

"So, thank you," she said, her gaze steady on his.

His mouth curved, even though his mind was screaming at him to drop his hand or step away from hers. "Did you just *thank* me? Did aliens abduct your brain but leave your body on earth?"

She rolled her eyes, but she stepped closer, and even though her mouth was curved upward, her gaze was serious. "I'm trying to get better at thanking you. At being there for you like you've always been there for me."

Gavin didn't know what to say to that. He could only stand there with her fingers on his face, and his on hers, paralyzed by the sincerity in her words, the gentleness of her touch, the sheer proximity of her.

Her gaze dropped to his mouth, lingered there. Every atom of being inside him sizzled to life and he felt something like a live wire watching her look at his mouth. Lou. Looking at his mouth.

He had to turn away. Self-preservation. But before he could, Lou moved up and pressed her mouth to his.

A kiss. Not prompted by anything other than . . . them. Unless there was some horse or ghost behind him she was putting on a show for. He let himself believe that for a moment. Let himself sink into the kiss, her mouth. Soft and almost timid, Lou of all people.

He wanted to wipe out that timidity. He wanted to pull her hard against him and do what he'd dreamed of doing too many times to count. Really kiss her. Devour her, from the outside in. His body was hard and hot, and for a blinding second, he figured it was fair. He could have this.

But something ice cold washed over him the minute he thought that. Have *this*? No. Christ, he couldn't let this happen. He couldn't let her convince herself this was some kind of option. It was convenient for her, and he couldn't bear it. He couldn't let her convince herself he was a means to more than one end, and have her wake up soon enough and realize he'd never be what she really wanted.

He pulled away, setting her firmly a few steps back. He looked her right in the eye, ignoring all the ways the kiss rattled through him and focusing on that awful certainty this would never be what he'd want it to be. "We're not doing this. Got it?"

He didn't wait for her to answer. He just turned on his heel and walked away.

* * *

Lou stood stock-still. She didn't move until she heard the door to the house slam shut, echoing across the large yard and into the barn where she stood.

She'd kissed Gavin. On purpose. A real kiss. She let out the shaky breath she'd been holding since he'd looked at her so darkly and essentially slapped her down for it.

Her hands were still outstretched from where she'd reached out to grab him and she forced herself to lower them to her sides.

Then, a laugh bubbled out of her from some unknown place. She laughed in the middle of the barn, all alone, like she was having some kind of psychotic episode.

Maybe she was. She'd kissed Gavin. On purpose.

It wasn't a particularly hot-and-heavy kiss, but she could still feel it in her toes. A warmth. A rightness.

We're not going to do this. Got it?

Except they *had* done it. He hadn't jumped away the minute she'd touched her mouth to his. He'd kissed her back. He'd . . .

It didn't make any sense, and maybe they shouldn't do anything, but she would not be ordered. She would not be slapped down like she was out of line. That had been a moment, and maybe he wasn't interested in pursuing anything farther than that, but she wasn't stupid.

Was she? Had she misread everything? She went around with a bandanna on her head, covering her scars. Maybe he couldn't possibly be interested.

She stopped laughing. Rex had always made it clear kissing wasn't her strong suit, and now she had scars to boot with the bad kissing. Maybe she'd totally grossed him out. Maybe he had to walk away so as not to have to look at her anymore.

She closed her eyes. They were stupid thoughts. Why would she believe what Rex said about her? And her scars didn't matter. They were what they were. She couldn't change them. Whether he felt that way or not was irrelevant.

He didn't want to kiss her, fine, but she wasn't going to be embarrassed. She wasn't going to act like it was a slap in the face or make up reasons. She wouldn't crawl back to her flowers and hide.

She was done with that. His reasons were his reasons, and she would just respect that he didn't want to kiss her. The end. But he didn't get to *dismiss* her.

She marched toward the house, embarrassment twisting in with the anger and hurt to make one potent motivator. She didn't even bother to knock, which she realized was stupid when she practically ran over Deb.

"Mrs. T. I . . . I . . . I'm sorry to barge in." Her cheeks heated, but she straightened her shoulders. "Where did Gavin go?"

"Oh, well, his room, I think. Stomping. Angrily." She nodded a little. "Now I see why. His room is upstairs. Second one on the right. Go head, dear."

"Thank you."

She'd been in Molly and Lindsay's room enough times she knew how to get to the back staircase and which room was Gavin's, though she'd never been inside it.

It filled her with a weird giddiness that went along with all this anger. She marched up the stairs, trying to order her thoughts. Trying to cement what she should say to him.

She paused at his door. She wouldn't insist they discuss the kiss or him being a big coward asshole about it. She'd act normal and in charge. Yes.

She didn't bother to knock, she just turned the knob and flung the door open.

"Jes—" He was clearly beyond shocked to see her as his eyes widened and his mouth dropped open.

And he was shirtless. Well, in the process of changing shirts or something. Because there was a T-shirt in his hands that he held somewhat in front of him.

Lou had to fight really hard to focus on her anger rather than the growing curiosity. She'd seen him with his shirt off when they were younger, but not so much in the past few years. Age had packed a hardness on him, filled in some of the lanky with a delicious kind of—

She shook her head and forced herself to look up at him. Imperiously, she crossed her arms over her chest. "What's your schedule tomorrow?"

"W-what?"

"We have to meet with Em to talk cake. We need wedding rings. There are lots of things to do and we need to get them done. So, I'm asking for your schedule so we can get some things knocked off the list."

He stared at her like she'd lost her mind, but she didn't care. She wasn't going to let anything change the course of the next few weeks. He wanted to be mad or weird over the fact she'd kissed him? Fine. Wasn't going to change the fact they were getting married.

Nothing changed that fact. He'd said that himself.

"Uh." He pulled on the T-shirt, which was a bit of a disappointment. "I'm supposed to meet with Gene and your grandmother tomorrow morning to go over some stuff. Then I have to help Shane with interviews for a new ranch hand. If we find a good one, we could put him to work on a trial afternoon and I could . . . whatever you need."

"Good. I'll text you what time to meet me at Piece of Cake."

"Lou."

She raised an eyebrow, waiting for him to bring up the kiss. Maybe he'd lecture her on line crossing again. Maybe he'd say they couldn't do this anymore.

She refused to entertain that last thought. He'd promised. Gavin wouldn't break a promise. Not to her.

"If we don't find a good candidate for a ranch hand, I might not be able to make it, but we'll reschedule if that's the case."

That caught her a little off guard, but she managed a nod and, hopefully, a rather unbothered expression.

"So, I'll probably see you tomorrow." A clear dismissal.

"I think you should spend the night tonight. Everyone's going to wonder why we got engaged and now barely see each other. Also, your mom saw us both barge in here angry as all get-out."

"I'm not angry."

"She said you were stomping. Angrily."

Gavin scowled. "I can't . . ." He trailed off and shook his head, his jaw working, and Lou realized in that moment how much Gavin kept locked down. It wasn't just the secrets, like with fake dating Em or proposing to Stephanie until the ultimatum. There were a legion of feelings he never let her in on, that she was beginning to suspect he didn't let *anyone* in on.

He hid anything soft with a joke or his temper, and realizing that all these years later than she should have, it softened her.

"Look, not tonight on the spending-the-night thing. But to make sure Mom doesn't think we're mad at each other, I'll walk you to your truck right now. I'll try to get away no matter what tomorrow afternoon for the bakery thing, and then we can go see a movie or something. I'll drop you off at your place late, come home late, everyone will be all convinced we . . . You know. That everything's fine."

Everything was definitely not fine, but Lou wasn't quite sure how to go about dealing with that yet. So, she let him walk her to her truck. She fake smiled as he kissed her stiffly on the cheek, and then she drove back to her place.

She spent the rest of her day working with her flowers, rearranging her schedules for Saturday's wedding, and trying to figure out what feelings Gavin was hiding.

Chapter Sixteen

"Maybe we should just start without him."

Lou looked away from the door of her sister's bakery. "He said he'd be here." Of course, it was all via text, but he'd said he'd be here.

"Yeah, like a half hour ago. I can work while I wait. Don't you have things you need to do at the farm? It's not like Gavin to keep you waiting."

"He had a lot going on today." Lou glanced at Em, who was refilling her cookie tray. She'd worked damn hard to keep this bakery afloat over the past few years, when the population decline of Gracely had made it hard to find customers. But Em had been smart and careful, and she might struggle to make ends meet but she hadn't given up.

Mile High Adventures, a local wilderness company, had done a lot over the past year with their chamber of commerce and attempts at making Gracely more of a tourist destination, and while the progress was slow, a lot of businesses like Em's bakery and The Slice Is Right were starting to see a difference in their profits.

"Why are you staring at me like that?" Em asked, her eyes still on the cookie she was frosting.

"I'm just really proud of everything you've managed to do."

Em looked up at that. "Okay, Gavin's late. You're being sappy. What's going on?" She pointed the spatula at Em. "Oh my God, are you pregnant?"

"Emily!"

"Is that a no?"

"It's a hell no, you psychopath." Her cheeks warmed at the thought. Sex and babies and . . . Everything inside of her panged with something she couldn't name and didn't want to delve into in front of her sister.

"Are you two having a fight, then?"

It wasn't a fight exactly, but Lou couldn't explain to Em what it *was*. So she had to smile ruefully. "I guess."

"What are you fighting about?"

"He's being grumpy."

"Maybe he has cold feet."

"Probably." Though the possibility made her sick to her stomach. He'd promised not to back out, but did she want him to do this if he came to the conclusion it was the last thing he wanted to do? He would, for her, but would she want him to?

"You know what's an excellent cure for cold feet?"

"Because you're an expert?" Lou replied sarcastically.

Em put one of the cookies on a bright, floral plate and slid it in front of Lou. "Hey, how many brides have I worked with over the past few years? I know a thing or two about cold feet. Including the cure."

"Okay, lay it on me."

"Sex," Em said firmly. Almost exactly at the moment the bell tinkled as the door opened and Gavin stepped in.

If he'd heard any of that, he didn't react, but Lou's cheeks heated all over again against her will.

It was one thing to pretend they'd done certain things. It was another thing to have kissed Gavin and actually think about those things in a real sort of way. *Pregnant.* God. She couldn't entertain that insanity.

"Sorry I'm late. Been a day. Phone's dead. Truck died. Boone had to jump it. So on and so on."

Lou didn't know that she necessarily believed all that, but at least he'd apologized.

"Well, let's get started," Em said enthusiastically, clapping her hands together. "Now, obviously I'm too excited, but if you don't like anything or want to try something else, don't be afraid to burst my bubble. This is *your* wedding."

Your wedding. To Gavin Tyler. She wanted to laugh maniacally, but instead, Lou smiled at her sister.

"Is this one of those things where I'm asked what I think, and no answer is ever going to be right, because men are stupid? I have two sisters. I know how that works."

Lou and Em both glared at him.

"In my experience," Em said imperiously, "while some grooms may not care much about the cake design, *all* grooms care about the taste of the cake." She went back behind the counter and fiddled around, getting things together.

Lou watched Gavin. Something was off about him. These past few days, he'd been muted and moody, and that wasn't usual for him at all, but it was starting to remind her of something. She just couldn't put her finger on what it was.

"Did you guys hire a new ranch hand?" she asked, watching the way his eyes looked around the shop or at his hands, but never at her.

"Yeah, I think so. He agreed to do a little test run, which I'm hopeful means he knows what he's doing.

Seemed laid-back enough to get along with everyone. Shane will promote from within to replace me, so it's not like . . . Well." Gavin shrugged. "Just typical hiring stuff."

It dawned on her then that no matter that having his own place was his dream, he might still be a little sad about leaving his family's place. Maybe *that* was what was so wrong with him. He was busy dealing with that and she was the jerk throwing herself at him. Gavin was more a one-emotional-upheaval-at-a-time kind of guy.

She reached over and put her hand on his forearm. He glanced down at it, his expression as blank as ever. She considered making a joke to offset the emotion in the room, but maybe it was time to start facing those things when it came to Gavin. Maybe that was the only way they got through this bumpy territory between them. "It's okay to be sad about leaving. It *is* your family's ranch, and it'll be lonely not working with your brothers anymore."

Gavin kicked back in his chair, scoffing. "I'm fine. I'm hardly *leaving*. I'll be right next door. Plenty of opportunities to be irritated by my brothers. I'm finally getting my own place. I'm ecstatic."

"It's . . . you can be ecstatic and sad. It's complicated."

Gavin shrugged. "If you say so."

God, she hated when he did that, and she used to just chalk it up to him being a man and all men being jerks, but in this new world where she looked deeper at what Gavin said and did, where she realized he wasn't the simple, easygoing, good guy token she'd made him out to be, she thought it was just . . . deflecting from a painful topic.

God knew she had some experience with that. "I'm not insulting you, Gav. I'm just trying to be understanding. I think there's room to be happy and sad."

"There's nothing to understand. No sad. Just excitement." He smiled a smile that probably would have fooled her a few weeks ago. She would have let it fool her.

Not anymore.

Em returned with a tray full of cute little cupcakes. She put it on the table in between Lou and Gavin and set two forks on the table as well. "I went ahead and chose my cupcakes for the day based on things, so I didn't have to do a whole tasting cake for each one, but if these don't work, I have other flavor options we can taste on another day, and of course if you like one frosting and one cake, I can mix and match."

She grabbed a sketch pad off another table and then sat down with them. "I couldn't sleep last night, I was so excited about the design I came up with." She glanced up at Lou. "But if you hate it, tell me, promise?"

"Promise."

Em opened her sketch pad and held it up so both Lou and Gavin could see. Em's design drawings tended to be a little more fanciful than practical, but she always did a great job of translating the dreamy feel of her drawings into the cakes.

But this . . . It was beautiful. The entire top of the cake was covered in a field of violets, each carefully sketched just as Lou knew Em would carefully pipe the flowers on the cake. There was a drawing of a truck sticking up from the side of the cake, a truck that looked exactly like Gavin's. Parked right in front of a three-dimensional barn that looked like Lou's.

Lou's Blooms was scrawled over the top of the barn doors, something Lou had planned for the barn but hadn't accomplished yet.

Lou had no idea why her emotions were getting the best of her, but she was completely choked up over how beautiful and perfect it was. If she and Gavin were actually in love and getting married, she'd probably actually break down and cry.

But they were only fake getting married, so she managed to blink back the tears and swallow down the lump in her throat.

"I haven't quite figured out what I'll make the truck and the barn out of, but it'll just take some experimenting. What do you think?" Em asked eagerly.

Gavin was staring at the cake as though it had mortally wounded him, which made the lump in Lou's reappear.

Was she forcing him into this horrible thing he didn't want to do? He was sacrificing himself just because he was a good friend, and now he was regretting it. She'd convinced herself that because he got something out of it, it didn't matter if he had cold feet, but the more he acted weird, the more she started to worry that she had done something terribly, terribly wrong by agreeing to this.

"Can someone say something, because the silence is really weird. I know you're fighting, but—"

"Fighting?" Gavin said, looking from the cake to Em with a frown. "We're not fighting."

Em's eyebrows rose and she glanced at Lou. "Well, you two have very different definitions of what you're doing. So, maybe you should talk."

Gavin shook his head and reached for his hat. "I should get back."

"Sit your ass down," Em ordered, causing Gavin to pause his movements. "No one is leaving until you've both tried every cupcake and made a decision. Now, I'm going to go in the back and work on some things. You call me once you're done. If a customer comes in, I'll hear the bell." With that, Em got up and flounced off to the back of the bakery.

"Why did you tell her we're fighting?" Gavin demanded.

"Because we *are* fighting. Well, no, I don't know what we're doing, but fighting was the only word I could use," Lou hissed, nodding toward the back, where Em had gone. "You want to be stoic and keep every emotion or thought you've got whirling around in that head of yours, fine. Don't tell me anything, but that only means I have to tell people we're fighting."

Gavin's expression was stormy, but there was no time to consider that when she looked out the big window and saw who was standing there gaping at her through the spaces in the bright cupcake with a face painted on Em's storefront window.

Gavin must have seen her pale, because his head turned, and in a flash he was on his feet. Whatever storms had been in his eyes before had turned into a full-blown hurricane.

Lou scrambled forward, grabbing onto his arm with all the strength she had. "I need you to promise me you won't fight him."

"I can't promise you that," Gavin said through gritted teeth, his gaze on where Rex was still standing outside, looking at them like he'd seen a ghost.

"I'm the one he hurt, don't I get some say into how you react to him?"

Gavin clearly struggled with that. "Fine. But I'm only promising not to fight him as long as he doesn't barge in here."

Of course that was the moment Rex decided to move forward. He jerked the bakery door open, sending the bell tinkling in overdrive, then looked at her and Gavin as if he'd caught them murdering people.

"What the hell is this?"

Gavin moved forward, but Lou still clutched his arm. "Please," she whispered.

Gavin held her gaze, and she held his arm, so she could tell the moment he acquiesced, because some of the tension drained out of his arm and she felt less like she was grasping pure metal.

In an easy move, Gavin pulled his arm forward, and because she was still holding on to it she moved with it, closer to him. He shook her grasp off, then slid his arm around her shoulders.

"I think what we're doing is absolutely none of your damn business."

Rex reached for her, and she wished she had the wherewithal to stand firm or reach out and slap him, but she reflexively flinched away from his outstretched arm.

But Gavin angled himself between her and Rex anyway.

"Touch her, ever, and you won't live to regret it," he said, his voice so low and full of violence, it gave Lou a cold chill.

"I'm calling the police," Em said, and though her voice was loud from behind Lou, she could hear the wavering fear in it.

"It's all right, Em," she assured her.

"You're wearing a ring," Rex accused, pointing at her. "An engagement ring. I asked you three times and you said you never wanted to get married."

"To a cheating asshole," Lou reminded him. Because he only ever proposed after he'd done something stupid.

"You . . ." He turned his gaze to Gavin. "You can't marry her."

"I think I can."

"You can't marry *him*," Rex said to her.

"Oh, the man who burned down my barn and nearly killed me says I can't marry you, Gavin. I better call it off."

"That fire was Allie's fault. She's in jail, isn't she?"

"I know, Rex. Nothing is ever your fault. You're always the victim or the innocent bystander." It was weird. She didn't have the same anger toward him anymore. Oh, she still hated his wimpy guts, but it wasn't violent. He was an idiot. A mostly harmless idiot, until he got mixed up with someone who wasn't harmless. He'd never hurt her with anything other than carelessness, and even with the scars . . . She just felt kind of sorry for him.

She didn't forgive him. Didn't wish the best for him. But she didn't . . . hate him in quite the same way she had. She couldn't muster up the energy to hate him when he was this pathetic.

"So, how many years were you trying to fuck her while she was with me?"

"If you don't turn around and crawl back into whatever hole you came from—"

"You're going to what? Feel my elbow in your face again like in the bar?"

Gavin tensed next to her, but he didn't move forward. He was keeping his promise. This man would always keep his promises, and eight years she'd wasted on the other, who'd never kept one.

It used to make her feel like such a failure, and such a fool, but with Gavin's arm around her she only felt *right*. Safe. Good.

"Well, you finally got what you always wanted, Gav. Congratulations. Enjoy the one or two years that lasts.

Between you not having the balls to do a damn thing and her being a frigid bitch—"

Gavin moved so quickly, Lou couldn't grab a hold of his arm to stop him, but where she expected him to reach back and punch Rex as hard as he could, there was no crack of impact. Gavin simply took Rex by the shirtfront, opened the door, and shoved him out. He closed the door and locked it, turning his back on Rex's screaming face in the window.

"You didn't punch him," she breathed, because she still couldn't believe Gavin had kept his temper under wraps for the most part.

He flung his arms in the air. "You told me not to! You want me to? Because say the word, I'd be happy to go out there and punch him until my hand breaks."

"He isn't worth it. He really . . . God, he's just pathetic, isn't he? Barging in here years after we've even been together. After he was part of the reason my barn burned down and I was hurt and . . . Delusional and pathetic and not worth the energy."

Lou sank into her seat. She couldn't wrap her head around that whole scene. Not just that Rex apparently thought he had a right to comment on who she married, but some of the things Rex had said about Gavin. They didn't . . .

She looked up at him standing there, hands still in fists. Rex had walked away, but Gavin still stared at where he'd been, something like murder in his expression.

"What did Rex mean by . . . finally got what you always wanted?"

Gavin didn't move. "Are we listening to delusional assholes now?"

"Gav. Explain that to me."

Em cleared her throat, though truth be told, Lou

had forgotten all about her. "I'm just going to go into the backroom and you two can talk."

Lou barely registered her sister saying anything. She simply stared at Gavin, waiting for some kind of explanation. Some way to make sense of it all.

"Look," he said, raking his hand through his hair. He didn't look at her, and everything about him was pure discomfort, from the way he held himself to the way he stood with his back half to her. "Rex is a dipshit. Yeah, I had a thing for you back in high school. He beat me to the punch. But it worked out." He shook his head. "I mean, it didn't work out for you exactly, but we wouldn't have worked out either. We were fifteen and stupid and it probably would've ruined our friendship. Maybe I would have ended up being the one burning down your barn."

"That's not funny," Lou said, hugging herself against all this. Maybe she'd kind of suspected Gavin had had a crush on her, but Rex had known? Gavin was admitting it now? *Now?* And he had all these things to say, like he'd thought about it all enough to have these explanations and excuses ready.

"I know. Look, it was a *long* time ago. We were fifteen. He thinks I've been harboring some secret crush for the past fifteen years? Come on. He asked first. He called *dibs.* It was just—"

"Dibs? He called *dibs.* I was a *dibs* to you two assholes?"

"We were fifteen." He turned to face her fully then, and she could all but see he jumped on that anger, cloaked himself in it rather than deal with the more delicate parts of this situation. "We did stupid shit all the time. Don't you dare get mad at me over something I thought when I was fifteen. I'm not the one who dated him for eight years."

Even though he was absolutely right and probably

had every right to say it, it still felt like he'd struck her. Hard.

She *was* the one who'd gone out with him for eight years. The one who'd put up with Rex because she didn't know . . . She didn't know anyone else who would make her feel as bad as she felt about herself. She had never said that out loud to anyone, but maybe . . . maybe Gavin needed to understand that about her. Maybe there were some things they both really needed to understand about each other.

She swallowed against all the fear and embarrassment and those reasons she'd never told anyone this. Never admitted this. She wouldn't be as pathetic as Rex, stumbling through life blaming everyone else. No. Not anymore.

"You know why I said yes to Rex?"

"Because he was fun and charming and exciting and all the things fifteen-year-old-girls want in a boyfriend?"

"No." She took a deep breath. This was it. She was going to tell him some of her darkest inner secrets. Not all, but some. If he ran, well, she'd know the truth, and if Gavin stuck through it like he always did, then maybe . . . maybe there was some way to forgive herself in all this.

"I came to my grandparents' house knowing I was the reason we had to live with them. Every time they struggled financially, struggled to put clothes on our backs or afford ranch equipment or put food on the table, *I* was the reason."

"Lou, you know that's not true."

"Whether I know it's true or not is irrelevant, because I was nine. That was how I *felt*. I felt it well into my teens. Rex was the kind of boy who treated me like crap. And for a very long time, I just sort of believed that I deserved it."

"Lou."

"I'm just barely getting to a point where I think I was wrong. And the fire, weirdly, had something to do with that. I didn't deserve that. I didn't deserve . . . a lot of things I thought I did."

"Of course you were wrong," Gavin said, his voice as scratchy and low as hers. "First of all, nothing *you* did is why you had to live with your grandparents. Second of all, you know they don't resent you. Your grandmother loves you. Your grandfather worshipped you."

"There are the things we know and the things we feel." She shoved her shaking hands into her pockets and forced herself to meet his somewhat horrified gaze. "They don't always match up."

He stood there for the longest time, just staring, but she knew something was going on behind that stare.

"I like the chocolate."

"What?"

He pointed to the table. "The double chocolate. You like chocolate. I like chocolate. Let's do chocolate."

"Chocolate. Cake. For our wedding cake."

"Yes," he said firmly.

And all Lou could do in her current state of being emotionally wrung out was sigh and agree.

Chapter Seventeen

They told Em chocolate on chocolate. Gavin drove them to Benson and went to the mall and found some decent wedding rings that weren't too pricey. They argued about who would pay for what.

He won.

They went to a movie. Some interminable drama that probably would have depressed him if he'd been paying any attention. He definitely hadn't been.

It was all very domestic and datey, and he was certain they were both so lost in their own thoughts and memories, neither of them would remember much of anything about it.

He took a meandering drive on back mountain roads on the way home, and Lou exclaimed over the sunset gilding the mountains gold. He'd planned on keeping her out late, but the day had exhausted him, and she looked a little tired herself.

So, even though it was only seven when they got into Gracely, he kept driving straight to the Fairchild property.

She didn't mount any arguments. He was tempted to ask her what she was thinking about, but if it was about finding out he'd had a crush on her in high school, he didn't want to know.

He'd told a pretty good story. Crushes and stupid fifteen-year-olds. And it wasn't a story really. It was the truth. All those things had been things he'd felt or had happened, and just because he'd acted as though it was all in the past didn't make it a lie.

He pulled to a stop in front of the Fairchild house. Lou turned to him, with this new expression he didn't know how to read but knew meant nothing but trouble for him. Like she was trying to read him. Fix him.

Not gonna happen, sweetheart.

She smiled. "Come inside."

"I think I should head back. Lots to do, what with essentially starting a new job next week. Your grandma has made sure to inform me this is probationary, and if I screw anything up there, or with you, I'm out on my ass."

"She didn't say ass."

"No, you're right, she said *keister.* But when I laughed, she hit me with a broom handle. I think she and Grandma Maisey have been spending too much time together."

Lou laughed at that, then she reached over and gave his shoulder a little shake. "Come sit with me for a little bit. Please?"

He couldn't say no to *please.* Not from her. He'd resisted punching Rex because she'd asked. He didn't think there was a limit to what she could say please to that he wouldn't immediately capitulate to.

So, he got out of his truck and followed her onto the porch. She situated herself on the swing, which was a little lopsided and creaked menacingly when she sat down on it. He eyed the chains holding it up.

"You'll be fine," she said, patting the spot next to her.

There was something different about her. A lightness he hadn't seen since before the fire. That might have brought him some joy if he wasn't so wary about where it came from and why she was directing it at him.

Still, he took the seat on the swing, though not where she'd patted. No, he thought it best to give them a little space until this weird . . . vibe passed. And he'd stopped using words like *vibe.*

The swing creaked ominously, even more so when she immediately slid over so she was shoulder to shoulder with him. "You should put your arm around me," she said resolutely.

"Why?" he returned suspiciously.

"In case Grandma looks out the window. We're supposed to look like a loving couple." She smiled up at him.

"What is up with you?"

She shrugged. "Seeing Rex was like a . . . a closure I didn't know I needed."

"How was *that* closure?"

"He's just pathetic. Why should he care anything about what I'm doing? He treated me like crap. I treated *him* like crap. We were a crap circle. He cheated on me. He didn't love me. He and his new girlfriend *set a fire in my barn.* And he still feels justified in being pissed we're getting married?" She shook her head. "It's just sad."

"And that makes you happy?"

She laughed, and took his arm and pulled it up over her shoulder herself. Then she nestled right in, as if she belonged pressed up against him.

"Maybe it does. Yes, it makes me very, very happy

he's sad and pathetic." She leaned her head against his shoulder. "And if that's petty, I think I earned it."

"You damn well did."

She wiggled in closer, adjusting her head so it was more her cheek leaning on his shoulder. She pulled her legs up under her and rested her hand against his chest. She was basically curled up against him, on a porch swing, in the middle of a pretty spring night.

It took him a few minutes to realize he was holding his breath, sitting as tense and still as a man waiting for a rattler to strike.

Lou wasn't a rattlesnake. Probably. He forced himself to breathe out, to relax his muscles. He focused on the night around them. Clear starry sky, a chorus of spring peepers the low buzz background noise.

And the smell of Lou's shampoo, something earthy to match the scent of turned soil that always seemed to be around her.

It was nicer than it should have been. The kind of dream he'd never let himself have about Lou. Sexual fantasies were one thing. A man couldn't control that. Domestic fantasies? That meant you were bad off, and he refused to be bad off.

Except now he never wanted to move. What was the harm? Just sitting here. Enjoying the moment. It wasn't sex, for God's sake. It was just sitting. Sitting after a long, draining day.

"Have you apologized to Shane?" Lou asked, her fingers fiddling with one of the buttons on his shirt.

He stared hard at the little crescent moon. "No, I haven't."

"You need to."

"I'm well aware," he managed to say, even though she was still playing with the button, every movement of her fingers sending a jolt of sensation where he could feel that little touch even beneath the fabric of his shirt.

"So, when are you going to?"

He could barely focus on anything when she flattened her hand back out over his abdomen. It was lower this time. Not obscenely low, but noticeably lower. *Purposefully* lower.

He shifted, trying to manage some distance between them both with the move and with his words. "You get engaged and suddenly it's nag, nag, nag."

She chuckled against his neck. "You should spend the night," she said, her voice low, throaty almost.

He had the very uncomfortable thought she was . . . Her hand was low on his abdomen, her other hand tracing patterns on his neck. No one was watching them, and she was looking up at him like he was . . .

"I don't think so."

"Why not?" she asked, and her face was the picture of innocence, but her hand was drifting lower and this legitimately could not be happening.

"Did you hit your head when I wasn't looking?" He grabbed her drifting hand and removed it from his person.

"No, but I have been thinking about yesterday's kiss."

He hopped up at that, uncomfortably hard, more than a little confused, and so tempted he could barely see straight.

He didn't know what her angle was, but he couldn't fall for it. "As I told you then, we're not doing this. Period."

"I want to talk about why."

"Well, I don't." He strode for the stairs, but she just kept going.

"We have chemistry. You can't deny that."

"I failed chemistry."

She was clearly following him as her voice was far too close for comfort. She jumped in front of him before he could reach out to his truck door.

"Why are you running away?"

"I've made myself perfectly clear. Don't you know how to take no for an answer?"

She crossed her arms over her chest and scowled. "Clear? You've proclaimed we shouldn't *cross any lines* and this *won't happen.* That's not clear. When we've been this . . ." She looked away, something like nerves creeping into her expression, the only reason he didn't physically remove her from blocking his truck.

Then she met his gaze again. "We've been having moments, Gavin. Chemistry moments. Why shouldn't we explore that? See where it goes?"

"Because I know where it goes," he returned, trying to keep a grip on his temper, not because he was afraid of it flaring out of control but because temper made it seem a bigger deal than he could let it seem.

"Oh really?"

"Yes, Lou. We've spent twenty years being friends. We can't let this fake . . . thing make us forget that. People don't magically change and . . ." He almost said *fall in love,* but he didn't want those words hanging in the starlight-laden air. "We can't let convenience or even chemistry make us think there could be something here. If there wasn't before, it's not going to magically grow now."

She watched him talk, her stubborn expression not lifting or lessening. "Okay, so it's convenience chemistry. There's no hope for Shrinky-Dink love."

"Shrinky Dink?"

"You said magically grow! Shrinky Dinks magically grow. Anyway, the point is, if it's only convenient we're having this chemistry moment, then it'll just disappear when this whole thing is over and it's not convenient anymore. It's a temporary situation, and it could be a temporary chemistry thing."

Gavin tried to understand a world where Lou Fairchild was suddenly trying to talk him into bed. And he was saying no.

He *had* to say no. For himself. Her convenience chemistry would kill him. Utterly destroy everything.

"It would be awkward, when all was said and done."

"We've had to kiss. Likely will quite a few more times. Isn't that going to be awkward?"

"Kissing is one thing. Knowing what each other looks like naked? That's a little more awkward territory." Lou naked. Was he dreaming? This was some kind of warped nightmare. Had to be.

"Oh. Oh, I get it." She leaned against his truck, looking up at the sky, some awful pain working over her expression.

"Get what?" he demanded.

"It's about my scars."

"No! What? Of course not. Lou—"

"They're ugly and gross. I wouldn't want to—"

He took her by the arms, furious she'd put that awfulness on him when he was just trying to save everybody some damn heartache. "They're you and nothing about you is ugly or gross. I . . ." Nothing was getting through to her, so he had to get as close to the truth as he could manage without embarrassing himself. "You're my best friend in the world. I think you know that. I love my siblings, but I've always felt I had to put up a strong front to be like my brothers, and an even stronger one to protect my sisters. I know you're the same with Em. There isn't anyone who knows us better than each other."

She blinked, but some of that fear or self-disgust or

whatever awful thing had been in her eyes was gone. Replaced with a kind of softness.

"Lou, I don't want anything to risk that. Ever."

She lifted her arms up, cupping his face. "Couldn't we just promise each other it wouldn't?"

He took her hands, giving them a squeeze as he pulled them off his face. "Are you trying to kill me? Do you really think I want to say *no* when we're facing, you know, an undetermined number of sexless months? I'm thinking of the greater good here, and you're going to have to stop trying to undermine that."

"Or what? I'll get what I want?"

That . . . that definitely made him speechless. Which apparently was some kind of sign for her to kiss him again.

Lou. Lou had kissed him twice of her own volition, and resisting once had been one thing. This was . . . another.

Her hands were on his face, and his were on her arms, and why not slide his hands down the length of her sleeve, then back up? Why not angle his head so he could take the kiss deeper, so he could run his tongue against her bottom lip and get a hint of what Lou's mouth would taste like?

Why not sink into this damn fantasy come to life? To cup her neck and draw her closer, to feel her sigh against his mouth. To nearly black out when she pressed against him.

"Come inside," she whispered against his mouth. "Please."

Well, she did say please.

"I can't sleep with you with your grandmother in the next room," he replied, but instead of breaking the kiss like he should, he started it all over again. Her lips parted for him this time, and he swept his tongue inside the sweet warmth of her mouth.

This was . . . everything he'd imagined and somehow more, because it was Lou. Sweet, perfect Lou, and she wanted this from him, and all those certainties and reasons had deserted him. There was only her, and when he managed to pull away this time, her big blue eyes were luminous in the moonlight.

"She already thinks we slept together with her in the next room, so why not actually do it?" she offered with a smile.

Hell. "Lou."

"I have an empty barn."

"I don't have condoms. And neither do you." He was talking about condoms with Lou. Making out with Lou. The potential of having sex with Lou was right here and right now, and . . .

"How do you know I don't have condoms?"

He raised an eyebrow.

"Okay, no I don't, but I am on birth control for some health-related reasons, so I take it religiously."

It was like blinding insanity where he was having trouble seeing the problem with what he was doing. Why would it be wrong? Or bad? Why couldn't they just . . .

Sex. Yeah, no. No. Noooo.

"This can't happen."

She groaned in frustration. "Gav, I just want to . . . I want to have fun. To do something enjoyable, for me. I don't think I ever have, except my flowers. Everything I did with Rex was self-destructive, ninety-five percent of what I do here is some warped need to feel like I've earned my keep. For once, I want to let all of that go and just . . . enjoy something out of life."

That was the problem with *sex*, because all that sent a wave of tenderness through him. He wanted to carry her inside and . . .

But he'd known all that. Well, not *all* that, but there were things he'd known all this time and she had never, ever looked at him in a romantic light. Why would he trust it coming out of nowhere now?

"I had the shittiest year of my life, and I've had some shitty years. Everything has felt hard and oppressive. Grandma wants me to forgive my father. I have to marry someone to ensure my farm survives. I've put in my dues, I think, at this point. Now, I want something for me."

"And that's me?"

She smiled, and it was the prettiest damn thing he'd ever seen. "It could be, if you say yes."

Chapter Eighteen

Lou held her breath and counted. She'd never propositioned someone before. She might have spent eight years with Rex, but she didn't remember ever being the one who initiated what they did. She'd just . . . done what he wanted.

Penance.

For her father's mistakes and her mother's. She'd made herself pay for the adults who'd betrayed her, and it was in seeing Rex burst into the bakery, probably a little drunk in the middle of the day, pathetic and empty, thinking he had any right to talk to her.

She didn't know her father, but that was what she pictured him like. Pathetic and empty. Her mother was worse.

She'd let herself pay for their cowardice and selfishness for too long.

"So?" she asked, trying to brazen forward so she didn't have to deal with all these nerves sneaking through her resolve. Every kiss they shared was bigger and more potent, and cemented her certainty that she wanted this.

If Gavin had to believe it was convenience, that was fine. There would be time to figure things out and work through how they felt. It wasn't wrong to want this first. She . . . she deserved it.

"So." He fiddled with the edge of her bandanna. "Will you take this off?"

She froze. "No." The word escaped her mouth quick and final. *No.* "I can't . . . It stays on, and so does my shirt."

He cupped her good cheek, rubbing his thumb lightly across her cheekbone. She knew it bothered him on some level, but she couldn't bring herself to change her mind because someone was bothered by how she dealt with her scars. It was her pain. Her thing.

You keep saying that, but I'm having trouble buying it.

She pushed Em's voice out of her head.

"It's just the convenient thing. Okay?" He searched her face, a naked vulnerability there that shook some of her certainty. "We're clear on that. And we promise it changes nothing when the time comes. We're not going to lose each other."

"You'll never lose me." A promise. A vow. Like when he'd promised they'd go through with the wedding no matter what. Gavin didn't break promises, and neither would she.

Was he really going to give in? Was he really going to . . .

"Say *please* again."

He said it in a tone she'd never heard Gavin use before. Dark and a little edgy. It gave her a delicious thrill. She wanted to draw that out, the intensity in his dark eyes, the way Gavin was looking at her like she was the answer to all his prayers.

No one ever looked at her like that.

"Please," she whispered.

"Hell." His mouth crushed to hers, wild and a little rough, and she reveled in it. She clutched his shoulders and opened for him, and somehow kissing Gavin like this felt exactly *right.* Like for once in her life, everything had aligned to make something perfect.

She slid her hands up his neck and raked her fingers into his thick hair. Arching her body against his, she took his bottom lip between her teeth and scraped. Then laughed when he groaned.

"Where?" he demanded darkly.

Another one of those amazing little shivers that stopped and pooled low in her belly. "Barn."

He didn't even give her a chance to move. He simply linked his arms under her butt and lifted, easily striding across the yard and to the barn. She laughed against his neck, holding on to him.

They reached the door. "Key?"

"Put me down," she said, poking at his shoulder.

Her let her down, but a long, slow slide down his body that had them both panting. With a shaky hand, she fished her keys out of her pocket. Struggling just a little, she managed to get the padlock undone, and then once that was out of the way, used another key to unlock the mechanism she'd had installed with her new door for the extra security.

She pulled the door open and it gave with a squeak, and then Gavin's arms were around her again, kissing her right into her barn. The barn he'd helped rebuild. He'd built so many foundations in her life, it made it hard for this to feel weird. Everything in their twenty years of friendship seemed destined to move to this point eventually. She hadn't seen it for most of the time, but she saw it clearly now.

It made the kiss, Gavin's arms around her, all feel weightier. Bigger and more important, and yet that didn't feel scary. No, it felt exactly right.

His hands inched under her shirt at her sides, and even as her skin broke out in anticipation goose bumps, she tensed and immediately grabbed his wrists to stop him.

"Just to touch," he murmured, kissing under her ear. "I won't take it off. I promise." Gently, tenderly, he kissed her neck, her jaw on her good side, until she relaxed and let her hands fall off his. He trailed his fingers up her side, around her back, working off the clasp of her bra.

She winced a little as the straps brushed against the sensitive skin of the scar on her shoulder, but then his hands were drifting forward, the delicious rasp of his calluses against the nonscarred skin of her sides making her sigh against his mouth.

She could feel his mouth curve under hers before he kissed her again. She wanted light, and she would have stepped back to turn some on if his hands hadn't chosen that moment to cup her breasts, brush his thumbs across her already peaked nipples.

She wasn't sure *what* noise escaped her mouth, but it made Gavin laugh. Which spurred her on to stop standing here just taking his attention and give some of her own. She reached for his shirt, and for every button she managed to unbutton, he moved lightly across her nipples, a jolt that shot straight to the core of her every single time.

By the time she had his shirt undone, she was something like desperate. She pushed it off him, ran her hands down the dips of his muscles, the delicious friction of the trail of hair.

She didn't stop to enjoy. Desperation was starting to claw at her. She wanted more, and now. She undid the button of his jeans, slowly pulling down the zipper, and then she traced the length of him.

Even as his body jerked, he didn't stop touching her, teasing her. He was so hot and hard even with the barrier of his boxers between her fingers and him. *Him.* She wanted him. Now.

"Gav. I . . ." He moved his mouth to her breast, over her shirt, but still he unerringly found her nipple and nibbled.

She downright squeaked at that, her knees practically going weak with want and *need.* Yes, need. She needed him. Inside of her. As soon as possible.

"Just . . . *geez* . . . hold on." She disentangled from him, shivering a little from the cold without his heat wrapped around her.

Once her eyes adjusted to the dark, she made her way to her worktable by feel and the dim starlight coming in through the windows. She flipped on the lamp she kept on her table for when the days were cloudy and the overheads didn't quite give her what she needed for more meticulous work. She pulled a blanket out of the chest. Usually, she only used it for background for bouquet pictures, but this was a much, much better use.

She spread it on the floor, then looked over at Gavin. He stood exactly where she'd left him, shirtless, his pants undone but still on his hips. The lamp didn't illuminate much beyond the table, but she could see the somewhat increased rise and fall of his chest. She could *feel* the way his gaze never left her body.

Gavin.

A good man you don't deserve.

No, she wasn't going to let old thoughts like that derail her. She had a chance at this, at him. She was going to take it. For once, she wasn't going to aim low, not just think big but insist on it.

Tonight she was going to demand more, and she'd reckon with the consequences of that flight of fancy tomorrow.

Determined, Lou straightened her shoulders and toed her shoes off. She watched Gavin reach down and pull off one boot, then the other. Lou undid the snap of her jeans and pushed them and her underwear down. Her shirt was long enough that it covered pretty much everything.

But that didn't stop him from pushing his own jeans down, though he left on his boxers. He was so . . . muscle. The kind clothes could hide or at least play down, but with nothing but boxers on, she could take in the corded muscles of his forearms, those delectable ridges of abs.

She knelt down on the blanket and raised an eyebrow at him, doing her best to make her voice come out strong and confident instead of whispery and awed. "Well?"

"Well." Slowly, he crossed the space between them. He looked down at where she was kneeling on the blanket, and though she could read the *lust* in just about every inch of him, there was some foreign softness in his expression. That whole answer-to-his-prayers thing like from before, and she didn't know how to breathe through the way her chest clutched hard and painful at that.

You know you can't—

She refused to let her brain entertain those old feelings. Just refused. So, she smiled up at him and motioned for him to drop the boxers. His mouth quirked, but he hooked his fingers in the waistband.

She made another one of those squeaking noises

that made him laugh because, just, wow. *Wow.* Naked Gavin was the kind of fantasy she'd never even allowed herself to have because it felt like cruel and unusual punishment to believe it existed.

Now he was here. Naked. With *her.*

Someone who looks like that is going to want to look at your mess?

She blinked at *that* awful voice, harder to fight because this was new. She was used to her own self-worth issues from childhood. Being ashamed of her scars, that was something she hadn't had to deal with because she just kept them covered up. She hadn't anticipated being naked with anyone.

Most especially Gavin. Her best friend, one of the few people she trusted, and what if he couldn't handle it? Why should he handle it? *She* couldn't handle it.

"Lou." His voice was suddenly close, and she realized he'd kneeled next to her without her even fully realizing. He took her chin and forced her gaze to him. "Hey, what is it?"

"Nothing. I just . . ." She focused on his face, his dark eyes, that surprisingly soft mouth. "You're very good-looking," she said seriously.

He looked at her dubiously, but he trailed one single fingertip from her ankle to her knee, and the shivery, shuddery feeling inside her did a hell of a job getting rid of the ugly doubts. Besides, she'd keep her scars covered and everything would be fine.

His finger kept tracing her leg, so she kissed him, lost herself in the meeting of their mouths, let him move her onto her back, and when his finger trailed up her leg, he didn't stop.

She gasped, but he only used it as an opportunity to deepen the kiss with tongue and teeth, a direct opposite to the light, gentle teasing below.

She didn't know what this was. How anything could feel this amazing and desperate all at the same time. How she could survive the way pleasure built but never unleashed. Even as she writhed under him, arched against his fingers, it wasn't enough. She needed that enough, but she found she wanted more than just teasing, more than any precursor.

She wanted him. Fully. Wholly. Didn't want to lose herself until he was deep inside her, joined and fully hers. She cupped his face and pulled his mouth from hers, looking him right in the eye. "Gavin. I want you. *You.*"

His gaze locked with hers, almost pained for some reason. He paused there, on that last precipice, so close she could feel him, something like concern chasing over his face. She touched that downward-point mouth at each corner.

"It doesn't have to change anything," she whispered, hoping she was reading his concerns correctly. "We're still us."

She could tell he didn't believe her, but he lowered his mouth to hers anyway. She thought for the briefest second about taking the dumb bandanna off, but . . . But she just couldn't bring herself to think about him having to look at that.

Then Gavin was sliding into her, slow and agonizingly perfect. He rested there, holding on to her, breathing hard, completely joined.

Okay, maybe it did change some things, because this . . . this was right. Them together filled her with hope and a million dreams that for once she didn't allow herself to push away as *silly* or *not for her.* Maybe in the morning. For tonight, she wanted to believe in miracles and happily ever afters, and most of all herself. And him. Them.

He withdrew, slow and intense, and the rock forward was just the same. She tried to keep her eyes open, wanting to watch the way his face was so intense, so absorbed in them. *Them.*

"Look at you," he murmured, like she wasn't laying here with her top still on and a bandanna covering half her face. Like she was perfectly beautiful no matter what.

Then she couldn't keep her eyes open, couldn't face the way any of that made her feel like some kind of fraud. She squeezed her eyes shut, wrapping her arms around his neck, moving with him at just the right angle to have every thrust feel like fireworks.

He whispered her name, all awe and need, one hand tangled in her hair, the other holding himself up. They moved together, the pleasure and desperation cinching tighter and tighter, increasing the pace.

Gavin murmured something that sounded like *always,* and finally the moment broke, joy spiraling out to every inch of her body, while wave after wave of climax weakened her grip on his neck and she felt limp and lax and *perfect* even as Gavin still moved in her. Every inch of his body tense, his movements becoming erratic, and she watched him, glittering eyes, tensed muscles.

"Gav," she whispered, not sure what she was trying to impart, but his gaze met hers in the same moment he pushed into her, holding there, a moan escaping his lips.

They lay there, him collapsed on top of her, limbs tangled, holding on to each other despite any discomfort. Slowly, their breathing returned to normal, and still Lou couldn't bring herself to move or ask him to.

She wanted to live in the perfect aftermath where

nothing was complicated and she could still feel tiny shocks of pleasure when he breathed.

Eventually, he rolled off her and let out a long, careful breath. He didn't say anything, but she didn't want him to. She didn't want to say anything either. It would mean the moment would be over, and as much as she hoped to do it again, and again, how could anything match or beat this?

"It's cold," he finally said, his voice low and raspy. "We should get dressed," he murmured, handing her her jeans.

Was it cold? She couldn't feel anything aside from what could only be described as *sparkle.* Still, she pulled on her pants and got to her feet, while Gavin did the same. He pulled on his shirt and glanced at her as he began to button it up.

She smiled at him, because it was all she could seem to muster. Smile goofily, because her brain felt like it was dead, but who cared when she was this happy. She held her hand out to him. "Come to bed." *Our bed.*

There was a hesitation as he finished buttoning his shirt, and she felt as though something sharp was being shoved through her chest. He was going to say no, he was going to—

Then he smiled back and took her hand, giving it a squeeze. She let out a breath of relief, that giddy happiness soaring back into place.

"Yeah, let's go to bed."

Chapter Nineteen

Gavin woke up to some obnoxious beeping sound, and someone moving around next to him, and none of this was normal or his life.

His eyes flew open and he looked around. Lou's room. Lou's bed. Lou all curled up next to him.

Lou.

It came back to him in a rush, along with twin feelings of joy and horror.

She groaned, flinging her arm over and slapping the alarm clock on the nightstand on her side of the bed.

Her. Side. Of. The. Bed. Because he had a side of the bed and she had a side of the bed and . . . Sex. They had had *sex*. Real sex. Sex sex. Sex.

He'd had sex with Lou. Despite all his promises to himself, despite all his attempts at self-preservation. She'd said *please* and all that stuff, and what was there to *do*?

Hell, he wanted to do it again.

He scrubbed his hands over his face and tried to think. But how was he supposed to think when Lou was curling right into him as if this was normal? As though this was the way things were supposed to be.

He might have lost his mind last night, but not enough to let himself sink into that fantasy life.

She groaned into his side. "I have so much to do today. Wedding bouquets for tomorrow and annoying emails and ugh. Not enough coffee in Colorado to get me out of this bed." She nuzzled closer.

Lou.

Lou Fairchild.

Curling up and nuzzling into him like this was normal and their life. All Gavin could think to do was lie here and take it.

She groaned again. "Must get up." With much groaning and moaning and theatrics he didn't usually associate with Lou, despite knowing she wasn't much of a morning person, she rolled out of bed on her side.

Her side of the bed. Him still in her bed. On his side. He scrubbed his hands over his face again and tried to make sense of any of this. When he dropped his hands and looked at her, she was standing there staring at him, a lump of material that might be a robe in one hand.

She studied him in complete silence, and he tried not to fidget. "What?"

"I don't know. You're in my bed. That's . . . new."

"Well, actually, this is the second time I've been in your bed."

"You were just kind of on top of my bed then. Now you're in my bed, and have been in other things."

"Jesus," he muttered, letting his head fall back and thunk against the headboard.

"It gets me thinking, though, we should talk about when you're going to move in."

"Uh." Somewhere in the back of his mind, he'd known that was happening sooner or later, what with a wedding hurtling toward them, but the whole *sex* thing suddenly made actually moving in far more weighted than it had been.

"Shouldn't we, ah, wait till after the wedding? Or ask your grandmother? Or—"

"I'll talk to her about it today. Grandma Maisey is coming over so they can see if they can make Grandma's dress work."

Her grandmother's wedding dress. For their wedding. More things made all the weightier by his weakness, because last night was *his* weakness. He could have said no. He could have walked away. But the promise of what he'd always wanted, even knowing it would probably destroy him, had been too tempting.

He knew what all those people who sold their souls to the devil felt like. The moment had been worth his soul and his life, but now the twisting was going to start. Lies and vows and heirloom dresses.

"It doesn't bother you?" he asked, sitting up in bed and raking a hand through his hair.

"What?" she asked, shrugging on the ratty old robe she'd been holding.

"Getting married in your grandmother's dress when it's just a fake marriage to me?"

She adjusted her bandanna, and something in her expression dimmed, but she just shrugged. "No. No, it doesn't bother me."

"Okay."

She waited a beat. "Does it bother *you*?"

"It doesn't bother me if it doesn't bother you." He looked down at his boots. He needed to get home and away from her. Just to get a grip on things. And not talk about this.

"Okay."

"Okay."

"God, I need coffee." She pulled the door open,

but once they left this room, that was it. Any actual conversations they had would have to be couched in fake.

"Um."

She stopped at the door, watching him expectantly. He stood up and grabbed the jeans he'd left in a lump next to the bed. He pulled them on, then shrugged into his shirt.

He should just let her go. Deal with this himself. Except she'd initiated this whole crazy thing and he had to understand some of her expectations or he'd just drive himself crazy. "Is this just a normal thing we do now?"

One side of her mouth curved, and damn how he wanted to kiss the other, to talk her back into bed.

"I'd like it to be."

"Okay."

"Wouldn't you?"

"I just . . ."

"I'm not one to look the best-sex-I've-ever-had gift horse in the mouth."

He paused in buttoning up his shirt. "The what now?"

"I mean, I wouldn't get a big head about it. You're only beating out Rex. I'm sure you, ah, well you know . . . had more . . . Just that you don't have to . . . Rex was never all that impressed with me either, so you've probably had bet—"

"Stop." Any pleasure he'd gotten over her original comment died at the thought of that little asshole putting any crap ideas in her head. "You already know this, I know you do, but let me reiterate—anything that moron said about you was a damn lie. You're warm and beautiful and . . ." *Everything I've ever wanted.* He almost said those words too. It was hard not to, the fight between wanting to make sure she understood how *amazing* she was and the fight to keep some semblance of *I haven't loved you forever and this isn't slowly killing me.* "Last night was great."

"Best-you-ever-had great or just great great?" she asked, head cocked, amusement sparkling in her eyes. It'd been a long time since he'd seen that in her. Since before the fire, since before her grandfather died. When she'd talked about the shit year weighing on her, he'd understood. Because he'd watched that light dim and then disappear.

He'd had some part in putting it back and that was . . .

Dangerous.

"Are you seriously postmortem quizzing me?"

"Yes. Seriously. So?"

It was worse, somehow, that she was smiling and enjoying herself. It twined into his heart and created too many hopes to dash all at once. He'd brought the inevitable pain upon himself, but he had to make sure she didn't get caught up in that. He didn't want her convincing herself there was something here just because he felt something. Every step had to be careful. He wouldn't crush her the way Rex had, even if it meant saving himself from being crushed. "Yes, best-I-ever-had great. But—"

"And you're not just saying that?"

"No, Lou. But . . ." He sighed, wanting to kiss her and forget everything else. But everything else was going to kick him in the ass eventually. "We have to be able to walk away from each other."

She looked down, her hair hiding her expression, but she nodded. "Yeah. I know."

"It's important."

She lifted her chin again and smiled at him, though it was a kind of blank smile. "Yes, it is."

"This is just friends with benefits for the duration of our marriage, or the duration of how long you want to put up with me, and then we end that part." It would haunt him for the rest of his life, but hell, it might be worth the haunting. "We don't go getting any funny ideas, right?"

She shrugged. "Sure." And then, before he could reiterate it just one more time, she rose to her tiptoes and pressed her mouth to his. She looked up at him from under her lashes.

"You know what you need to do today?"

And because this was some kind of dream world, he figured he might as well go with a joke. "Be your sex slave?"

Her peel of laughter was too amazing to worry about what it did to his heart.

"You need to apologize to your brother for this." She tapped his lip, which didn't hurt much anymore but was still a tad swollen. "You can be my sex slave after."

"I could be your sex slave now *and* after."

She glanced at the staircase, then back in the room. Then she grinned up at him. "Deal."

Lou's least-favorite days were the ones before a wedding. They were hectic and stressful and full of hiccups she couldn't anticipate.

None of it seemed to bother her today. She'd had to redo all the ribbon because the lacier spool had run out, made a last-minute change to the boutonniere at the groom's request. By the time she had everything finished and in the cooler all ready to be delivered in the morning, her back and limbs ached.

And she whistled all the way inside.

Good sex was amazing.

Grandma and Grandma Maisey were in the living room when Lou entered. They had Grandma's wedding dress spread out on the couch and were arguing about sleeve length, of all things.

"Well, here she is. Get it on, girl."

Lou was in too much of a good mood to be irritated by Grandma Maisey's rough greeting. She took the dress and went into the bathroom to change. The sleeves were a definite problem, but the rest of the dress fit rather well. A little tight, but doable, especially once the grandmas worked their magic.

She couldn't see herself because the first-floor bathroom only had a small sink over the mirror, but when she stepped back into the living room, the grandmas had arranged a little step stool and a full-length mirror.

"Up you go," Grandma said, measuring tape already in hand, the little wrist needle holder on her arm. Grandma had tried to teach her to sew once.

It hadn't gone well.

Lou stepped up onto the little stool and turned to face herself in the mirror. She looked at her reflection and all that giddy happiness evaporated.

She looked like a bride. A real bride. The dress was old-fashioned, but simple enough it didn't feel out of place. It didn't feel wrong at all.

Her eyes stung with tears, worse when she heard Grandma's little exhalation of joy.

"Take off that bandanna, girl. Those scars can't be worse than that ugly thing," Grandma Maisey said.

Lou blinked, managing to pull herself out of the emotional moment. "No, thank you."

"Humph."

Grandma cleared her throat and began to fuss with the hem. "So, what can be done, Maisey?"

"Hmm. Those sleeves will have to go."

"No. No, I need sleeves," Lou said. She wouldn't be showing off her scars at her wedding. Period.

"Could make a fur stole," Grandma Maisey suggested.

"For a spring wedding?" Grandma said dubiously.

Maisey shrugged. "I got plenty of squirrel."

"I'll pass on the squirrel fur wedding dress."

"Suit yourself."

The door swung open and Em rushed in. "Did I miss it?" She dropped her purse. "Oh my *God, Lou.* You look . . . oh my God."

"I . . ." Lou didn't know what to do with Em's outburst of emotion because it was all positive and she couldn't fix positive emotions.

But Em had moved on to the grandmas. "You look amazing. Even better if you take the sleeves off."

"No."

All eyes turned to her in the mirror. "I like the long sleeves," she said, which was stupid. Why not just admit she didn't want to show off her scars at her wedding?

Fake wedding. Gavin has made it very, very clear this was super fake, no matter how good the sex was.

But surely she could change his mind? Time would change his mind. She was almost certain. They were best friends. They had chemistry. Serious, serious *amazing* chemistry and sex. Why couldn't they have a romantic relationship built on that?

Gavin was just being cautious, surely because they

were getting married and it'd be hard and weird to *start* a relationship when you were already married.

"The sleeves are too short as is," Grandma pointed out gently, breaking into Lou's thoughts.

"What about a plaid shirt?" Em suggested. "I've had brides do that. A plaid shirt over the top. It'd cover up your arms and let you keep the rest of the dress as is."

Lou about cried at that. "That's a good idea."

Em smiled and winked. Then they spent a half hour fiddling with the dress, the grandmas making notes and Em giving Lou little squeezes of encouragement.

Finally, Grandma Maisey left and Grandma began to pack up her sewing supplies.

"Why don't I go fix us some dinner?" Em suggested.

"That'd be fine, Em. First, though, I want to talk to you both."

Lou exchanged a glance with Em, all the weird emotional upheaval of dresses and scars sinking into dread.

"Your father's coming into town next weekend," Grandma announced. She sounded regal and in charge, but Lou noticed her hands shook before she clasped them together. "I told him we don't have the room for him here, but I've gotten him a hotel room in Benson."

"Grandma, you don't have to do that. He can come here," Em said.

It wasn't exactly a surprise her sister was more soft-hearted than Lou herself, but it still made Lou a mix of angry and guilty. Who was Em to say? She didn't live here.

"No, I don't think I'm ready to have him here, and I don't think he's ready for that either. He had a tough relationship with your grandfather. We'll need to work up to healing some of those scars. I'm going to have dinner with him in Benson on Saturday. You're welcome to join us, or abstain, or make your own plans with him." She looked right at Lou. "He'll only be here Saturday and Sunday. One night. Two days."

"Where . . ." Em cleared her throat. "Where is he living?"

"Idaho. He's working on a ranch there. Hard to figure when he hated this one, but he says he's been clean for a year and working there and happy." Again, her gaze slid to Lou. "Mostly."

Lou looked away. She couldn't stand the weight of that gaze, even more so now because she didn't have the anger she quite did.

Talking with both Gavin and Grandma the other day about it, and understanding maybe for the first time that Grandma's relationship with her son was complicated by a mother-son dynamic Lou couldn't understand.

So, instead of just being mad and betrayed, she was mad, betrayed, and guilty.

"I'm going to go put these away. You go ahead and start dinner, Em."

Lou and Em stood in the living room as Grandma went up the stairs. Lou knew she should say something, reassure Em in some way, but boy was it emotional whiplash to go from giddy happy hopeful to . . .

This.

Without saying anything, Em moved for the kitchen. Lou trailed after her. She had to say something. She couldn't just let all these years of protecting Em from their parents go down the drain.

"You don't have to see him. Grandma said so herself."

Em opened the fridge, pulled out some ground hamburger. "How does spaghetti sound?"

"Em."

Em took a deep breath and let it out. She didn't stop her preparations, but Lou got the impression she was at least thinking about everything.

"I think I want to see him," Em said once she had a pot of water on the stove to boil and the hamburger in a pan to brown.

It was painful, but Lou knew then and there she would do whatever it took to protect her sister. Even see that man.

"Okay, so we'll see him."

Em turned away from the stove and looked at Lou, so uncharacteristically grim. "I want to do this myself."

"What?"

"I don't want you going in there trying to protect me. I want to have a meeting with him by myself. If you want me to go with you when you—"

"I'm not going to see him."

Em was silent for a moment. "Well, that's your choice. But I don't want you coming with me."

For the second time in as many hours, Lou blinked back tears.

"I know you've tried to protect me forever. You've always been my knightess in shining armor, or whatever female knights are, but I'm not a little girl anymore. It affected me too, what he did. It hurt me, but in different ways. I need to work that out on my own, and I can't have you sweeping in trying to fix it." Em squeezed her hand. "I don't say that to hurt you, even though I can tell you're hurt."

"I'm not hurt."

"Lou."

"I'm not hurt," Lou insisted.

Em studied her. "I hope you don't do this to Gavin."

"Do *what* to Gavin?"

"Pretend your feelings away. I'm your sister. I can see through it. I don't know how good husbands are at reading through bullshit."

Husband. Gavin. Feelings.

Em's expression softened. "Sit down. You're looking pale."

"I'm f—"

Em raised an eyebrow and Lou sank into the chair.

"I'm Lou and I suck at emotions," she muttered, thunking her forehead against the table.

Em laughed, perching on the seat next to Lou. She patted her back. "We'll work through it. Together. Just because I need to do this one thing alone doesn't change that we're always in this together and have each other's backs, okay? It doesn't mean I won't talk about it with you. I just need to face him on my own at least once. But you've got my back and I've got yours. Always."

Lou looked up, and even though she believed Em wholeheartedly, she leaned her head on her sister's shoulder. "Promise?"

"Promise."

Chapter Twenty

Gavin worked all day at the ranch without catching a glimpse of his brother. Frustrating, because he did want to get the apology off his chest, and even more so because he'd probably only spend one more full day working their ranch before he moved full time to the Fairchild place.

It was . . . weird. He was days away from this thing he'd always wanted and there was more dread than excitement. Maybe it was a mistake. He should stay here where he knew how to do things. Here where his mistakes wouldn't ruin people's lives.

He tried to breathe as his chest tightened against his will. He looked out over the Tyler Ranch. This was home. His *ancestors* had worked this, his father. Why shouldn't he stay here, right here?

When he turned toward the truck engine and saw Lou's truck bumping toward him, the riot of a spring sunset pink and lavender behind her, his question seemed to be answered.

She pulled up to where he stood, rolling down the driver's side window.

"Hey," he greeted. "What are you doing here?"

"Want to go for a ride?" she asked.

"Yeah. Sure. If you tell me why now? Don't you have a wedding tomorrow?"

"Yes. And I'd like to not obsess over it until tomorrow morning's deliveries. I thought you could distract me." She fluttered her eyelashes at him and made him laugh.

"Go park over by the stables."

She nodded and drove her truck over while he walked. He glanced at the house. The downstairs lights glowed in the fading daylight, and he imagined his family was in there chatting over dessert.

He looked at Lou getting out of her truck by the stables, and it was a very strange thing to want both. He wanted to go hang out with his family. He wanted to take Lou with him. He wanted to take Lou back to her farm and do what they'd done last night—and not just the sex, loathe as he was to admit it, but to sit on the porch and talk.

What was he supposed to do with all those different wants? He didn't have a damn clue. A life of getting second place in the wants department and now they were something like overflowing.

It was terrifying. So, he focused on Lou. She was pretending to be cheerful, but something was eating at her. "So, why'd you really come over?"

She studied him for a second. "Do you always see right through me?"

"Not always, but I pay attention every now and again."

She seemed to mull that over as they walked into the stables. They worked in tandem to saddle Templeton and Bodine because they were the horses who wouldn't have been working today.

"My father's going to be in town next weekend," she finally said on a loud exhale.

"Are you going to see him?"

"I don't know. Grandma is. Em is. Em didn't want me to go with her, though."

Gavin thought that over, both the information and the disappointed way Lou said it. It was kind of funny. Lou was a lot like Shane. She wanted to protect Em from everything, even when Em didn't need protecting. Shane had always been like that with his younger siblings too. Something about being the oldest, he supposed.

"So," Gavin said, leading Templeton outside, Lou right behind him with Bodine. "My take. Em wants to face him on her own. Sometimes we younger siblings need to do that."

They stepped out into the chilly dusk, and Lou wrinkled her nose at him. "What's so wrong with letting someone be with you and there for you and—"

"And not let you deal with your own stuff. She's an adult, Lou. I know you want to protect her, but she'll ask if she needs that. Em isn't afraid to ask you for help."

"Why do I feel like that means, *unlike you, Lou.*"

He grinned at her. "I don't know. Are you feeling insecure about your actions?"

"Humph."

"Well, I hope you know if you want to meet with him, even for a screaming session, I'll go with you if you need someone."

She stood there, holding the reins to Bodine, looking at him like he'd handed her some grand prize and slapped her all at the same time.

She let out a breath. "Em offered the same, but . . ."

"But you wouldn't want her to watch you cuss him out if you wanted to. Her or your grandma. Meanwhile, I'd be happy to applaud from the sidelines."

She stepped over to him, wrapping her free hand around his neck and pressing her mouth to his. Sudden, yes, but so damn sweet it just about shattered him to pieces.

When she pulled back, she looked right into his eyes. "You're the best man I know. Do you believe that?"

He took a slightly cowardly step away. "Based on the shitty men you know . . . maybe."

It didn't make her laugh or even chuckle, as he'd hoped it would.

"Come on. Let's ride."

She didn't say anything, but he went ahead and got up on the horse. Eventually, she did too, and he waited for her to get situated in the saddle before he nudged his horse forward. They rode in silence at a slow pace, out around the east pasture. He hadn't really been thinking about it, but pretty soon they were getting close to the field where he'd proposed. *Fake proposed.*

He didn't want to face that right now. "Ready to head back?"

"Sure."

They turned their horses, and Gavin had to pause here on this ridge, the Tyler Ranch spread out before him in the light of sunset. The pasture glowed green, the house and stables gold. The barn a bright, gleaming red.

"You're going to miss it," Lou said softly.

Gavin shook his head, but he couldn't shake away the emotion coursing through him. "Yeah. Stupid. Be right next door."

"But it's not yours."

"This isn't either. It's Tyler land, but it's Shane's . . . I don't know. I used to think that was because of bad luck or birth order, but it's not mine the same way it's his. I love it, I do, but it's like you have a role. Shane's is steward. Mine's . . . I don't know. Maybe I don't really have one. Maybe that's why I always wanted my own piece."

"Have you apologized to him yet?"

He shifted in the saddle, his gaze still on the house in the distance. "No."

"Gavin Tyler."

"He was scarce today. I'll round him up tonight."

"Is that what's bothering you?"

If only.

"You sure you trust me with your place? I know the alternative isn't much better, but I've never had to prove myself."

She was silent for a minute, and he didn't dare look to check, but he had the feeling she was studying him.

"I have the upmost confidence in you, Gav."

He looked down at the reins in his hands, doubts and fears and a million things working through him to make him downright stupid. "What if I . . . mess it up?" he asked, so low it was a miracle she managed to hear it over the spring peepers and the wind in the trees.

"Of course you'll mess up." When he whipped his head to look at her, she smiled. "It's a *ranch.* You're not God." She reached over and patted his thigh. "Making mistakes isn't failure. It's part of the process. I make mistakes with my flowers all the time."

"Shane doesn't mess up."

"Bullshit he doesn't. You go ask him. I bet he can think of mistakes he made every month for the past twenty-five years."

"He's too hard on himself."

"And so are you, but at least Shane is too hard on himself for thing's he's *done.* You're predicting failure before you've even given yourself a chance."

I love you. It wasn't fair that it was a sharp slice of

pain to have those words in his head. To be this close and to even be able to *act* on them, but not say them.

You're predicting failure before you even give yourself a chance.

But that was for things like ranches, not people. Not life.

"Let's get back."

Lou nodded, and they trotted at a meandering pace back to the stables. They were both quiet as they took care of the horses and cleaned everything up. Gavin glanced outside when he heard an engine, Shane's truck coming into view on the drive as it pulled up to the garage off the house.

"Well, here's your chance," Lou said, giving him a nudge out of the stables. "Go apologize."

"Nag, nag, nag," he muttered, but he moved. Much as he dreaded the apology, he knew he needed to give it. He walked with Lou over to her truck, though.

She climbed in, but paused before closing the door. "You coming over tonight?"

He shouldn't. He should avoid it as long as he could. Every night spent together was a memory he wasn't going to be able to erase when this whole thing was over. But maybe that just meant he should soak up all the memories while he could. "Yeah, if you want."

"I want," she replied with a smirk. "But only if you get that apology in."

"Yes, ma'am."

"I think he's waiting for you."

Gavin looked over at the porch. Cora and Micah were walking inside, closing the door behind them, but Shane and King sat on the porch.

"I'll see you later, then."

He grunted, but before he could turn and walk for

the house, she leaned down and gave him a quick kiss. Like they were a couple.

A very temporary couple, dipshit.

"Later then," he muttered, pulling his hat low and starting the long walk to his brother.

He reached the porch, something other than dread pooling in his stomach. A weird kind of resignation instead.

"Hey," Shane greeted.

"Hey." Whereas Gavin expected to feel pissy, defensive that Shane seemed to be waiting for an apology, the usual emotions never materialized.

"Last day tomorrow?"

Gavin nodded. "Be right next door if you ever need a hand, though."

"Same goes."

Gavin still stood on the bottom step, and Shane stayed seated on one of the porch chairs. They didn't look at each other.

Gavin wanted to resent going first, but he'd thrown the first punch, hadn't he? "Sorry about the shiner."

Shane rubbed his cheek. "Had to sleep in the doghouse for that one."

Gavin thought about last night and tried not to grin. "I didn't."

Shane huffed out a laugh. "Well, I'm sorry too. You know I don't often lose my temper, but it's hard to watch someone you love think less of themselves than they are. It gets frustrating, because there's nothing I can do to fix that for you. I want to, but I know even if I could, you wouldn't want me to."

Much as he was close to his brother, they weren't sentimental, I-love-you close. "No, I wouldn't," Gavin managed to say.

"You'll do a fine job with the Fairchild place," Shane said seriously. "I hope you believe that."

"And if I don't?" Gavin asked, not daring to look at his brother's expression. Likely disappointed or some other uncomfortable thing Gavin didn't want to face.

"You've got a lot of people to lend a hand until you do."

Gavin looked at Shane, then. Serious, dependable Shane. Gavin had always figured he couldn't live up to that. Who could?

But his brother believed in him, and would be there for him even if he screwed up. Gavin knew that, but there was something about saying it too.

It was funny. He'd spent his whole life being resentful of those hands, that support, and for maybe the first time at the mention of help, all he felt was grateful.

The week was a blur of her customer's wedding, then plans for her own. She threw her days into those wholeheartedly, and Gavin at night wholeheartedly, because then she didn't have to think about what the weekend would bring.

But it was Saturday, and Lou had arranged to meet with her father. Not because she wanted to, but because Em was meeting with him tonight and Lou wanted to warn him off. Em would be pissed, but Lou had to make sure her father wasn't planning on doing something that would hurt Em.

In the end, she'd decided she didn't want Gavin to come with her, much as she'd been touched by the offer. She needed to do this alone. But when she came back home, he'd be there, trying to make sense of a cattle operation that had fallen off considerably in the last year.

It was such an amazing comfort. She knew he always would have done that for her, but knowing he was here, knowing he was hers, and trusting that she got to have that without worrying if she was *good enough.* There was a miracle wrapped up in that.

She took a deep breath as she drove into Benson. She'd refused her father's offers to meet somewhere in Gracely. She didn't want to think about him in the town that had become her home.

She pulled into the little fast-food restaurant's parking lot and took a deep breath in and out. She could do this. For Em. She couldn't stop trying to protect Em, even if she didn't want it anymore.

She stepped out of the truck and walked up to the rundown restaurant with a pit of dread in her stomach. She didn't even know if she'd recognize him, but the minute she stepped inside, a grizzled, skinny man in a corner booth stood, looking straight at her.

She wanted to turn and run, but she would be stronger than him. Stronger than this. It was for Em, after all. Standing up to him. Making sure he didn't cause any more damage.

She approached the man, not sure she could see any similarities to the picture of him in her head. But his eyes were familiar. The same shade of blue as hers. She remembered those eyes.

"Louisa."

She didn't know what to call him. He wasn't her *dad* and Father sounded so formal. "Hi."

"Do you want something to—"

"No."

He nodded, clearly nervous and uncomfortable as he sat back down in the booth. She slid into the seat across from him. She didn't look directly at him, couldn't bring herself to.

"What made you change your mind?" he asked in a quiet, raspy voice.

"I know you're meeting Em later." She lifted her gaze to his. Because this was all about protecting Em. Nothing else. "I want to make sure you don't say anything to upset her."

"I suppose there's not much hope of that."

"Let her guide the conversation. Don't ask anything of her. Give her the space to do what she needs. That's all I came here to tell you."

Her father frowned a bit at that. "There's nothing you wanted for yourself out of meeting me?"

It was so strange to be cut in half by the question. Part of her recoiling away from the question. For herself? No. Never.

But words bubbled up inside part of her. She shoved them away. "Don't ask Em for anything. Don't talk about the past. Like I said, you let her guide the conversation, and you don't ask for more than you deserve. Which is nothing."

He didn't say anything to that. She didn't know if that was good or bad, but she'd said her piece, so she should just leave. That was all she needed to tell him.

She stared at her hands and wondered why her feet weren't moving, why she felt rooted to this seat and this spot. "I'm getting married."

"Your grandmother told me. She said she liked him."

He's a better man than you'll ever be. It was true, and yet it felt unnecessary to say to the man wilting in the booth across from her.

"Why are you here?" she demanded, not sure she wanted to hear any answer, let alone a truthful one. Yet she stayed rooted to the spot, looking at her hands.

"I'm fifty years old. I have nothing to show for it.

My life has been a waste, and I couldn't bring myself to come home for my own father's funeral."

"So you thought you'd arrive a year late?"

Her scathing tone didn't change anything about the way he spoke. Slowly and methodically. Soft and uncertain inside of that. "The day after his funeral, I walked into a church."

"And you were magically saved and changed?" she said with a sneer, wanting to find some anger, something to fight against.

"No. But the people there pointed me in the direction of some state-funded rehab programs. I went through the program, got a job, fell off the wagon, started going to AA. It's been . . . I'm not perfect. But I've kept my job for six months and I enjoy the work. I've been clean for four months. I can't make up for anything I've done, but I wanted . . ."

"To what? Have a magical family reunion? You know what words I haven't heard you say? *I'm sorry.*"

"Well, I am, but—"

She jumped out of the seat, furious and hurt somehow because even that wasn't an apology. "You're a coward and a worthless bastard."

"I know."

"And you blamed a little girl for your own failures."

"I never blamed you, Louisa. I—"

"You told me it was my fault. When the police were taking you away, you kept yelling it at me. *This is all your fault. Couldn't you keep your mouth shut?*"

He sat there, slack-jawed and wide-eyed. "I . . . I don't remember that."

"It happened."

"I believe you. I do. I'm sure it happened. I was . . . pretty high. I'm sure I did a lot of shitty things I don't remember."

None of this was going right, and she was digging into *her* things when this was supposed to be about Em. This was a mistake. A disaster. She had to leave.

But he stood, and she was frozen in place, looking him right in the eye, because they were the same height. Same eyes. So many similarities, she wanted to cry or run away, but all she managed to do was stare at this man who was the reason she even existed. The reason for so many things, because she'd *let* him be. Despite his complete and utter absence for years, she'd let him determine how she felt about herself and other people, and much like seeing Rex in the bakery the other day, she right here did not know *why* she ever let this man determine how she felt about anything.

"Louisa, I . . . I can't be your dad. I can't make up for all I've done wrong. I don't think you'd want me to try."

"No, I don't."

"But Mom wants me to. I want to make some things up to her. So, I'll be here. For her, if not for you girls. I don't expect anything from you, but if you ever need anything from me, I'm going to try to give it."

It solved nothing. She didn't feel soothed or healed, not that she'd expected to, but so much worse than not feeling those things was not being able to hold on to her anger or her fury.

Because he was just a sad man who'd wasted years, and even though she'd wasted a few of her own, she'd always had Grandma and Grandpa and Em. She had the Tylers. She'd been given hope and love and support and been able to come to this point in her life.

And she was meeting her father in a fast-food restaurant, surrounded by the realization of all the time he'd wasted and the bad choices he'd made, doubled down on, allowed to ruin so many years. His years.

"That'd be a good thing to tell Em," she managed to say. "I hope you'll do everything Grandma asks of you."

"What about what you hope I'll do for you?"

It was strange to realize, but a kind of weight lifted. "I don't wish you harm. I hope you stay clean. I don't need anything from you. I don't want anything from you. I don't hate you." But that was kind of . . . it. There would be no great, lasting bond here, and Lou found she was okay with it. And okay if Em chose a different course.

Somehow, this anticlimactic thing was life as much as the rest, and in this small moment in a fast-food restaurant, she found some peace with that part of her childhood, and she laid it to rest.

"If Grandma ever wants you to come out to the ranch, I hope you'll do what she wants."

Her father looked extremely uncomfortable at that, but he nodded rather than argued.

"Well, goodbye."

"Goodbye, Louisa."

Lou left and drove back home, numb sort of, but not that awful numb after something terrible happened. Just sort of dazed. It was a lot to process, and as she sifted through it, she didn't know how to accept the emotions assaulting her.

Then, as she drove up to the house, she saw Gavin on the porch with Grandma, laughing about something. The sun was shining and her bright red barn was a beacon in the midst of her growing flowers and greening pasture in the background.

Her home. Her life. Even her man. All hers for the having and tending. Grandma stayed on the porch and Gavin walked over to greet her.

Feeling robotic, she turned the ignition off and slowly got out of her truck. Gavin stood right there, as if he'd been waiting for her, his cowboy hat low on his head.

"Go okay?"

She nodded, but when he pulled her into a hug, everything fell apart. The numbness dissolved and she cried. Hard and loud and unabashed, right into his shoulder. She let it all out. The uncertainty, the confusion, the uselessness of not having anything to fight, and the relief at having this weight lifted from her shoulders that she hadn't been fully cognizant of carrying.

Gavin held her through it all, rubbing a hand up and down her back, murmuring soothing words. He would have done it whether they were getting married or not. He would have done it in the middle of a fight or if he was mad or upset about his own stuff. He would have done this no matter what.

That was love. The true kind. The kind you trusted. The kind you reciprocated.

Chapter Twenty-One

"So, I have a surprise for you," Gavin managed to say once Lou's crying had lessened in strength and volume.

It physically *hurt* to see her so upset, especially when he couldn't do a damn thing about it. Even offering to punch the guy wouldn't help, and Gavin didn't have much else in his arsenal.

So, he had a distraction up his sleeve because it was the best he could muster.

Lou took a deep breath and slowly untangled herself from him. He couldn't read the expression on her face. It was serious and searching and something else that had him tugging her toward the surprise because it would get him out of trying to label *that.*

He led her behind the barn, where he'd set up a little makeshift fence to keep his surprise wrangled and out of trouble for the time being.

Lou glanced down at the puppy who was currently running mad, stumbling circles around the enclosure. The dog caught sight of both of them and started yipping excitedly.

Lou didn't move. She stood there, tearstained and rather stun-expressioned.

"Now, if you don't want her, I've got plenty of takers lined up. It turns out Ben's dog is quite the little fiend and did a number on Cal Barton's sister's dog. The puppies are cute and all that, and Sarah's giving them away for free, so this little girl is the last one. But if you don't want—"

"Don't want? Look at her." Lou kneeled at the little fence and picked up the wriggling mass of puppy joy. "Isn't she the sweetest?" Lou cuddled the puppy and murmured sweet, soothing words.

Gavin had been jealous of dogs a few times in his life, but he supposed this was the most jealous he'd been. Even with their weird situation, he rarely got sweet, soothing words from Lou.

But he was more than relieved she looked happy after crying like that. The puppy licked her face and she laughed as she stood, still cradling the dog. "What kind is she?"

"Mutt, through and through."

"Well, isn't that just about perfect," Lou said, rubbing her cheek against the dog's head. "Does she have a name?"

"That's all you."

She looked at him, studying, considering. It made him itchy, and a little close to bolting. He didn't trust that look, not that he could work out why.

"Shouldn't we choose it together?"

The discomfort dug deeper. "She's your dog."

"She's *our* dog."

"No. I got her for you."

"But, we're a we right now."

A we. But not a real we. He could have argued that, maybe should have, but Gavin didn't trust this new way she had of looking at him lately. "Whatever name you want," he said, forcing a careless smile.

"Blossom?"

"Sure. Flowers. Blossom. It works."

"And you aren't embarrassed to have a ranch dog named Blossom?"

"She's a flower farm dog."

Lou's eyebrows drew together, and she put the puppy back down in its makeshift pen. She stepped close to him, studying him with eyes he was afraid saw far too much. "Why are you being weird about this?"

"I'm not being weird."

He expected her to argue, but she just stared at him for a few seconds, that same consideration mixed in with a softness he never associated with Lou. A softness that scared him down to his bones, because she was trusting him with it, when she never trusted anyone with it. He might know it existed—her sweetness, her care with people, and the genuine goodness about her—but she kept it hidden under a lot of things.

He didn't know what to do with it standing here naked all over her face, like she'd dropped all masks and pretense when it came to him.

She looked back at the dog. "Brenna," she said firmly. "We'll call her Brenna."

"Where'd you get that?"

"A book."

"A book about what?"

Something in her smile went mischievous, which gave him absolutely no comfort whatsoever.

"Your mother lent it to me when I was in the hospital. Well, she lent me lots of books. Romances. All hope and love. She said I needed that, and she was right. I gave them back to her when I got home, except one. It sits on my bedside table. I wasn't sure why I liked it so much, but now I know."

"What's it got to do with the dog?"

She laughed. "Nothing."

"Now who's being weird?"

"Thank you. For Brenna. For you." She stepped into him and brushed her mouth against his. She curled her fingers in his shirt, keeping him there, her eyes blue and serious, even with her mouth smiling.

"When'd you get so . . ."

"So what?" she asked, still not letting go of his shirt, so he had to be close and smell her shampoo. A scent he knew intimately now that they shared a bathroom more nights than not.

"Happy," he realized. For the first time since losing her grandfather and dealing with the fire, Lou seemed well and truly happy. A realization that made his chest tight, with emotion and then with something a little closer to panic.

She held his gaze, and it was as if she was searching for some kind of confirmation of something there in his eyes.

"I guess I found my hope again."

It felt as though his heart shuddered to a stop, a car losing its engine.

He was letting himself get in too deep. Worse, he had the sinking suspicion she was convincing herself she was in deep too. He had to do something. He had to fix this. They should stop having sex. That was all there was to it.

Tonight, he'd be strong. He'd draw the line.

She kissed him again, and this time it was no simple brush of lips. Her free hand cupped his cheek, her mouth pressed to his, searching and sweet.

Draw the line. He was supposed to . . .

Okay, maybe tomorrow he'd draw the line, he decided, sinking into her and the kiss. Wrapping his arms around her and bringing her close. No matter how much he got of her, he wanted more, and more, and more.

What was the harm in waiting until tomorrow to draw the line? Or even Monday. A new week, and they'd start on the right foot. She'd had a rough day, so they could enjoy a weekend together. He could have a little more for a little while.

"Gav," she murmured, but he wasn't ready to let go. He kissed her again, deeper, a little more desperate than she was, but she moaned appreciatively. Yeah, he could stand a little more of this.

Next week, though, it was going to be clear. Friends only. Doing a favor for each other. All funny business had to be set aside. Or at least in a few weeks when they got married. They could fool around a bit now. What was the harm? They both enjoyed it.

But once the rings were on, they had to be serious about why they were doing this. No more fantasies about it being real for either of them.

The thought of rings had him pulling back, stepping away. Rings. Marriage. "I should get to my chores," he said, because any more of this and he would forget he existed for her for one thing and one thing alone: to keep the Fairchild Ranch running, and hopefully profitable again.

He wasn't here to kiss Lou, or make love to her, or bring her puppies or be her shoulder to cry on. He was more than happy to do those things, though, and that was the problem.

He was prone to make mistakes, to let himself believe in the unbelievable. He might be able to stand that, if he didn't believe she was convincing herself this might work out.

Because it was easy. Because it was convenient. But she'd only regret that. Him. He didn't ever want to be her regret, or the thing holding her back, or the reason she wasn't happy.

So, he turned and left. Went to his chores and ignored Lou and Brenna, convinced himself he wouldn't share her bed that night.

But that was exactly where he ended up that night, and the next.

The weeks flew by between ranch work and flower work and plans for her own wedding and trying to train Brenna the overzealous, adorable puppy.

Her wedding. To Gavin. Tomorrow she was going to marry Gavin. Every time she thought of it, a giddy little laugh bubbled up. Half the time it escaped too.

The grandmas had altered Grandma's dress and made it fit perfectly, and Em had found her the perfect plaid shirt to wear over her arms. Grandma had made her a veil that was thick enough on one side to cover her scars. Lou had made a bouquet for herself, and a bout for Gavin. Em was doing all the cake finishing touches in the morning, but it was mostly ready. Cora was in charge of getting the officiant to the right place at the right time, along with the chairs.

They weren't going to do a rehearsal dinner because the wedding was so small and casual, but Lou had gotten it in her head she and Gavin should do something special tonight.

Not just special, but alone. A moment before the wedding to sit down and talk and . . .

She was going to tell him she loved him. She was going to tell him she wanted this marriage of theirs to be real. Gavin had been weird these past few weeks, but he'd been *here*. He kissed her like she was precious and he made love to her like she was the center of his universe.

She just had to believe he felt the same about her as she did about him. His weirdness had to be nerves, or maybe worries she didn't feel the same way. He'd been the one to bring up lines all those weeks ago so they didn't get hurt. Which meant there were feelings to hurt.

She inhaled shakily, surveying the table she'd set. She lit candles, rearranged the plates and glasses. Then she went ahead and poured herself some wine because this was nerve-racking as hell.

"He loves me," she whispered to herself. "I love him. He loves me. No nerves needed." She believed that. Her *heart* believed that, but it seemed some other parts of her body weren't quite on board yet.

They'd get there. They would.

The backdoor swung open, and Gavin stepped in. It had become habit. Routine. And every day Lou couldn't believe this was real, but it *was.* And hadn't she suffered enough to deserve it? To deserve him?

A good man to love her, support her, and she would do the same for him. Tomorrow, their vows would be real. *Real.* She was sure of it.

He stopped there in the doorway, eyebrows halfway up his forehead. Slowly, he hung his hat on the peg and wiped his boots on the rug. "Er, what's all this?"

"Dinner."

"You're in a dress."

She moved her hips so the skirt fluttered around her legs. "Do you like it?"

"I, uh . . . You look . . . Yes, I like it, but . . ."

"I made dinner too. I thought we could have a nice, quiet dinner together. Grandma is over with Maisey, arguing over the food they're making for the reception, so we have the house to ourselves." She couldn't believe how nervous she sounded, and how stupid to be nervous it was, and how no amount of telling her to stop seemed to work.

"I was . . . I was going to go have a drink with Shane and Boone."

That threw her off a moment, but it made sense. A drink with his brothers before he got married tomorrow. But that didn't mean they couldn't talk first. "A drink. Not dinner. You can have dinner with me, can't you?"

"Right. Sure. Okay."

"You're not having second thoughts, are you?" She said it in a teasing manner, but there was a part of her a little terrified that was what was really bothering him.

"Of course not." He smiled at her. "But did *you* make dinner or did your grandmother make dinner? Because that's an important distinction."

"I can cook."

He grinned. She scowled.

"Oh, fine, Grandma put it together, but I made the salad."

He finally moved into the kitchen, though he looked uncertainly at the candles and her glass of wine. She couldn't let that bug her. One step at a time. Once they got this all out, they'd both feel a lot less weird.

She filled their plates and tried idly chatting about flowers and the market, but he didn't keep the conversation going. Every time she stopped, he stopped. When she sat down across from him, he was looking down at his plate of food as if it was something . . . dangerous.

"Did you want wine?"

"No. No, water is fine."

Then they ate in silence. Lou couldn't even come up with something to talk about, because with every moment of ticking silence her throat got tighter, and her heart beat its panicked beat harder, and she started overthinking every bite she chewed and every breath she took.

Don't tell him.

You have to tell him.

This is pointless. You're getting married anyway. Let it happen naturally.

You should both go in with eyes wide open.

You love him. You love him. You love him.

It wasn't strange to accept that simple fact after twenty years of not, because there *had* always been love there. It had ebbed and flowed, changed and altered, but it had always been there. In the past year of Gavin being there every step of the way, in the past few months of learning to forgive herself, to believe she might be worth more than an asshole like Rex or the self-punishment she'd given herself for years, she'd allowed herself to fully explore that love.

She wanted all of it. More of it. Honestly and openly, before they uttered a single *I do.*

Before he'd even finished everything on his plate, Gavin scooted his chair back. "You know, I should go have that drink. Last night as a single man and all. Least for a bit." He got to his feet, and she did too.

"Gavin."

He looked at her a bit like she was a snake that would inevitably bite him and inject him with venom.

Rethink. Abort. He doesn't want this. But she knew Gavin. She knew him better than anyone. He was definitely acting weird and she hadn't figured all that out yet, but she was certain he loved her. She didn't have to know why or how to know he did.

She took a deep breath and then forced herself to rip off the Band-Aid. "Gav, I love you."

He didn't stiffen exactly, but there was next-to-no reaction. "I . . . Well, as a friend—"

"No. Not as a friend. I love you. I'm *in* love with you. When we say our vows tomorrow, I want us to mean them." She tried to smile, but his reaction was so . . . so . . .

Blank. She could have dealt with horror, maybe. But blank just left her feeling like she was falling off some kind of cliff, no clue if she'd be able to grab something and save herself or if she was going to crash on the rocks below.

"Lou, I don't know what you think . . . I don't . . . We aren't . . ." He raked both hands through his hair.

Her heart beat too hard against her chest. Maybe this wasn't going the way she'd planned, but she knew . . . she knew. "You love me. I know you're in love with me."

He stood there, staring at her like she'd somehow stabbed him instead of told him she loved him. "Yeah. Yeah." His whole demeanor changed, then. Not nervous or squirrelly or even panicked. His expression went dark, hard. Her heart stopped its frantic beating and just froze, sharp and painful.

He'd never looked at her like this before. Not ever.

"I've been in love with you most of my whole damn life," he said, as if it was some kind of admission of guilt. Something to be ashamed of.

But that was silly. So silly. "Then—"

"Which is how I know you're wrong. You don't love me. You aren't *in love* with me. This is convenient, and there's a physical . . . thing there. But you don't love me."

She blinked at him, shocked beyond measure. "You're telling me how I feel. You're standing there telling me I don't understand my own feelings. You."

"Yes. Twenty years of watching, I think I know a thing or two."

"Thirty years of *feeling*, I think I know a thing or two."

"I don't want to fight about this with you. Not tonight. We'll follow the plan. Get married tomorrow. Get divorced once the papers are all figured out. Let's not complicate it."

"I'm standing here telling you I *love* you, that I want to marry you for *real* tomorrow, and you're afraid of complicating things."

"Be reasonable."

Reasonable. He was telling her how she felt—that her feelings were *wrong*, and *she* was supposed to be reasonable. She wanted to run away or cry, but she wouldn't let him see her do that. No. She'd rather be mean. "How about you don't be such a coward. Oh, but that's the Gavin Tyler way, isn't it?"

He laughed, caustic and bitter. Candlelight and nice dinner completely and utterly ruined. Lou wished she could take off this stupid dress and burn it. Right here, right now.

"Okay, you love me. Didn't for twenty years, but you suddenly do now. So prove it."

"Prove it?"

"Take off your bandanna."

Her hand flew to her bandanna in a kind of self-defense movement. She wouldn't take it off. What did that prove? What was he even talking about? "What does my bandanna have to do with anything?"

"We've been sleeping together for weeks and you sleep in that. You won't take off your shirt. You say it's about you, but that's shit. Love would make that different. You'd let me see it."

She could barely breathe and could only manage to shake her head. No, he was wrong. About it all. About everything.

Chapter Twenty-Two

Gavin stood, every muscle tensed, including his hands into fists. She shook her head, back and forth, and twin feelings of relief and pain shot through him as she refused his request. Well, demand.

He'd known she wouldn't take it off. It hadn't even been a gamble to ask. She didn't love him and she wouldn't let him in. He knew that. He'd always known that. It was why he'd asked her to take it off, because he knew it would prove his point.

It was disgusting to realize there'd been some tiny inkling of hope he'd be proven wrong. How had he let things go so wrong?

"I'm going."

She stepped between him and the door, angry and defiant. Which was good. He could fight that so much better than the way she'd been when he'd first come in. All sweet and hopeful. Dresses and candles. For him.

She'd lost her damn mind.

"We're not done here."

"I'm done here."

"Because it's easier to run away. Easier to decide it's not worth it, or that you'll fail, than it would be to try and fall and have to dust yourself off."

"How loving of you to point out all my failures and weaknesses to me," he returned, hoping his voice was devoid of all the emotions roiling around inside him. "Now, if you'll excuse me . . ."

"Was that not quite it? Not so much cowardice as comparison holding you back? Maybe it's Shane's fault. He's such a good husband to Cora. You know you can't measure up. So why try?"

Gavin clamped his jaw tight. He wasn't going to argue with her. He'd made up his mind, and any nasty thing she came up with was only further proof he was right. So, let her poke at him.

"Or is it Rex's fault? He got here first and now I'm tainted."

"Don't call yourself that," he snapped, kicking himself as the words tumbled out despite his attempt to keep his mouth shut.

"Or maybe it's my fault? You've been in love with me for *how long* and never done a damn thing about it. Maybe I was too mean to you. Too hard on you. Maybe all that love isn't so much love as it is an easy place to lay your blame, because you do love to blame everything except yourself, Gavin."

"That I do. I should probably go, then."

"You could fight for once. For once you could be brave enough to fight for the thing you wanted. For once, you could stop worrying about whether you're as good a rancher or brother as Shane. You could *trust* my feelings, because I'm telling them to you and you trust me, love me. I know you have all that fight and bravery and trust in you, Gavin. I know you do."

He couldn't pull in a breath. There was some heavy, sharp thing cutting the oxygen off. He couldn't breathe and he couldn't move and he couldn't find it in him to make her stop.

She reached out, her fingers curling around his arms. "You don't think *I* know you. You don't think *I've* paid attention the past few years. Gavin. You said it yourself. We lean on each other more than anyone else. We let each other in because we aren't worried about protecting each other or saving face. How can you not believe that means something?"

"Because feelings don't change, Lou. You never felt that way until it was convenient. If you can't even show me your scars, which I've *told* you don't bother me, what is this supposed to look like? Feelings don't change. The end."

"That's a fucking lie and you know it. I'm not the same girl I was when I was nine, or nineteen, or hell, twenty-nine. Everything I am, right here and right now, has been a hard-ass fight, and I refuse to believe I'm the same as that neglected, hurt, scared, depressed little girl who came to my grandparents' house quite certain they were going to grow to hate me."

She just had to cut him in all his softest places. He'd known that girl, and yes, he'd seen her grow and change, but that didn't mean—

"Do you want to know what happened at my mom's house?"

She almost never, ever mentioned her mother. When he'd asked about this a few weeks ago, she'd refused to talk about it. He knew, he absolutely knew he should leave. Push her out of the way if need be. He couldn't listen to this because she was pulling out every last stop and he only had so much strength in him.

He stood rooted to the spot.

"Mom had a boyfriend. He didn't like me much, but boy did he like Em."

Gavin's skin went cold.

"I knew it wasn't right. It made me feel all wrong,

and after everything with Dad, I knew it was my job to protect Em. I hadn't before, but now I had to."

"Lou."

"So, I wouldn't let him near her. No matter what they did. No matter what. If he was there, I wouldn't leave Em's side. I'd take her to the bathroom. I'd sleep in her bed. I knew something wasn't right, and he hated me for that."

Gavin opened his mouth to tell her this didn't have to do with anything and he didn't want to hear it, but no matter that it shredded him to ribbons, she'd convinced herself she was in love with him, that didn't change how much he wanted to know her, heart and soul.

"First time he hit me over it, Mom told me to stop being so annoying." She dropped her hands from his arms then, and he wanted to reach out, pull her into him. Whisper soothing words like she was forever whispering to Brenna.

But she turned away, hugging herself. Because she was strong enough to hold herself up. She didn't need him, and he wouldn't allow himself to get fooled into thinking she did. She was stronger than him, just like everyone.

"I told a teacher what had happened, and thank God for that woman, because she took it very, very seriously. I should find her and thank her. Do you know what that stranger did that my own parents wouldn't do?" She turned to face him, and though her blue eyes were shiny she wasn't breaking down like she had after she'd met with her father. No, this was warrior Lou, and she absolutely floored him, over and over again. "That teacher who barely knew me pushed every agency she could find, and when they said there wasn't enough evidence to step in, she called as many family members as she could until she found one who cared."

"Your grandparents."

"They sued my mother for custody. Mom didn't have the money to fight it, or the desire, and we got moved here. Em was upset with me. She didn't understand . . . I thought it was all my fault. If I could have taken care of Em when we were with Dad, we never would have had to go through that. I blamed myself, not the monster who wanted to molest a little girl. Not the worthless father who expected a *child* to be able to care for another child all on her own. For years I blamed myself."

"I don't . . . Lou."

"Still want to lecture me on how feelings don't change?"

"It isn't . . . You can't compare us or this to that."

"Can't I?"

"You were a kid. You went through . . . You've had it rough, Lou. You're strong and you're brave and you've come out of all that and I . . ."

"You what?"

I love you. More than I've ever loved anything. I would give up just about anything for you. But I will fail this in all the same ways I always do. Except he couldn't say any of that. It just jumbled around in his head sounding like a kind of desperate gibberish he didn't have the first clue how to articulate. "You don't love me."

She rolled her eyes and shook her head. "Keep telling me how I feel, Gavin. Keep telling me how I'm wrong and only you know the true right way, as if that changes anything. *Anything.* Why would I listen to you when I know what I feel?"

"I promise you, Lou. I am doing this for our own good. For the sake of our friendship. For the sake of—"

"Bullshit. You're doing it for the sake of your own damn fear of failure, so you make sure you do. You don't think I know the different ways you've done it?"

"It's weird, this doesn't sound all that much like love. It sounds a lot like insults."

"I love you more than any damn thing. You, who have always been there for me. Who have sacrificed and been there no matter what, for me, when I didn't feel worthy or lovable. When I wasn't nice. You were *there.* Yes, I see your flaws, Gavin. Because I know you. But I also know every last inch of goodness in you. Feelings don't change?"

She flung her hands in the air. "Bullshit! I watched how hard your dad dying hit you, and I was just a little girl and you were just a little boy. I watched how you fell into the much easier role of second to Shane because you were afraid of disappointing his memory. You were afraid of hurting your mom. But you didn't dwell in those ways you felt less. You kept doing the important things and you found ways to be there anyway. You *have* let it hold you back from things you deserve. Don't do that anymore. Please. For me. Believe in us. Believe *me.*"

Believe. Believe that something might work out. That he might be worth something.

"I'll only disappoint you," he managed to say despite the tightness in his throat. "And I can't bear the thought."

She touched him again, grabbing him hard and fierce, and he tried to pull away, but she wouldn't let him.

"I love you. I think we'll probably disappoint each other now and again. But we'll love each other despite it."

"Take off your bandanna."

She released him again, stepping back, just like he'd known she would.

"It's one little thing, Lou. One little thing and you can't give it to me. Is that a love we should really risk our friendship on?"

"It's *my* thing," she whispered. "It isn't about love."

"It is to me." He stepped around her, pulling the door open. "Bye, Lou."

"Are we still getting married tomorrow?"

He didn't know how to answer that, so he just left. Walked out the door, ignored Brenna's barking from her runner, where Mrs. Fairchild insisted she be when they were eating. He went straight to his truck and drove back to the Tyler Ranch.

The sun was setting by the time he got home. He parked his truck in his usual spot on the concrete pad in front of the garages. By the time he found the wherewithal to get out of the truck and head toward the house, Mom was outside sitting on the porch with King and the new puppy.

"Got a name yet?" Gavin asked, hoping his voice didn't sound as wrecked as he felt as he stepped onto the porch.

Mom smiled, patting both dogs on the head. "Micah insists on LeBron. Cora insists on MacKade. Shane insists on not being the tiebreaker."

"Sounds about right."

Mom stood. "Let's go for a ride."

Uh-oh. Mom only ever went on rides when she was after a heart-to-heart, and boy did Gavin not have that in him tonight. "Near dark."

"We'll risk it."

Gavin edged toward the door. "I'm not in the mood."

Mom linked her arm with his and spun him around back toward the stairs. “Exactly.”

“Mom.”

“Now, are you really going to waste your breath arguing with me when you know I’ll keep poking and poking and pok—”

“Okay, okay. You win.”

Mom smiled broadly as they walked into the stables. They worked in a companionable silence to saddle the horses. Since Gavin had Genevieve over at the Fairchild spread now, he saddled Stan.

They walked the horses outside and mounted, Mom immediately urging her horse forward so Gavin had to follow wherever she was going.

They rode a while, in the spring evening that was starting to edge toward summer. Peepers and a lack of icy cold even as the sun went down. She meandered around pastures until they reached a swell of land on the north end of the property between pastures.

“You know, it was just last summer I took Shane on a ride out here,” Mom said as Gavin’s horse pulled up next to hers. “Took him to the cemetery. Talked some sense into that boy.”

“Is that where we’re headed, because you took a wrong turn.”

“Not the cemetery, but the sense part. Yes.” She clicked at her horse and guided Templeton to turn around. Gavin did the same. They stood on a crest of a hill, looking down over the fence that separated the Tyler Ranch from the Fairchild one. He could see the Tyler house fully, and hints of the Fairchild house through the little grove of trees.

“Haven’t been yourself these past few weeks,” Mom said conversationally.

Gavin wasn't stupid enough to think this was a conversation. "I haven't been around."

"But a mother notices these things. Not worried about handling things on your own, are you?"

"No." The funny thing was, as much as those doubts had plagued him on the days leading up to his taking over the Fairchild Ranch, once he'd started the work, there'd been so much of it, there'd been little time to worry or second-guess himself.

"So, it's Lou, then."

"What's Lou, then?"

"The reason for your brood. The thing you've got yourself all twisted up about. Have a fight?"

"Lou . . ." He didn't know how to explain the whole thing to his mother. "I think she'd be happier . . . I think . . . I just . . ."

"Cold feet?"

"I guess." It was the only reason he could give, because even though he was mad and hurt and scared, he'd marry her tomorrow. For her ranch, for her farm. He'd made a promise.

You also promised to stay friends.

Well, he'd stay friends with her, but maybe give her some space until she realized she didn't love him. He'd sleep in the barn. He'd do whatever. He honored his promises, no matter how much he hated himself for it right now. So, he'd find a way.

Tonight, he'd prefer to, as his mother had said, brood.

"Can't imagine you not wanting to marry her after all this time."

Because of course he was that transparent. Always had been. The only surprising thing about his mother knowing he'd been in love with her forever was the fact Mom hadn't meddled any over it.

But maybe that told him what he needed to know. Even his mother hadn't tried to push them together. They didn't suit. "She needs someone . . . stronger. Someone better."

"Better than my son?" Deb demanded.

She didn't say it as a joke either. She said it like she was offended. Which only made Gavin determined to be honest.

He'd been honest with Lou. She didn't love him. He wasn't made for her the way he needed to be. So, he might as well admit all his failures to his mother. What was the point in hiding them anymore? Everyone saw through him anyway.

"I'm a coward, Mom. I always have been. I always will be. I don't want to fail. You or Dad's memory or anyone. So, I . . . hide. I run away. Whatever it is. It's the way I am. So, yes, someone better than me and that." Because Lou *did* know him. Much as he didn't want to admit it.

Maybe you should trust her feelings, then.

"You know your father only married me because he knocked me up."

Gavin nearly fell off his horse. Not because Mom had been pregnant when she'd married Dad. They all liked to joke Shane had been at their parents' wedding. What shocked him was Mom saying Dad wouldn't have married her.

"I know I was a kid, but you two loved each other."

"Oh, we did. Ridiculously and endlessly. He had this idea in his head he was being noble. He was my first, and he was worried I should experience more before settling down."

"This feels really personal and like information you don't need to share with your son."

"Oh, don't be such a baby. He didn't want me to feel like I'd missed out on something. He wanted what was best for me, and in a way, watching you grow up and learning the man you are, I think I can look back and realize clearly he was afraid. Afraid he and this ranch wouldn't be enough."

Mom took a deep breath, squinting as she looked out over the Tyler house at dusk. "The thing was, I didn't want to experience the world. I knew what I wanted without a shadow of a doubt. Him and this place. Do you know how infuriating it was that he didn't believe me?"

He thought of the fury in Lou's blue eyes. "I might have an idea."

"I know you're afraid of failing, Gav. The one thing that was nice about having kids is, it was nothing but failure after failure, and your dad and I had to get over that right quick. But I understand wanting to protect yourself from that feeling. I do."

"But?"

"But it's a choice you make. You call yourself a coward like it's just what you are. Like you can't change it. But it's all on you. Whether you decide to run away from a life you've always wanted, or you decide to work your ass off for it. You have your father in you. You have me in you. Shane and Boone, Molly and Lindsay. Even that crazy grandmother of yours. We're all cut from the same cloth, and that cloth has a lot of damn goodness in it."

Gavin looked down at the reins in his hands. "I want her to have everything, and I know I can't give her that."

Mom reached over and squeezed his arms. "No one

could. No one wants you to. She'll want to give herself some things on her own, after all."

"Mom."

"Gavin. If you love that girl as much as we suspect you have, and if she loves you even half as much as she told you she did, you've got a leg up on a lot of people. And my God, the stubbornness between you two? I think you'll make a good thing work."

"Even if we only started the whole thing so Lou could keep her place?"

Mom laughed. "That isn't why."

"Um, yes it is. We—"

"No, you started the whole thing because you love her. And she accepted the whole thing because she loves you. The two of you don't accept help from anyone else. You can tell each other all the stories you want about how this started, but at the end of the day, you helped and she let you because of love."

"I don't know if I believe that."

Mom squeezed again. "Try."

Chapter Twenty-Three

It was a very strange thing to put on a wedding dress when you weren't sure there was any reason to do it. Maybe it would have been weird even if she'd been sure, but at least there would have been some excitement.

Right now, all she felt was dread. Em and Grandma chattered around her, zipping this, rolling lint off that. Lou could only stand there feeling like cotton shoved into a body.

"I really didn't expect you to be *this* nervous," Em said, grinning and giving her a little nudge.

Lou ran her hands over the front of her dress. It was really beautiful. The grandmas' work had created something that fit her like a dream, and Lou appreciated that Grandma had worn it to marry Grandpa.

Well, she wanted to appreciate it. Right now, she felt mostly sick. She'd never dreamed she'd have a marriage like Grandma and Grandpa's. Until the past few weeks, when she'd allowed herself to dream. To hope.

She should have known better.

She squeezed her eyes shut as Em fiddled with her hair and adding the veil that Grandma had specially made thicker on the right side to cover her scars.

"What's eating you, girl?" Grandma asked, setting out Lou's shoes so she could step into them.

Lou looked at her grandmother and tried to lie. *Nothing. It's great. Just nerves.* But what if Gavin didn't show? Maybe they needed some forewarning. "He might not . . ." She cleared her throat. She didn't want to say it out loud, but it would be good if they knew . . . "What if he doesn't . . ."

"You aren't seriously worried *Gavin* isn't going to show up to your wedding? Gavin of all people." Em laughed as if it was insane.

Lou wished she could find it quite so funny. "We had a fight," she said quietly.

"Oh, well, not the best timing, I suppose, but there will be more fights and more bad timing. That boy wouldn't miss this," Grandma assured her.

"I love him," Lou whispered.

"Well, isn't that the point?" Em asked.

Lou supposed she was being a little nonsensical, considering they didn't know anything. Considering this was all backward and jumbled up.

"It wasn't at first, though, was it?" Grandma asked softly.

Lou looked at her grandmother wide-eyed. "You knew?"

"Not until these past few days. You seemed so much more . . . Well, easy with each other than you were in the beginning. Hopeful. Well, you anyway. Got me thinking maybe things hadn't exactly been on the up-and-up." Grandma reached out and touched her cheek under the veil. "It's been good to see you happy."

"I'm sure he'll be there, Lou," Em said, though she clearly looked worried now. "Gavin wouldn't . . . He wouldn't just not show up."

Except Molly was supposed to text her when he got there, and she hadn't yet. He was supposed to have been down at the wedding site *thirty* minutes ago.

"I agree with Em," Grandma said firmly. "Fight or not. Love or not. That boy wouldn't hurt you that way. I just can't imagine it."

Lou looked at her grandmother, still fiddling with her dress and her hair and expressly not looking at Lou. "You could have told me you'd figured it out."

"For what? You were getting married, falling in love. Why would I interrupt that with a silly thing like telling you I'd figured it out? Knowing you two, that would have ruined everything. Stubborn cusses, the both of you."

"What if *I'd* been the one marrying Gavin, because Lou and I talked about that?" Em asked, looking something like angry.

Grandma's eyebrows raised. "Whatever for?"

Grandma's feigned ignorance hurt. "So I could keep this place," Lou said gravely.

"You were never in danger of losing this place. What are you even on about?" But Grandma turned away, not meeting either of their gazes.

"Why'd you do it?" Lou asked softly. "I blamed grief. Em blamed senility."

Grandma shot a look at Em, who straightened defiantly.

"What were we supposed to think? You raised us to be strong and independent and go after our dreams, then suddenly we couldn't handle a ranch without a man around? It didn't make sense unless you'd lost it a little."

Grandma snorted. "You were both lonely. Don't argue. I know you are and you were," Grandma said, pointing to Em and then Lou. "You have friends, so it couldn't have been a lack of that. It had to be something more. Deeper. And . . . I needed a reason to contact your father. To try to mend that bridge."

"Couldn't you have just said that? Told us you wanted a relationship with your son? Told us you were worried about us? Couldn't you have just *told* us instead of putting us through this?" Lou asked, so hurt it was hard to be angry.

"I suppose I could have. You could have told me you were going to marry Gavin for all the wrong reasons."

"I was afraid I'd lose this place if I didn't lie. You basically said I would!"

"You could have told me that too, that you were afraid, what it would have meant to lose it, instead of arguing with me that I was just wrong. You could have told me how you *felt*."

Lou blinked at her grandmother. Was it possible they'd never really . . . communicated? Lou expected her grandmother to know everything she was thinking or feeling because she'd always seemed something like magic in that department. But maybe . . .

"Come, sit," Grandma said, sounding exhausted. They all sank onto the couch cushions, Grandma sandwiched between Em and Lou. "I suppose I mishandled it."

"Suppose," Em muttered.

"Yes, suppose, Emily." Grandma heaved out a sigh. "And I think you were right a little, Lou. I acted out of grief. You know how we used to have to . . . Well, your grandfather was so stubborn, and he never wanted to talk about feelings." Grandma took Lou's hand, then Em's. "In retrospect, I may have tried maneuvering you girls like I used to maneuver your grandfather."

It made a warped kind of sense, and in the grand scheme of things *none* of them were too keen on talking about their feelings. Never had been. *Feelings* were meant to be kept under wraps—good or bad.

"I miss that man," Grandma whispered, and it was the most honest she'd been about any feeling since they'd lost Grandpa. Usually, she didn't speak of him, or she did in some matter-of-fact voice. There were no memories or laughing over something he used to do. It was all grim marching on from that loss.

"I miss him too," Em said, staring at her lap, her voice scratchy.

Lou could only nod because her throat was too tight to speak.

"He'd *hate* us sitting around crying over him," Grandma croaked, dropping Lou's hand and using her fingers to brush tears from her cheeks.

Lou couldn't remember ever seeing her grandmother cry, even at the funeral. "He would, but you know, we get to anyway."

Grandma blinked at her, and for the first time in Lou's life, she realized her grandmother wasn't some perfect paragon of every good, smart, right thing. It wasn't just grief that had caused her to make a bad decision in giving her and Em an ultimatum over the ranch, it was the fact she was human, and humans made mistakes.

She was always so aware of her own, she tended to miss other people's, including Gavin's.

He'd been afraid last night. She knew that, understood that. It wasn't about loving or not loving, it had been about fear. So he'd used her fear against her, and she'd fallen into the trap.

Her text message sound went off, and Lou grabbed

her phone off the table and read the text message from Molly.

He's here! See you soon :)

She'd mishandled things last night, but she wouldn't mishandle things at her wedding.

"Where the hell were you? I was starting to worry," Molly said, scowling at him.

"We're all off schedule now," Cora added, clearly irritated with him.

"Sorry," Boone offered, clapping Gavin on the back. "Just had a celebratory last moment-of-freedom drink and lost track of time."

It was a lie.

Gavin had been in the stables when Boone had found him. Apparently, Boone, Ben, and Shane had been searching for him for half an hour before Boone had thought to look with the horses.

Gavin had been dressed and ready to go and just . . . frozen. Dread had kept him rooted to the spot. When Boone had told him they had to go, Gavin had only been able to shake his head.

"You're going to stand Lou up? Embarrass her in front of everyone she loves?"

That had gotten him moving, but he didn't feel any more . . . present or in charge. He felt weighed down by a million contradictory thoughts, and the only reason he was here, in the little field of wildflowers that now included rows of chairs, a white runner between them that led to some wooden altar thing decorated with flowers, was because he'd made a promise.

No matter how afraid he was, no matter how sure of

failure he was, he'd made a promise. He wouldn't go back on it.

"What the hell is wrong with you?" Molly hissed, grabbing his arm and squeezing tight.

He could have shrugged, but something about his sister's fierceness had the truth tumbling out. "Probably making a mistake."

He wasn't at all prepared for his little sister to slap him across the face. Hard.

"Hey!"

"I hope that knocked some damn sense into you, and quick. There's nothing about Lou that's a mistake, and if you ruin this with your self-pitying bullshit, I'll do a lot more than slap you." She stormed off.

When he glanced around at the small crowd, most of his family looked away from him, pretending they hadn't seen Molly slap him. Except Mom.

She didn't come over and give him a pep talk. She didn't smile or frown or do anything other than stand there next to Ben and look at him.

Disappointment clearly etched across her features.

He turned away, walked over to Cora, so she could situate him where he was supposed to be. The officiant smiled at him, and Cora told him to stay put here, standing in front of his entire family like a monkey on display.

It was awful, and he shouldn't go through with it. But he would, because he'd promised. They'd stay friends because they'd both promised. The rest was difficult, but they'd muddle through one way or another. They always did.

Then the truck approached. Mrs. Fairchild got out first, followed by Em and the puppy. Brenna barked and frolicked, chewing on her leash, which was decorated with flowers, as Em and Mrs. Fairchild walked to the setup before taking seats.

They both looked at him, and he couldn't read the expressions on either woman's face, but he had a feeling they weren't exactly *positive* looks.

Gavin wanted to bolt. At least that's what he told himself this expanding feeling in his chest was. The desire to run away and not try to do anything that might require failure or sacrifice.

But he didn't move. Lou stepped out of the truck, fancy lacy dress, a veil obscuring a lot of her face. She stood in the midst of a patch of yellow flowers that had grown to overtake the purple of spring and the sun shone down on her like a spotlight.

She was the most beautiful, wonderful thing he'd ever seen.

She walked down the aisle, and though she smiled happily at the small group of people in seats, he saw that she clutched her bouquet with white knuckles as she approached.

She reached the end of the runner, then handed Em her bouquet before stepping up to face him in front of the officiant.

Her blue eyes were uncertain as she met his gaze through the gauze of the veil.

Love slammed through him so hard, it nearly toppled him over. He loved her. Always had. Always would. She was one of the bravest, strongest, best women he knew, and he knew a lot of brave, strong, good women. He didn't think he'd ever be able to live up to it.

But she wanted him to, and the truth was, he didn't want to believe her because he knew love was hard. Relationships were hard. It was easier to hide it, keep it under wraps, than have to deal with all the hard things love did to people. Easier not to try rather than fail at something so important, so soul-changing.

But maybe if he took his mother's advice and *tried*, he'd actually manage to do something good and right. For her, and the love she'd bravely found. For himself, and the life he deserved if he stopped being such a damn coward.

Because it was a choice, wasn't it? He could choose to listen to the fear, or he could choose to fight it.

He held out his shaky hands, palms up, and she smiled, sliding her hands over his.

Gavin made his choice then and there.

"Good afternoon," the officiant greeted. "And welcome to a celebration of love, and the bringing together of two good souls in marriage. Marriage. A precious institution, one of love and partnership, one of hope and comfort. But the beauty of marriage isn't so much in weddings and frills, it's in the day-to-day promises. The making up after fights, the supporting each other through crises of faith and hope. It's loving through the hard times, and making the good times that much sweeter for it."

Gavin watched Lou through all those words, and she held his gaze. Her hands held on to his for dear life, and he supposed his hands were doing the same. Because they were getting married, and even if that hadn't started as any kind of soul promise, that was exactly the promise they were making today.

"Louisa Jane Fairchild, do you take—"

She cleared her throat and interrupted the rote words they'd agreed on. "I want to say my own vows."

"But, we were just going to—"

She shook her head at Gavin. "I have some things I want to say." She looked at him, then their families sitting in front of them. She cleared her throat again, her hands clammy in his. "If you all could put your cameras down while I do this, I'd really appreciate it."

"Lou—"

But she shook her head again and slipped her hands out of his, tugging when he reflexively held on.

Once he got it through his head to release her fingers, she reached up to her veil. She pulled out a few hairpins, and then took the veil out of her hair, revealing her entire face.

Emotion clogged his throat, stung at his eyes. The side of her face that had been burned was a pinkish white, abnormally smooth. Somehow, her expression was one of both misery and determination.

She hadn't just shown him her scars, she'd revealed them to everyone, even if her right side faced the officiant, not the crowd. Gavin couldn't begin to fathom how hard this was for her.

And she was doing it for him.

He very much doubted he was going to get through this without crying in front of his entire damn family.

For her? He didn't care.

Chapter Twenty-Four

It was hard to breathe, but Lou had to figure out a way to get the words out. Putting emotions to words was important. It would take her some time to really embrace that, but she knew, most especially after talking with her grandmother about Grandpa, that this was one of those moments when she had to do the brave thing. The heart-revealing thing.

She realized part of her had been waiting for Gavin to flinch at the revealing of her scars. But his expression was one of awe, and his eyes were even shiny, and she wanted to sob right there at the thought she'd brought Gavin to tears.

But she had things to say, promises to make. None of which could be done with the prescribed words the officiant had been instructed to give them.

She gently placed her veil on the ground and then held out her hands for Gavin's. He took them, and she forced herself to smile.

"I love you, Gavin." Because that was the center of all her truths. She loved this man. "You're one of the best men I know, and you've always been there for me. No matter what. Even today, when I wasn't sure you'd show up, here you are. And I think that's love. The kind you build a life on. Because at the end of the day, if we keep being there for each other, not much else matters."

She could tell he was gearing up to say something back, but she wasn't ready to hear his voice just yet. She had some more to say. "I don't like my scars. I can't imagine that'll change. But they aren't *me.* They're just a mark on my skin, and I . . . I won't be afraid to show you those things anymore. The scars, the things I feel. I've survived a lot worse than baring my soul. I might as well stop being afraid. So, that's what I promise you, Gav. Not just to love you or cherish you till death do us part, but to show up every day and try. To tell you when it hurts, and when it doesn't. To always show you my scars, even if I don't want to show them to the world."

She stepped closer, losing the battle to keep her voice steady and her eyes dry. "I can't promise not to be afraid, but I'll tell you when I am. And you'll tell me when you are, and we'll help each other not be afraid. Okay?"

He didn't answer, but when his mouth crushed to hers, she figured that was answer enough. She gave herself over to the kiss, even knowing both their families were watching.

"Er, did you want to say some things, Gavin?" the officiant asked, and by the way he said it, Lou had a feeling he'd asked once or twice while the kiss had been going on and neither of them had heard it.

Gavin laughed as he pulled away, shaking his head, but his words contradicted that movement, and he didn't let her hands go. "Yeah, I'll say some things. I'll say some things." His gaze searched her face, and she kept waiting for it to linger on her scars, to trace the ugly line of normal skin to damaged, but it never did.

He saw her as whole. He always had, and in that she'd learned to see herself as whole too.

"I've loved you for as long as I can remember. I didn't always know what to do about that. I convinced myself there wasn't anything *to* do because I'd always be there if you needed me. But I was a coward, because I never tried to be more than your soft place to land. It was . . . safe there. I guess as much as I didn't want to fail, I also wanted to stay in that safe place where I didn't have to be uncomfortable or upset or hurt or sad."

He tugged one hand out of her grip, then reached out and cradled her cheek. The scarred one, as if it didn't matter where he touched, she was precious to him.

"I think I had to learn a few things about life, and I think I had to learn a few things about sacrifice. And most of all, I had to learn how to fight, fight the fear and step outside those safe places. And I learned that watching you. No matter how bad things were, you always fought. No matter how you got knocked down, you'd get right back up. You awe me, every day, and I've always loved you for that, but it took me time to figure out how to fight too. But I know how now, and I'm going to fight every day to be the man you deserve."

"Just be you. Just be there and be you, like always."

"I will. I promise you I will."

"I promise too."

Then he was kissing her again. Fierce and determined, with everything she knew he'd had in him even when he'd been so sure he didn't. She forgot they were in front of their families, forgot this was a wedding, she just poured herself into the kiss. All her love, all her hope, and all that strength he was so certain she had, she gave to him.

And he gave it all back.

Eventually, they seemed to remember where they were. Lou figured it was from the fact that half their little crowd was cheering, the other half booing or groaning. They pulled away from each other, though Gavin held her face with his hands and she still had her fingers curled into his shirt.

The officiant cleared his throat. "Well, I'd say those are some pretty powerful vows. So, I'll now pronounce you man and wife. You've already kissed the bride a few times, but if you need to—"

Gavin kissed her again before the sentence was even out of the officiant's mouth. She laughed against his mouth, and they managed to break away from each other before Boone started booing again.

"Ladies and gentlemen, Gavin and Louisa Tyler."

They turned toward their families, who started getting up to surround them with hugs and congratulations.

"Louisa Tyler," he murmured into her ear. "I like that."

"Well, you're only ever going to see it on official documents. Lou Tyler suits me just fine."

He grinned at her. "It'll do."

"Oh my God, you two, if you don't stop kissing, I'm going to puke." Em wrapped her arms around both of them. "But that was beautiful."

Then Molly was hugging them. "I'd apologize for slapping you, but I'm pretty sure it worked."

Lou looked wide-eyed up at Gavin. "She slapped you?"

"Hard too."

"He deserved it. Trust me." Molly hugged them both with a little sniffle. "Oh, I'm so happy for you two. I've been waiting so long for it, I was starting to think it'd never happen."

Gavin grinned at Lou. "Me too."

"Good things come to those who wait, and have family machinations requiring a fake wedding, and then finally have to face their feelings. I think that's how the saying goes."

Gavin chuckled into her hair. "Definitely how it goes, Mrs. Tyler."

Mrs. Tyler. Yeah, life turned out okay sometimes.

They ate at picnic tables in the front yard of the Tyler house. Lou barely left his side, and when she did, it was hard not to watch her. Laughing with Em, dancing with Lindsay, whispering something with her grandmother. His wife.

His wife. Somehow, a dumb-ass coward like him had gotten his act together and had the wife of his dreams, quite literally.

"Well, you pulled that one out of your ass," Boone said, clapping him on the back as he perched himself on the edge of the seat.

"Don't be jealous."

Boone slid a look toward where Em, Lou, Molly, Cora, and Lindsay were laughing on the makeshift dance floor. "Not even a bit."

"A nice woman would do you some good," Shane said, grinning at Gavin as he slid onto the bench.

"I ain't got no use for a *nice* woman," Boone returned with an exaggerated drawl.

"I'm going to be a bachelor forever, like Skeet at Mile High," Micah said, stuffing his face with another piece of cake.

"Sure you are, kid," Shane said indulgently.

"Why don't you all bother Cal?" Boone said, nodding toward where Cal sat at the opposite end of the table. "He's the one who better be marrying our baby sister right quick."

"Be there soon enough," Cal muttered in his taciturn way, but Gavin didn't fail to notice the way the man looked at Lindsay like she was the center of the universe.

He knew the feeling.

"Where'd Mom disappear to?" Gavin asked. "She's not cleaning, is she?"

"That'd be my bet," Shane said. "Want me to go find her and drag her back out?"

"No, I'll get her." Gavin had a few things to say to his mother, and now was as good a time as any.

He found her in the kitchen, sneaking all three dogs—King, LM (LeBron MacKade), and Brenna, scraps from the paper plates she'd collected and brought to the trash.

"What are you doing when the party's outside?"

Mom turned to face him and smiled sheepishly, very carefully hiding the fact she'd been feeding the dogs people food. "Honestly? Makes me a little teary to see all of you so grown and happy. Just figured I'd cheer myself up by getting a head start on cleaning and get some one-on-one time with these little guys."

The dogs looked up at her adoringly as she patted each of their heads.

"I think the lesson of the day is, it's okay to be a little teary."

Mom chuckled. "I know. Some lessons are harder to learn than others, though." She heaved out a sigh and crossed to him. "I'll come back out. If you don't mind Ben and me doing a little dirty dancing."

Gavin groaned. "That's just mean."

Mom laughed. "I know."

She started to walk out of the kitchen, but he stopped her by blocking her way. "Mom?"

"Hmm?"

He wrapped his arms around her and squeezed. "Thank you."

"Oh hell," she muttered, squeezing him back, and though his mother almost never cried, he was pretty sure that was exactly what she was doing.

"I needed that ride and that talk last night. I wouldn't have been able to do this right, to make it count, without that. Without you. So, thank you."

She pulled back, definitely some evidence of tears on her cheeks, but she smiled. "You're a good boy. Be good to that wife of yours."

"Wife," Gavin echoed, walking back toward the front door with his arm around his mother's shoulders. "Somehow, I got me a wife."

"Somehow, you did. And I know, just like your father was, you'll be an excellent husband."

It choked him up some, but he cleared his throat. "Plenty of Tyler women to kick my ass now if I don't."

"And don't you forget it."

He walked back outside with his mother, and as they stepped off the porch, Lou was walking up to them.

"You're pretty as a picture, sweetheart," Mom said, sounding a little emotional all over again.

Lou smiled, and though he didn't think she realized it, she touched the side of her face that was scarred before she dropped her hand. She smiled. "Thanks, Mrs. T."

"Here's your husband. I'm off to find mine."

Mom went over to the picnic tables and Lou took her place next to Gavin. He slid his arm over her shoulders and she slid her arm around his waist.

His wife. His actual, in name and deed and love wife. Hell, that was weird. Amazing but weird.

"Ready to go home, cowboy?" she asked, leaning into him.

He raised an eyebrow at her. "Don't we have to collect your grandma first?"

"She's spending the night here. She said newlyweds should be free to christen their home alone on their wedding night."

Gavin grimaced. "She didn't."

"I'm pretty sure Grandma Maisey got her drunk," Lou said, sounding far too amused. "There was talk of signing her up for Tinder."

"Please tell me that's a joke."

"I think so, but with your grandma, I'm never quite sure."

"Yeah, me neither."

Gavin stopped their forward motion, taking in the sights around him. Tylers and Fairchilds, laughter and food, family and hope.

He looked down at her, and she was taking it all in too, with a big smile on her face. His wife.

When she glanced at him, her smile softened. "Let's go home."

"Yeah, let's."

They said their goodbyes, were hugged approximately ten times, more by the family members who'd indulged in a little too much champagne. Gavin realized he hadn't managed a drop of liquor the whole evening.

When they got home and Lou led him upstairs, he was glad there wasn't a thing clouding his mind. She was more than enough.

She pulled him into her—*their* bedroom—then turned to face him. She watched him as she reached behind her, and he heard the slow, quiet rumble of her pulling down her zipper. She let the dress fall, then took off her underwear, so she was standing in front of him completely naked.

He barely registered the scar marks on her shoulder or her arm, because she was the most beautiful thing he'd ever seen, and she was completely naked. For him. Gavin could only stand there and hold his breath.

"I want you to know," she said, placing her hand over his thundering heart, "I'll probably still wear my bandanna a lot." She started to undo his buttons. "But I'll always take it off at bed." She looked from the buttons to him. "I'll always take it all off for you."

"I love you," he said, because it was all he had, and sometimes the simplest thing was enough. He'd believe that now.

"I know." She grinned up at him. "And I love you. You believe me now, don't you? Trust me?"

He had to clear his throat to answer her. "You're one of the smartest ladies I know, so I guess I better."

"Good. Now, why don't you show me just how much?"

So, that was exactly what he did.

Epilogue

As spring turned to summer, and summer to fall, the Fairchild-Tyler residence was a whir of activity. Gavin had his hands full trying to bring the ranch back into the black, and spring and summer were Lou's busy season, with both the florist arm of her business and the flowers themselves. Grandma had taken to running her flower booth at the farmers market, which had allowed Lou more time to work the flowers and given Grandma something to do outside the ranch.

Dad visited sometimes. Not often, and Lou wouldn't say she was particularly comfortable with his appearances, but she was learning to weather them. And it made Grandma so happy, that was the important thing.

Lou sat on the porch, Brenna at her feet chewing on a rope bone, watching the sun set as she waited for Gavin to return from the Tyler Ranch. They'd been working on some building project on the house and needed an extra hand, so he'd headed over after dinner.

Grandma was inside cleaning up after dinner, and Lou was content to enjoy a little quiet. There wasn't much of it to be had these days. Gavin liked to talk, and chatter, and narrate. She loved the man, but some days he about drove her nuts.

But she always woke up with the same wave of love and amazement that she'd somehow landed in the middle of all this *good.*

The same wave that swept over her as Gavin's truck appeared on the horizon. He drove over to the gravel drive and parked where Grandma preferred the cars to be. He hopped out and strode toward the porch.

"Get everything done?"

"Few finishing touches yet, but they got a lot accomplished with my help." Gavin took his seat on the rickety rocking chair. He almost always refused to sit on the swing with her because he was sure it would come tumbling down at any minute.

Lou always trusted it to hold both their weight.

Despite Brenna's ever-increasing size, she jumped right up onto Gavin's lap.

"For supposed to having been my dog, she sure likes you best."

Gavin scratched behind her ears. "Oh, don't be jealous, sweetheart. Women can't help loving me." Brenna stared at him adoringly before carefully licking his cheek, proving Gavin's point.

"You want dessert? Grandma made cobbler."

"In a bit. Wanted to talk to you first."

"About what?"

Gavin nudged Brenna off his lap and stood. He came over to her, and she had to raise her eyebrows at the fact that Gavin was voluntarily sitting on the porch swing with her.

"You know one thing we never talked about before we got married?"

"What's that?"

He slid his arm over her shoulders. "Kids."

"Kids?" Kids. Children. Having . . . kids. Not that she'd never thought about it, she just hadn't . . . thought about it enough to know how she felt about it.

"Yes, ma'am. So, what do you say?"

"About kids?"

He grinned at her. "Yeah. Want to have a whole passel with me?"

He was so cute. So good. Such a good, hardworking husband, and she just couldn't think of any reason her answer would be *no.* "Maybe not a passel. Let's start with one."

"You sure?"

"Yeah. A little boy with your bad temper and my sheer stubbornness. What could go wrong?"

He chuckled, pulling her closer and resting his chin on her head. "A little girl with your blue eyes and strength and my bad temper, so she can fight off any boy that looks at her sideways? Sounds good to me."

She didn't know why, but it did sound good. It sounded perfect. "Yeah, me too."

"Want to start now?"

"Now?"

"We have to hurry. I get the sneaking suspicion Cora and Shane beat us to the punch."

"Cora's pregnant?"

"Shh. I don't know for sure. Just a feeling I get."

"We can't beat them if they're already pregnant. And oh my God, why are we trying to beat them anyway? They've been married longer and it's hardly a contest."

"Okay, so it's not a contest and I'm just trying to talk you into bed. You got a problem with that?"

She laughed. "No, not at all." She pulled back so she could study his face, that crooked brawler's nose and the soft smile and all that *love* in his eyes he wasn't afraid to show anymore.

"You'll be a really good dad."

He pulled up the flap of her bandanna so he could look into both her eyes. "You'll be a hell of a mom."

"Come on, let's go to the barn."

And they laughed the whole way across the yard, racing for the future hand in hand.

Don't miss any of Nicole Helm's
Mile High romances:

Brandon's story in *Need You Now,*
Sam's story in *Mess With Me,*
Will's story in *Want You More,*
Shane's story in *A Nice Day for a Cowboy Wedding,* and
Lindsay's story in *Santa's On His Way.*

Now on sale in bookstores and online!

Read on for a preview of *Need You Now* . . .

Brandon Evans stood on the porch of his office and stared at the world below him, a kaleidoscope of browns and greens and grays, all the way down the mountain until the rooftops of Gracely, Colorado, dotted into view.

Across the valley, up the other side of jagged stone, the deserted Evans Mining Corporation buildings stood, like ghosts—haunting him and his name. A glaring reminder of the destruction he'd wrought while trying to do the right thing.

He wished it were a cloudy day so he couldn't see the damn things, but he'd built the headquarters of *his* company in view simply so he could remind himself what he was fighting for. What was right.

"Are you over there being broody?"

Brandon looked down at his mug of coffee balanced on the porch railing, not bothering to glance at his brother. He *was* brooding. They were outvoting him and he didn't like it. He took a sip of coffee, now cool from the chilled spring air.

He leveled a gaze at his brother, Will, and their business partner, Sam. This was his best *I'm a leader* look, and it usually worked.

Why the hell wasn't it working today?

"Hiring a PR consultant goes against everything we're trying to do." Of course, he'd already explained that and he'd still been outvoted.

"We need help. The town isn't going to grow to forgive us. We can do all the good in the world, but without someone actually making inroads—we're not getting anywhere. We can't even find a receptionist from Gracely. No one will acknowledge we *exist*."

"We have Skeet."

"Skeet is not a receptionist. He's a . . . a . . . Help me out here, Sam?"

"His name is *Skeet*," Sam replied, as if that explained everything.

The grizzled old man who answered their phones for their outdoor adventure excursion company and refused to use a computer *was* a bit of a problem, but he worked for cheap and he was a local. Brandon had been adamant about hiring only locals.

Of course, Skeet was a local that everyone shunned, and he seemed to only speak in grunts, but they'd yet to lose an interested customer.

That they knew of, Will liked to point out.

Brandon set the offensive cold coffee down on the railing of the deck. He needed to do something with his hands. He couldn't sit still—he was too frustrated that they were standing around arguing instead of Sam and Will jumping to do his bidding.

Why had he thought to make them all equal partners?

"She's local. Great experience with a firm in Denver. She can be the bridge we need to turn the tide." Will ticked off the points they'd already been over, patient as ever.

"She's recently local—not native—and she can't change our last name."

"Well, even lifer townies working every second at Mile High can't do that."

"Can we cut the circuitous bullshit?" Sam interrupted with a mutter. "You were outvoted, Brandon. She's hired. Now, I've got to go."

"You don't have a group to guide until two."

Sam was already inside the cabin that acted as their office, the words probably never reaching him. Apparently his time-around-other-humans allotment was up for the morning. Not that shocking. The fact they'd lured him from his hermit mountain cabin before a guided hike was unusual.

Brandon turned his stare to his brother. They were twins. Born five minutes apart, but the five minutes had always felt like years. He'd been George Bailey born-older, and any time Sam sided with Will, Brandon couldn't help but get his nose a little out of joint.

He was the responsible, business-minded one, not the in-for-a-good-time playboy. They should listen to him regardless, not Will. Brandon had spearheaded Mile High. It was his baby, his penance, his hope of offering Gracely some healing in the wake of his father's mess of an impact. The fact that Will and Sam sometimes disagreed with him about the best way to do that filled him with a dark energy, and he'd need to do something physical to burn it off.

"Go chop some wood. Build a birdhouse. Climb a mountain for all I care. She'll be here at ten. Be back by then," Will ordered.

"You know I'd as soon throat punch you as do what you tell me to do."

Will grinned. "Oh, brother, if I kept my mouth

shut every time you wanted to throat punch me, I'd never speak."

"Uh-huh."

Will's expression went grave, which was always a bad sign. They both dealt with weighty things and emotion differently—Brandon acted like a dick and Will acted like nothing mattered. If Will was acting like something was important . . .

Well, shit.

"Don't think we don't take it seriously," Will said, far too quietly for Brandon's comfort. "Trust, every once in a while, we know as well or better than you."

"My ass," Brandon grumbled, feeling at least a little shamed.

"She'll be here at ten. I have that spring break group at ten-thirty, and you, lucky man, don't have anything on your plate today. Which means, you get to be in charge of paper—"

"Don't say it."

"—work and orientation!" Will concluded all too jovially.

"I could probably throw you off the mountain and no one would ask any questions."

"Ah, but then who would take the bachelorette party guides since you and Sam refuse?" Will clapped him on the shoulder. "You'll like her. She's got that business-tunnel-vision thing down that you do so well."

Brandon took a page out of Skeet's book and merely grunted, which Will—thank Christ—took as a cue to leave.

Regardless of whether he'd like this Lilly Preston, Brandon didn't see the usefulness or point in hiring a PR consultant. What was that going to accomplish when the town already hated them?

If even Will's personality couldn't win people over,

they were toast in that department. The only thing that was going to sway people's minds was an economically booming town. Mile High had a long way to go to make Gracely that. And they needed Gracely's help.

Hiring someone who had only cursory knowledge of Gracely lore, who couldn't possibly understand what they were trying to do, wasn't the answer. Worse, it reeked of something his father would have done when he was trying to hide all the shady business practices he'd instituted at Evans Mining.

Brandon glanced back over at the empty buildings. If he wanted to, he could will away the memories, the images in his mind. The pristine hallways, the steady buzz of phones and conversation. How much he'd wanted that to be *his* one day.

But then he'd told his father he knew what was going on, and if Dad didn't change, Brandon would have no choice but to go to the authorities.

The fallout had been the Evans Mining headquarters leaving Gracely after over a century of being the heart of the town, his father's subsequent heart attack and death, Mom shutting them out, and everything about his life as the golden child and heir apparent to the corporation imploding before his very eyes.

A lot of consequences for one tiny little domino he'd flicked when his conscience couldn't take the possible outcomes of his father's shady practices.

So much work to do to make it right. He forced his gaze away from those buildings into the mountains all around him. He took a deep breath of the thin air scented with heavy pine. He rubbed his palms over the rough wood of the porch railing.

It was the center—these mountains, this place. He believed he could bring this town back to life not just because he owed it to the residents who'd treated him like a king growing up, but because there was something . . . elemental about these mountains, this sky, the river tributaries, and the animals that lived within it all.

Untouched, ethereal, and while he didn't exactly believe in magic and ghostly legends of Gracely's healing power, he did believe in these mountains and this air. He was going to give his all to fix the damage he'd caused, and he was going to give his all to making Mile High Adventures everything it could be.

So, he'd put up with this unwanted PR woman for the few weeks it would take to prove that Will and Sam were wrong. Once they admitted he was right, they could move on to the next thing, and the next thing, until they got exactly what they wanted.

Lilly took a deep, cleansing breath of the mountain air. The altitude was much higher up here than in the little valley Gracely was nestled into, but even aside from that, the office of Mile High Adventures was breathtaking.

It was like something out of a brochure—which would make her job rather easy. A cabin nestled into the side of a mountain. All dark logs and green trimmed roof, with a snow-peaked top of a mountain settled right behind to complete the look of cozy mountain getaway. The porches were almost as big as the cabin itself. She'd suggest some colorful deck chairs, a few fire pits to complete the look, but it took no imagination at all to picture groups of people and mugs of hot chocolate and colorful plaid blankets.

The sign next to the door that read MILE HIGH ADVENTURES was carved into a wood plank that matched the logs of the cabin.

If it weren't for the men who ran this company, she'd be crying with relief and excitement. She *needed* a job that would allow her to stay in Gracely, and this one would pay enough that she could still support her sister and nephew even with Cora's dwindling waitress hours and low tips.

Cora and Micah were doing so well, finally moving on from the abusive nightmare that had been Stephen. Lilly couldn't uproot them, and she couldn't leave them. They needed her, but her Denver-based PR company had refused to let her continue to work remotely when they'd merged with another company and kept only those willing to relocate to Denver.

So, here she was, about to agree to work for the kind of men she couldn't stand. Rich, entitled, charming. The kind of men who'd hurt her mother, her sister, her nephew.

Lilly forced her feet forward. This was work, not romance, so it didn't matter. She'd do her job, take their money, do her best to improve the light in which their business was seen in Gracely, and not let any of these rich and powerful men touch her.

Shoulders back, she walked up the stairs of the porch. There was a sign on the door, hung from a nail and string. It read *Come On In!* in flowing script. She imagined if she flipped the sign there'd be some kind of WE'RE CLOSED phrase on the back.

Impressive detail for a group of three, from what she could tell, burly mountain men hated by the town at large.

Her stomach jittered, cramped. She really didn't want to do this. She *loved* Gracely. Even for all its problems, it was charming and . . . calming. She felt cozy and comfortable here. More than she'd ever felt in Denver, where she'd grown up.

Working for Mile High would keep her here, but would it still be cozy and comfortable if the town looked at her with contempt? If they considered her tainted by association with these men she'd never heard a good word about?

Well, as long as Cora and Micah still needed her, it didn't matter. Couldn't.

She blew out a breath and lifted a steady hand. She opened the door. Will *had* instructed her to come on in, and the sign said as much.

Upon stepping into what was an open area that seemed designed as both lobby and living room, she wasn't surprised to find more wood, a crackling fire in the fireplace, warm and worn brown leather couches pushed around the hearth. The walls were mostly bare, but there was a deer head over the mantel, a few framed graphics with quotes about going to the mountains and the wilderness.

A grunt caused Lilly to jerk her attention to the big desk opposite the entryway. She wasn't sure what she'd expected of the other employees of Mile High, but she'd assumed they'd all be like Will. Young, athletic, charming, and handsome.

The man sitting behind the desk was *none* of those things. He was small and old with a white beard and a white ponytail. A bit of a Willie Nelson/*Dirty Santa*-looking character in a stained Marine Corps sweatshirt.

Not what she expected of a receptionist . . . anywhere.

"Hello. My name is Lilly Preston. I'm supposed to be meeting Will Evans and his broth—"

The man grunted again, a sound that was a gravelly huff and seemed to shake his entire small frame.

What on earth was happening?

"Ah, Lilly!" Will appeared from some hallway in the back. "Skeet, you're not scaring off our newest employee, are you?"

The man—Skeet, good Lord—grunted again. Maybe he was their . . . grandfather or something.

She returned her attention and polite business smile to Will and the man behind him. It wasn't any stretch to realize this was Will's brother, Brandon Evans. There were a lot of similarities in their height, the dark brown hair—though Brandon's was short and Will's was long enough to have a bit of a wave to it. They both sported varying levels of beard, hazel eyes, and the kind of angular, masculine face one would definitely associate with men who climbed mountains and kayaked rivers.

There were some key differences—mainly, Will was smiling, all straight white teeth. Brandon's mouth was formed in something a half inch away from a scowl.

Well. She forced her smile to go wider and more pleasant. She wasn't a novice at dealing with cranky or difficult men. About seventy-five percent of her career thus far had included dealing with obstinate and opinionated business owners. The Evans brothers might be different, but they weren't unique.

"You have an absolutely lovely office. I'm so impressed."

Will gestured her toward the couches around the fireplace. There were rugs over the hardwood floor, patterns of dark red and green and brown. It was no lie, she *was* impressed.

"Have a seat, Lilly. I have a group to guide rock climbing shortly, so Brandon will conduct most of your orientation. We've got the necessary paperwork." He placed a stack of papers on the rough-hewn wood coffee table. It looked like it had probably come from Annie's—the furniture shop in Gracely. Furnishing and decorating from local vendors would be smart.

Smart, rich men with charming smiles and handsome scowls. It didn't get much more dangerous than that, but Lilly never let her smile falter.

"Once we've done that, Brandon will show you around, show you your desk, and you can ask any questions."

"Of course." She leaned forward to take the paperwork, but Brandon's hand all but slapped on top of the stack.

"One thing first."

Will muttered something that sounded like an expletive.

The stomach jittering/cramping combo was back, but she refused to let it show on her face. Nerves were normal, and the way she always dealt was to ignore them through the pleasantest smiles and friendliest chitchat she could manage until they went away.

"I'm at your disposal, Mr. Evans," she said, letting her hand fall away from the papers as she settled comfortably into the couch. At least she hoped she was exuding the appearance of comfort.

His expression, which hadn't been all that friendly or welcoming, darkened even further. "You will call me Brandon. You will call him Will. There are no misters here."

Ah, so he was one of those. Determined to be an everyman. She resisted an eye roll.

He leaned forward, hazel eyes blazing into hers. "Do you believe in the legend, Ms. Preston?"

"The . . . legend?" This was not what she'd expected. At all. She quickly glanced at the door in her periphery. Maybe she should bolt.

"You've lived here how long? Surely you've heard the legend of Gracely."

"You mean . . ." She hesitated because she didn't know where he was trying to lead her, and she didn't like going into unchartered territory. But, he seemed adamant, so she continued. "The one about those who choose Gracely as their home will find the healing their heart desires?"

"Are there others?"

Lilly had to tense to keep the pleasant smile on her face. She didn't like the way this Evans brother spoke to her. Like he was an interrogating detective. Like she'd done something wrong, when Will had been the one to convince her to take this job.

Because working with the Evanses was going to put a big red X on her back in town, and she didn't trust men like them with their centuries of good name and money.

But she needed a job. She needed to stay in Gracely. So, she had to ignore the way his tone put her back up and smile pleasantly and pretend he wasn't a giant asshat.

"So, Ms. Preston." Oh she hated the way he *drawled* her name. "The question is: do you believe in the legend?"

This was a test, a blatant one at that, and yet . . . she didn't know the right answer. Would he ridicule her for believing in fairy tales if she said she believed the first settlers of Gracely were magically healed when they settled here and all the stories that had been built up into legend since? Would he take issue with her being cynical and hard if she said there was no way?

The biggest problem was her answer existed somewhere in between the two. Half of her thought it was foolishness. Losing her job and having to take this one hardly seemed like healing or good luck, but her sister and nephew had flourished here in the past year and, well, healing was possible. Magic? Maybe—maybe not. But possible.

So, maybe it was best to focus on the good, the possibility. "Yes." She met his penetrating hazel gaze, keeping her expression the picture-perfect blank slate of professional politeness.

"And what do you think is the source of that legend? What makes it true?"

"True?" She looked at Will, tried to catch his gaze, but he looked at the ceiling. She might not trust Will, but at least he was polite. Apparently also a giant coward.

"Yes, if you believe Gracely can heal, what do you believe *causes* that ability?"

She flicked her gaze back to his. It had never wavered. There was a fierceness to his expression that made her nervous. He was a big man. Tall, broad. Though he wore a thick sweater and heavy work pants and boots, it was fairly obvious beneath all those layers was the type of man who could probably crush her with one arm.

She suddenly felt very small and very vulnerable. Weak and at a disadvantage.

Which was just the kind of thing she wouldn't show them. Powerful men got off on causing fear and vulnerability. She'd seen her nephew's father do that enough to have built a mask against it, and she'd worked with and for plenty of men who'd wanted to intimidate her for a variety of reasons.

She could handle whatever this was. Chin up. Spine straight. A practiced down-the-nose look. "Do legends need a cause? A scientific explanation? Or are they simply . . . magic? Do I need to analyze *why* I believe in it, or can I simply believe it happened and continues to? And, more, what on earth does it have to do with my work here?"

"If you're going to work here," he said, his voice low and . . . fierce to match his face, "you will need to understand what *we* believe about the legend. Because it has everything to do with why we built Mile High Adventures."

"That's not what I heard," she muttered before she could stop herself. Okay, maybe remote consulting *had* dulled some of her instincts if she let things like that slip.

"Oh, and what did you hear, Ms. Preston? That we're the evil spawn of Satan setting out to crush Gracely even deeper into the earth? That we're bringing in an influx of out-of-towners, not to *help* the businesses of Gracely, but to piss off the natives? Because if you think we don't know what this town thinks of us, you don't understand why you're here."

"I know what the town thinks of you *and* I know why I'm here." She took a deep breath, masked with a smile, of course. "I'm here because I think this is an excellent opportunity." *To sell my soul briefly so I can stay where I want.* "I do believe in the legend, and I think it would be imperative you do too if you expect to sell the town on you being part of its salvation."

His eyes narrowed and she knew she was skating on thin ice. He was one of those control freaks who didn't like to be told what to do, only unlike most of the men she'd worked with like that, he wasn't placated by sweet smiles or politeness.

She'd have to find a new tactic.

"I believe, Ms. Preston"—that damn conceited drawl again—"in these mountains. In this *air.* I believe that, if people choose to look, they can find themselves here. I believe in this town, and that it can be more than what it's become. You'll need to believe that too if you want to work here."

"We've already hired her, Brandon," Will said, *finally* inserting something into the conversation. *After* letting this man act as though she were . . . well, unwelcome, unwanted.

Typical.

"*You* hired her."

"Did I walk into the middle of something, gentlemen? I can just as soon come back at another time when you're ready and willing to be in agreement." She even stood, picking up her bag to slide over her shoulder. Because she might be desperate, but she wasn't going to sell half her soul *and* be treated poorly.

That was not what she'd signed up for. She'd as soon move back to Denver. It would kill her to leave Cora and Micah, but she had some pride she couldn't swallow.

"Have a seat, Ms. Preston."

When she raised an eyebrow at Brandon the Bastard, he pressed his lips together, then released a sigh. "If you would, please." All said through gritted teeth.

Ugh. Men.

She took a seat. One more chance. He had *one* more chance.

"I apologize if I've come off . . ."

"Harsh. Douchey. Asshole spectacular."

Brandon glared at his brother, who was grinning. She didn't want to find it humorous. They were both being asshole spectaculars as far as she was concerned, just in different ways.

"This business and what it stands for is everything to me, so I don't take it lightly."

She met his gaze. Just as she didn't want to find them amusing, she didn't want to soften, but she realized in that simple, gravely uttered sentence, that he wasn't fierce so much as . . .

Passionate.

She met his gaze with that realization and her stomach did something other than the alternating jittery cramps. Her chest seemed to expand—something flipped, like when Cora drove them too fast down a mountain road.

She couldn't put her finger on that. The cause, what it was, and more, she didn't think she wanted to. If she was going to survive working for the Evans brothers, it was probably best to keep her polite smile in place and ignore any and all *feelings.*